Take Heart

Hart & Soul Book Series
Book One

CAROL CANNON

*"Be strong and take heart,
all you who have hope in the Lord. "*

Psalm 31:24 (NIV)

*I dedicate this book to my mother
who gave me her unconditional love
even when I was most unlovable.*

Other books by Carol Cannon

Forgiveness

Hope

Peace

Joy

CHAPTER ONE

Before the call that changed everything, the day had dawned as one of Nelli's better ones. She was awakened by glorious sunlight streaming through the curtains of her bedroom windows. After four long dismal days of enduring sunless, dreary weather, it was a sight she welcomed with a smile. She got out of bed and hurried over to the window that faced her backyard. She threw back the curtains and gazed out to the fields and woods beyond. It thrilled her heart to be greeted by such a brilliant, sunlit morning. The refreshed world outside her window seemed to shimmer with a newness of life. The budding leaves on the trees appeared a darker, deeper green. The grass seemed to glow with a rich emerald green. Her breath caught in her throat at the awe-inspiring sight of the deep purple hyacinths scattered among the rows of soft yellow daffodils. She wondered if her grandmother Topsy, who had planted the flowers two generations ago, had once stood at this window and marveled at such a sparkling, dew-drenched scene.

The landscape before her filled Nelli with more happiness than she'd felt in weeks, maybe even months. After staring out the window for several minutes, she felt the familiar lure of nature pulling her outside to be a part of God's magnificent creation. As fast as she could, she threw the quilt her grandmother made for her when she was a child over the bed and put the pillows with their shams in place. She hurriedly took off her pajamas and changed into jeans and a T-shirt topped with an oversized flannel shirt that had once belonged to her brother. Once dressed, she went down the back stairs and eased open the door to the back porch where she stepped into her knee-high black rubber boots. She grabbed her ICHS baseball cap off the hook and placed it squarely on her head as she walked down the back steps and into the splendor of the morning.

Stopping on the bottom step, she took in the freshness of a new day. She closed her eyes, breathing in the sweet perfume of blooming flowers along with the scent of the damp earth. She opened her eyes and watched as a squirrel climbed up the budding dogwood tree in its hopeless attempt to snatch some sunflower seeds from the squirrel-proof birdfeeder hanging from a limb. She laughed at its squeaks and barks of frustration as it scampered away. She called out, "That's what you get for trying to rob from the birds, you silly squirrel. There's plenty of food for you just over the fence."

After Nelli spent an hour or so weeding and tending to the flowers and plants in her backyard, she walked out through the field and into the surrounding woods, taking in the richness of the beauty around her. She wasn't surprised when she found her meanderings took her to where the edge of her woods met up with the plantation pond. Most of her wanderings led her back to this exact spot. It was the place where her husband Nicholas had placed the cypress bench he'd made for her over sixty years ago and where she'd spread his ashes nine years later.

As Nelli ran her hand over the smooth weathered wood of the bench, tracing their carved initials with her fingertips, the memory of why he'd made the bench came back to her.

As newlyweds, at the end of the day when their work was done, they'd walk to the plantation pond, enjoying the peace and beauty of their land along the way. Their evening walks soon became routine. When she became pregnant with their first child, as her pregnancy progressed, she found it more difficult to walk all the way to the pond and back home without needing to stop and rest. That's when he'd surprised her with this bench. He explained how he'd made it out of cypress so it would last a lifetime.

Nelli shook her head at the tragic irony of his words spoken so long ago. In one way, he'd been right. It had lasted his lifetime. That day when she'd first sat down on this bench was a precious memory she would hold in her heart forever.

She sat down and stretched out her legs. It wasn't until the moment she stopped moving that she realized her left knee, which had throbbed and ached through the rainy days, hadn't bothered her in the least this morning. Seated on her bench, Nelli took in the views and sounds around her. Her ears caught the soft whispering of the leaves in the trees as a cool breeze blew through.

As she looked out over the plantation pond, she recalled the days when she could swim all the way across and back five times without stopping. Even though those days were far behind her, she still held their memories close. It wasn't often she took the time to stop and think about her past life, but that's what Nelli did that morning as she sat on her bench where the woods met the pond before getting the phone call that would change her life. She leaned back and looked up at the blue sky above, allowing precious memories to come flooding back to her.

The plantation pond had once been a part of her family's grand Tucker Plantation. It was whittled down to only forty acres after the Great Depression. Her father, Edward, as the only surviving son, inherited the plantation house and remaining land. It was to that house he brought his bride Cora and raised his three children. Coranelia Mae, born in 1943 and nicknamed Nelli, was the youngest and only girl.

When Nelli was eleven years old, her mother died. Her grandmother Topsy—so called because she always wore her hair on top of her head—took on the job of raising Nelli and her brothers, Matt, and Jim-Jim, which she did with a stern, but loving hand.

Nelli smiled remembering how her two older brothers drove her crazy with their overprotectiveness, especially when it came to boys and dating. She begged her father to make them stop, but her father only chuckled and said, "Now, Nelli, one day when the right boy comes along, your brothers will know. That'll be when they'll leave you alone."

As it turned out, it was because of her older brother she met the right boy, or rather the right man, the winter of her senior year in high school.

CHAPTER TWO

The chill of the early morning air blowing across the plantation pond brought Nelli back to the present. Surprised to find her cheeks wet, she quickly wiped away her tears. She noticed how far the sun had risen in the sky while she'd been wandering through her past and realized it was well past breakfast time. With a loving touch, she rubbed her hands across the bench once more before pushing herself up. She walked back to the house, pulled off her muddy rubber boots and, leaving them on the back porch, stepped through to the kitchen in her stocking feet. She put two slices of her homemade raisin cinnamon bread in her toaster oven then padded her way to the stove to fix her usual breakfast of one egg over easy with two pieces of extra crispy bacon. The phone rang while she was buttering her toasted bread.

Nelli put down the knife and placed the toast on her plate next to her fried egg and bacon. She walked to her phone that hung on the kitchen wall. Not recognizing the number displayed on the caller ID window, she hesitated. She considered letting the call go to voice mail, but something deep inside nudged her to answer. Feeling optimistic about her day ahead and believing only good things would come into it, she picked up the receiver. "Hello."

A nervous male voice said, "Hello. I'm calling for Mrs. Coranelia Hart?"

Nelli frowned. No one who knew her would use her full first name. She'd gone by Nelli for almost eighty years. Her curiosity as to why this man had used her given name kept her from hanging up on him. "Who's calling, please?"

There was silence on the other end. Nelli couldn't tell if the man was still on the line. She was ready to end the call when he answered, "I'm looking for Coranelia Hart who was the wife of Chief Nicholas Hart."

Nelli couldn't imagine why someone would be referring to Nicholas by his rank after all these years. "You've reached the right person. You need to tell me right now who you are and why you're calling me, or I'm hanging up this phone!"

"I'm sorry, Mrs. Hart. I've gone about this whole thing the wrong way. Please allow me to start over." The man cleared his throat. "I had it all worked out in my mind and even rehearsed what I was going to say before I called. But now I've made the call. . .and I'm talking to you. . . I don't know how to tell you what I've called to tell you. . .what I think you should have been told by the army."

Nelli was growing tired of listening to his rambling. The irritation building inside of her came through her voice. "The army? What does the army have to do with anything? Sir, are you sure you've called the right person?"

The man's tone of voice changed from one of uncertainty to confidence "My name is Jake Albright. My father, Captain Steven Albright, served with your husband in Vietnam."

At his words, Nelli's annoyance drained away. She felt sympathy for this young man was reaching out to someone who might have known his father. She searched her memory but couldn't recall Nicholas ever referring to a Captain Steven Albright. "I'm sorry, but I don't believe I ever heard my husband mention your father's name in any of his letters. Was he a helicopter pilot with my husband?"

"No, ma'am." He paused. "He was a prisoner of war."

Nelli had heard stories of how the Vietcong treated their prisoners. She was about to express compassion for what his father must have gone though, when Jake interrupted her thoughts.

"He was a prisoner of war. . .with your husband?"

Nelli shook her head. This young man had been given the wrong information. "I'm sorry, Mr. Albright, but you have the wrong person. My husband, Chief Nicholas Hart, was killed in Vietnam in 1969 when his helicopter crashed. He was never a prisoner of war."

"You're right, about your husband's helicopter. It did go down in 1969, but you're wrong about him being killed. He didn't die in that crash." Jake hesitated. "He was taken prisoner by the Vietcong. That's what the army never told you."

Nelli's heart began to pound as her knees grew weak. With shaking hands, she reached for the nearest kitchen chair and pulled it to her. She knew if she didn't sit down now, she'd fall down. There was no way Nicholas had been a POW. The man on the other end of the line had to be mistaken. There was no way the army made mistakes as grave and heartless as that. After all, they had sent his body home for her to bury. They wouldn't have just sent home a random body. It wasn't possible her Nicholas could have been alive, held as a POW, suffering unimaginable torture the day they believed they'd put him to rest.

"Mrs. Hart." Jake's voice broke through her thoughts. "Are you alright?"

Nelli cleared her throat. "To tell you the truth, Mr. Albright, I'm not sure how I am right now. I am confident of one thing. You, sir, have been misinformed."

Jake didn't hesitate. "No, ma'am, what I've told you is God's honest truth. It's you who has been misinformed."

"If it's the truth, then why am I just finding out about this now from someone who's a complete stranger to me? If your father really was with my husband as a POW, why didn't he come to me years ago to tell me this?"

"That's a hard question to answer. I'd never heard your husband's name until a month ago while sitting next to my father as he lay dying."

"How can you know it's true if your father didn't tell you about it until he was close to his own death?"

"I know he was telling me the truth. He wrote it all down in a letter. He gives an account of everything that happened to your husband, including the truth of how he died."

Nelli wanted to believe this man's news was only the ramblings of an old man on his death bed. However, the sincerity of Jake's belief and the conviction she could hear in his voice made her reconsider. "Well, Mr. Albright, if what you're telling me is true, before I can even consider your outrageous claims, I need to see your father's letter for myself."

"Yes, ma'am, that's why I'm calling you now. I live in Huntsville, but I have business in Savannah next Tuesday. I'd like to tell you in person what my father told me and bring his letter to back up his story. Could we meet on the 29th?"

Nelli looked at the calendar hanging on the wall. The next week was clear. A part of her had hoped she'd find it filled with activities that would make it impossible to meet with him. She sighed. "Yes, I'm free on the 29th. We can meet at my house that afternoon. I'm only about thirty minutes from Savannah depending on which side of town you're staying. Bring the letter claiming my husband was a POW with you."

"Thank you, Mrs. Hart. I want you to know I'm sorry about all of this, but I promised my father I'd tell Chief Hart's family his story. It's something I need to do to fulfill my father's dying wish."

"I'll listen to your father's story, but I'm not making any promises about believing it."

"All I ask is that you listen. I'll see you on Tuesday the 29th."

Nelli hung up. She couldn't imagine what story Jake Albright had to tell, but she admired his determination to follow through on his father's request. Tears began to fill her eyes as memories of how she met Nicholas flooded her mind.

Matt had always been obsessed with helicopters. It began the day he saw one land in Ida's— their hometown's— town square when he was only seven. Nelli's brother's dream of one day flying a helicopter ended when he learned the same eyesight problem that had kept their father from serving in World War II would keep him from being a helicopter pilot. Instead of serving in the military, he enrolled in Armstrong State College, as his father put it, "to prepare for a professional career." His choice of attending Armstrong had everything to do with the fact it was close to Hunter Army Airfield where helicopter pilots were being trained. He would hang out at the airfield every minute he had free. It was there Matt met Tyler Holbrook, who was a helicopter pilot in training. Matt struck up a friendship with Tyler and began inviting him to his home in Ida. Then one day Tyler invited his flight instructor to come with him to see a true Southern plantation. As fate would have it, the instructor Tyler brought with him to the Tucker Plantation that chilly January day was Nicholas Conrad Hart.

Nelli wasn't sure she would call it love at first sight, but there was a definite attraction between the two of them from the very start. Nicholas was not a particularly handsome man. His bright red hair was trimmed too close to his head. His nose was a little too big for his face and off center—she'd later learn it had been broken in a fight during basic training. He was just over six feet tall and on the thin side. But it was his deep, azure blue eyes—by far his most attractive feature—and his easy-going, life-loving, good-hearted personality that captured and won over Nelli's heart.

When fate brought them together that cold winter day, both Nelli and Nicholas knew they'd met the person they were meant to be with for the rest of their lives. The problem they faced was that no one else in Nelli's family was convinced Nicholas was the right person for her. Both her father and Topsy made it clear that Nicholas being ten years her elder was far too much of an age difference. However, their words fell on deaf ears. Nelli didn't have one tiny smidgen of a doubt she'd one day be Nicholas Conrad Hart's wife, and she was determined to overcome any obstacle, including her family, to make it happen.

Nelli graduated valedictorian of her class that May and her family celebrated her accomplishment by giving her a surprise graduation party. They invited friends and relatives—including distant relatives Nelli didn't even know—as well as the entire town of Ida for a barbecue complete with all the traditional Southern fixings. Nicholas, the one person Nelli wanted there, hadn't been invited. But Nelli didn't mind. She had her own plans.

The day after her graduation, she waved good-bye to her family and headed off to Panama City, Florida, for what her family believed would be a celebration week of fun and sun with her high school girlfriends. When she got to Panama City, it wasn't her girlfriends she met. It was Nicholas. The two headed to the Bay County Justice of the Peace where they were pronounced husband and wife. Nelli would forever remember and cherish the love and laughter they shared that first week of their married life.

Nine months after their wedding at the Bay County Courthouse, Nelli gave birth to their first daughter, her father's first grandchild, Topsy's first great grandchild, and her brothers' first niece. They named her Kalliope Mae Hart. They called her Kalli. From the day Kalli was brought home to Tucker Plantation, Nicholas was treated as one of the family's own. As two more daughters— Nicola and Jillian— followed Kalli within the next two years, Nicholas had to keep changing his military housing request for more bedrooms. In the end, they decided the best thing for Nelli and the girls was to remain with her family on Tucker Plantation. As it turned out, it was to be one of the best decisions they would make.

Nicholas continued to instruct helicopter pilots at Hunter Army Airfield, where he was promoted two more times. They were sure his position as an instructor would keep him away from the Vietnam Conflict and out of combat. They were wrong. The girls were six, seven, and eight years old when Nicholas was notified he was being sent to Vietnam, not as an instructor, but as a helicopter pilot. He was given a month's leave before he had to ship out.

Those four weeks flew by faster than any other four weeks in Nelli's life. She and Nicholas were determined to create as many memories as they could with their three young daughters, hoping those memories would be enough to hold on to through the year they would spend apart. Little did they know the memories they'd created during those last four weeks their family was whole would need to last them a lifetime.

Only six months after she kissed Nicholas good-bye, Nelli received a telegram from his commanding officer informing her he was MIA—Missing in Action. He'd been on a rescue mission to transport wounded soldiers from a site where the soldiers had been ambushed when his helicopter crashed over a dense part of the jungle.

One month after receiving the MIA telegram, an army officer and chaplain came to the door to inform her that Nicholas was no longer MIA, but dead. His flag-draped remains were sent home three weeks later and his funeral was held two days after that. At Nelli's request, his casket was never opened. She had what remained of her beloved Nicholas cremated. She and her young daughters scattered his ashes around his favorite spot—the plantation pond and the bench he'd made for her. The flag that had once draped his coffin was still upstairs in her bedroom.

When Nelli and Nicholas met that cold January weekend, she'd believed in her heart of hearts that they were destined to live happily ever after. If only there had been a happy ending to their ever after.

CHAPTER THREE

K alli was sure if she had to answer one more senseless question, she was going to tear her hair out. Why was it so hard for college students to just do what they were instructed to do? She'd handed out her class syllabus at the beginning of the semester which outlined in complete detail the specifics of the course along with student expectations and responsibilities. If a student had hopes of receiving a high score on their research paper, they should be following the timeline she'd included with her syllabus and should be well past the halfway mark by now. The time for questions had passed weeks ago. There was only time now to hunker down and do the work. But there were always those who procrastinated and offered excuses of why they hadn't been able to start. She wanted to shout, "Just get it done, people!" Instead, she smiled through gritted teeth as she answered each inquiry with as much civility as she could muster.

The same thing seemed to happen every year. Yet Kalli was always so hopeful at the beginning of each spring semester that this class of seniors would be different. For a few days, she managed to hold on to the hope that these students might be the ones who would get it right. But she was most always disappointed. It was the same scenario with the top students in the class working hard to turn in excellent research papers and the rest barely getting by. She remembered what her mother had told her and her sisters so many times it was burned into their brains.

Insanity is doing the same thing over and over and expecting different results.

If this was true, then it was official. She was insane. She didn't know what else she could do to change the motivation, dedication, and work ethic of her students. Deep down in her heart, she knew the chances of the students changing were slim to none. All she could do was keep hoping it could be different with the next class.

When the class was over and all her students' questions had been answered, Kalli gathered her computer and papers and went down the hall toward her office. She was looking forward to fixing herself a soothing hot cup of green tea. She was about to open her office door when she remembered the weekly Journalism Department meeting. Her attendance at these meetings, although not a required condition of employment, was strongly encouraged if she was going to retain her good standing in the department. She looked down at her watch. She only had enough time to drop off her things before the meeting. Her cup of tea would have to wait.

It was still hard for Kalli to believe she'd been passed over as chair of the Journalism Department. She was the one who had a Ph.D. in Journalism and Mass Communications from Columbia School of Journalism and had taught journalism for over twenty-five years. The job should have been hers, but the college's good ol' boys had given it to Kip Kidman instead. If she'd gotten the job, she would have stopped the weekly meetings and communicated more through emails and texts. It seemed to Kalli that Kip—what kind of a name was "Kip" anyway— enjoyed the power of his position, but most of all he loved hearing himself talk. And talk he did. The meetings usually lasted an hour, too long in her opinion. She was confident she would be a better chair than Kip, who had limited experience and was young enough to be her son.

"Dr. Abbott, what about this?"

Kalli was brought back to the present by the question. Phoebe, one of her procrastinating students, thrust a paper at her.

Kalli put up both hands as she began walking away. "I'm sorry, Phoebe, but you'll have to make an appointment. I don't have time to look at this right now. I'm late for a meeting."

Kalli had taken several steps away when she was stopped by the sound of a heart-wrenching moan. She turned to find a red-faced, sobbing Phoebe standing in the middle of the hallway. At first, she wasn't sure how she was going to respond to what she considered a gross overreaction on Phoebe's part. Then a memory came flashing back to her of when as an undergraduate she'd been mistakenly placed in an advanced-level logic class. She'd never felt so stupid and lost in her life. She remembered when the professor passed out the final, she'd silently cried the entire ninety minutes without answering a single question. The professor had taken pity on her and instead of failing her, had given her a D. If only Phoebe had asked her if at the beginning of the class if she should withdraw. She could have told her she was in over her head, and this wouldn't be a problem she'd need to deal with now.

Kalli took a deep breath, turned around, and said, "Come on, Phoebe. Let's go to my office. We'll figure this out together."

Kalli could see the gratitude in Phoebe's glistening eyes as she looked up at her. Wiping away her tears, she said, "Thank you, but what about your meeting?"

"They'll just have to get along without me."

Kalli knew she'd get a nasty memo from Kip about missing the meeting, but she knew her student needed her more than she needed to be in Kip's meeting. An hour later Phoebe left Kalli's office with a clear plan on how to proceed with her research. Kalli knew she'd done the right thing by stopping to help. The feeling she had at this exact moment was the reason she hadn't retired from her position. At fifty-nine, with her years of service, she could have been done with the challenges of teaching. She'd had the opportunity to retire and either stay home or start a new career. She sat back and smiled, satisfied she'd made the right choice.

After everyone in the Journalism Department left for the day, Kalli remained, as usual. Never in a hurry to go home, she busied herself with checking and rechecking to make sure everything was set up and ready for the next day. She took care of her correspondence, both physical and digital. Satisfied there was nothing left she could do, she picked up her purse and headed out to her car.

There was a time not that long ago when she couldn't wait to get home to her husband Marshall and son Gabe. As she drove home, she thought back to when her son had been a small child. She'd go home after a long day of teaching to find the house a mess with his toys strewn all around. Later, in his teenage years when she'd arrive home, she'd find a bunch of his friends sprawled out around their family room watching television or playing video games as they ate anything and everything that wasn't nailed down. In those days, she believed it'd be heaven on earth if she could come home to a clean and organized house with fully stocked kitchen cabinets and refrigerator. She was now all too aware of how wrong her thinking had been. Now, she went home to a clean and organized house with fully stocked kitchen cabinets and refrigerator, but the empty house was the exact opposite of heaven.

Gabe, her only child, was now two thousand miles from home, pursuing a Bachelor of Science degree in Environmental Studies at Montana State University. Kalli knew it was her fault he hadn't stayed closer to home by choosing one of the universities in Georgia to get his degree. She'd been the one who'd planned the trip to Yellowstone and Glacier National Parks the summer Gabe turned sixteen. It was that trip that had set her son on an educational path with the end goal of becoming a national park ranger, and where better to start on that path than at Montana State.

Once she was convinced there was no way Gabe could be swayed from his career choice, her only option was to support his goals.

She missed him so much she could almost feel her heart breaking from his absence.

Kalli understood she wouldn't feel the deep heartache of Gabe's distance from home if she still had Marshall in her life. After eighteen years of her life revolving around her son, she was just beginning to adjust to the newness of being alone with her husband when he was taken away from her forever.

Kalli believed Marshall had been a rarity among men his age. He'd loved his family and his God with all his heart and soul. While other men were wrapped up in their careers and advancement in the world, Marshall was all about his family and friendships. He'd been well known in their community as a sincere, devoted Christian and a genuine all-around good guy. He'd had a heart for helping others through service, which led him to his choice of a career as a fireman. His unselfish willingness to help others, a trait Kalli had so admired in her husband, had eventually cost him his life.

Only thirty short days after Gabe left for Montana, Marshall was on his way home early in the morning after coming off a seventy-two-hour work shift at the fire station. Being the Good Samaritan he was, he stopped to help an elderly woman with a flat tire pulled off to the side of the road. Just before he finished changing her tire he'd been struck by a car going seventy miles an hour. The doctors assured Kalli he died instantly without feeling any pain. She wasn't sure if they were telling her the truth or if it was something they told every grieving wife.

Kalli still marveled at how her family had surrounded her with their love and support during the most horrific time of her life. Her mother, who had suffered through the tragedy of losing her own husband, had rushed to be with her. Her two sisters, Nicola and Jilli, along with their families, were there for her as well.

Knowing how devastating his father's death would be to Gabe, Kalli struggled with how she would break the tragic news to him. It was her sisters—to whom Kalli would be forever grateful—who'd flown to Montana to tell him. It was also Nicola and Jilli who convinced Gabe to return to college after the funeral even though he felt his obligation as the only child was to drop out of college and stay home to take care of his mother. And it was Kalli's mother and sisters who stayed with her to help her through the heartbreak and the legalities that come with the death of a husband.

Now home after a long day at work, Kalli pulled into the garage, turned off the car's engine, and sat, allowing the silence to surround her. She closed her eyes and recited a Bible verse she'd learned as a child and had repeated every day since the most tragic of all her days.

"I can do all things through Christ who strengthens me."

This had become her ritual. It gave her the courage to get out of her car and face her empty house. Taking a deep breath, she opened her car door, got out, pulled her shoulders back, and walked in her house ready to face another evening home alone.

CHAPTER FOUR

The last place Nicola wanted to be on a beautiful day like today was sitting at a conference table listening to these junior executives tell her how Sweet Hart Bakery could become a household name if she would sell it to the big conglomerate food chain they represented. As far as she was concerned, her maiden name in the middle of her bakery name said it all. Sweet Hart Bakery was hers. She was the one who'd started it thirty years ago. To the shock of her family and most of her friends, it had become a success. She'd opened her fourth store a little over a year ago, and all four stores were doing quite well financially. Now this guy wanted them to sell out to his company that would swallow it up into their big chain of stores.

Nicola was well aware her bakeries wouldn't be the success they were if it hadn't been for her brilliant, handsome business manager Alexandre, her husband. It was her sweet creations the customers craved, but all would have fallen flat if not for Alexandre's marketing ideas of getting the customers in the door to purchase them. He was the one who'd believed in her talents from the very beginning when others scoffed at the idea of her opening a bakery. She knew one of the smartest decisions she'd made was to trust her husband with the business part of running her bakeries. After all, he was the one who'd graduated from ESSEC Business School in France.

The love and respect Nicola had for her husband was why she was sitting at this long conference table listening to a man who didn't have a clue about how much of her soul she'd put into her bakeries drone on and on about the benefits of selling out. Her husband believed they needed to be looking toward the future by securing a good retirement for themselves instead of living the rest of their lives with the headaches and challenges of owning and running their own business.

At one time they'd hoped their daughter and son, Alexandra, and André, would want to join them in the business and eventually take it over. However, both children had made it clear they had other interests and ambitions. Nicola could respect their decisions, but she still found it hard to accept.

Nicola hadn't liked the idea of selling out from the minute Alexandre pitched the idea to her. Even after thirty years of getting up well before four almost every morning, she loved the trials and challenges each day brought. She felt it kept her alive and vibrant. She couldn't imagine retiring at only fifty-eight years old. What would they do with the rest of their lives?

She recalled how last year they'd decided that, instead of spending their usual two weeks in France visiting relatives, they'd extend their stay to four weeks. Alexandre's uncle offered them his villa in Sainte-Maxime along the Mediterranean Coast for the last two weeks of their stay. The first six days they filled with fun and sun, but the next eight they searched for something to occupy their time. She'd realized then they weren't ready for a quiet, relaxing life—at least not yet. If they couldn't find contentment and happiness at one of the most beautiful beaches in the world, what hope was there in finding it in

South Georgia? Had Alexandre forgotten so soon what it was like to have time on his hands?

Nicola uncrossed her legs as she shifted her body in hopes of finding a more comfortable position. She was tired of sitting. She glanced up at the clock on the wall, wondering how much longer it would be before she could leave. She'd lost interest a long time ago in what was being said. Plus, she already knew what her answer was going to be to selling her bakeries to these people.

Even when Nicola tried to give her full attention to the pitch, she found herself distracted by her husband's profile. It still amazed her that this attractive, charming, charismatic man had chosen her— a redheaded, blue-eyed, freckle-faced, hot-tempered young girl. She opened her notebook and began doodling as her mind traveled back to when they first met.

It was the summer between Nicola's freshman and sophomore year at Merritt Atlantic College. While attending Ida County High School, she'd worked hard to become the top girl's high school tennis player in Georgia which earned her a tennis scholarship at Merritt. She'd been playing tennis since the day her father put a tennis racket in her hand at the tender age of five. From the first volley, it was evident to all she'd been born to play tennis. Truth be known, tennis was the only reason she'd gone to college.

That summer, their tennis coach, Coach Cunningham, arranged for the Merritt Atlantic College Women's Tennis Team to play in several European tournaments. Nicola was beyond excited with the prospect of spending the summer playing tennis and traveling through Europe. Never having been more than one hundred miles from her home in Ida, Georgia, it was a dream come true for her.

Nicola knew the one obstacle standing in the way of her dream becoming a reality was her mother. Out of the three sisters, Nicola had the reputation of being the adventurous, try-anything-once sister. When the three sisters decided to be dare devils, it was Nicola who took the dare to roller skate down their playground slide for which she earned a broken arm. When the three sisters decided to become rodeo performers, it was Nicola who volunteered to rope the bull from the back of her horse. As soon as the rope went around the bull's neck, he'd taken off like a shot. Nicola was pulled from her saddle and drug thirty feet through the pasture before letting go of the rope. That trick earned her three broken ribs, a broken nose, and a total of twenty-four stitches down her back. Through most of Nicola's life, she'd heard her mother declare, "You're going to be the death of me!"

Nicola was aware she had a challenge ahead of her with convincing her mother she should be spending the summer in Europe playing tennis instead of going home to help at the Hart & Soul Inn, her mother's bed, and breakfast business. As it turned out, it was Coach Cunningham who approached her mother before she even had a chance to plead her case. Coach persuaded her mother the experience she would gain from playing top rated European opponents would be invaluable. In the end, with reservations— she wasn't sure Nicola was ready for Europe or Europe was ready for Nicola— her mother had given her consent for Nicola to travel with the tennis team under the supervision of Coach Cunningham. Nicola left Merritt Atlantic College for Europe the day after she finished with finals never to return.

The tennis team began their European Tour in England where they played in three tournaments. Their tournaments never started before one in the afternoon, which left the mornings to visit the places she'd never imagined she'd ever see in person. She decided if she had a choice to live anywhere other than Georgia, she'd choose to live in England. When they traveled on to Italy, she changed her mind deciding it would be there she would want to live with its impressive architecture and beautiful landscapes. That is how it continued for Nicola. She fell in love with each country they visited until they arrived in France, the last European County on their tour.

Their team's first tournament in France was scheduled to be played at the Tennis Club de Paris. Nicola was most excited about this tournament. She was to play Celeste Touchard, an up-coming French tennis star who had a following and had been featured in an elite French tennis magazine. Since starting the European Tour with her team, Nicola was the only one who had won every match she'd played. Her confidence level was high as she stepped onto the tennis court certain she'd be the winner once again. Two hours and thirty minutes later, she walked off defeated. She'd lost all three sets in quick succession. She'd never lost so profoundly. She was numb as she'd watched the matches that followed hers.

After the tournament when the team was back at their hotel, Nicola headed for her room hoping to crawl into bed, cover her head, and cry herself to sleep. Her teammates had other ideas for her. They were not going to allow her to feel sorry for herself when they were in Paris, one of the most exciting cities in Europe. Even though the last thing she wanted to do was go out with the team to see the sights of Paris, when they came pounding on her door demanding she come out, she reluctantly gave in to their demands. She'd go out with them if it would make her teammates happy, but promised she wasn't going to have fun.

As Nicola stood with her team outside the hotel waiting for the two cabs they'd arranged to take them to the Eiffel Tower, she felt a tap on her shoulder. She turned around to find a tall, well-tanned, dark-haired, attractive man with long, thick black eyelashes framing exotic olive-green eyes, smiling down at her with the most perfect white teeth.

"Pardonnez-moi, vous n'êtes pas Nicola Hart?"

Nicola was struck silent by this attractive stranger's question; she could only stare up at him wide-eyed. She had no idea what he'd asked her, but she liked how her name sounded coming from his mouth. After several seconds of gazing into his handsome face, she said the only thing she could think to say. "Do you speak English? I'm from Ida, Georgia, where there isn't much call for learning French."

The Frenchman gave a hearty laugh. "Please forgive me. I will ask again so a person from Ida, Georgia can understand. Are you Nicola Hart?"

Nicola put her hands on her hips. "That all depends on who is asking?"

As he looked down at her, she noticed how his eyes sparkled. He spoke with a lilting French accent. "I beg your forgiveness." He bowed deeply. "I am Alexandre Michel Giraud. I watched you play today against Celeste."

Nicola raised an eyebrow as she asked with an icy tone, "Are you here to remind me I lost to her?"

Nicola watched as a hurt look passed over Alexandre's face. "Never would I do that." He put his hand to his chest. "I came to tell you I watched your matches today, and I wanted you to know how much I enjoyed watching you. You play with such passion and... gusto."

"Gusto?"

"Yes. It is a word, yes?"

"It is, but not one I hear many people use, but I like the way you say it." Nicola smiled up at Alexandre offering her hand. "I am Nicola Hart. I thank you for the compliment."

Alexandre took her hand in his, but instead of shaking it as Nicola intended, he bent down and kissed it. When she felt his soft lips brush across her hand, she wanted the moment to last forever. "Bonjour, mon cher. I think I will not call you Nicola, but give you a French name." He stood, still holding her hand, he smiled at her. "I shall call you Nicolette."

Never in her life had Nicola felt an instant affection for anyone like she felt for Alexandre in that moment. The words she would use later in life when she told the story of how they met to their children were "he swept me off of my feet". That's exactly how it felt to her from the very moment he kissed her hand.

It was Alexandre who took Nicola from the hotel to show her the sights of Paris that evening. She'd been wrong. She had the most fun of her life that night. She spent every free minute she had with Alexandre over the next two days. Each evening they spent exploring Paris and getting to know one another. Nicola found the more time they spent together the harder it was to be apart.

When the time came for the team to leave Europe and return to the United States, Nicola realized there was no way she could leave Alexandre behind. She'd fallen head over heels in love with him. In the end, she made the decision not to return to the United States and Merritt Atlantic College with her teammates. Against Coach Cunningham's protests, she stayed behind in France to begin a whole new life with Alexandre. When she returned to the United States five years later, Alexandre was by her side.

"Nicola, wouldn't you agree?"

Hearing her name, Nicola jerked her head up. Her blue eyes darted around the room. Composing herself, she brushed her hair from her face and smiled over at her husband, hoping it was he who'd asked her the question. "Would you mind repeating the question, sweetheart?"

Alexandre smiled back at her. "I told these gentlemen we'd need to take a closer look at this proposal before making any decisions." His olive-green eyes met hers. "Wouldn't you agree, *mon cher*?"

Nicola sat up straight in her chair. "I most certainly do."

CHAPTER FIVE

Jilli glanced at her watch as she hurried from the Ida County Courthouse. A case she'd been confident would be settled by noon had taken twice as long as she'd expected. She had exactly fifteen minutes to go home, change out of her suit into comfortable clothes, and get to the Spartans' Baseball Field. She was determined she wasn't going to miss another game in which her youngest child, sixteen-year-old Drew, was scheduled to be the starting pitcher. It still bothered her knowing she'd missed too many of Morgan's softball games and Hazel's tennis matches when they were in high school. During those years, her focus and energy had been on building a successful law practice. She hadn't realized how consumed she'd been with her career while those fleeting, growing-up years of her two daughters had slipped by and were now gone forever. That's why she'd made a promise to herself to be there for as many of the important events in Drew's life as possible. She wished she could slow down the time she had left with Drew, but was aware it wasn't within her motherly powers.

Jilli made it home in under five minutes. She pulled her long, blond hair back into a ponytail, changed into jeans and Spartan sweatshirt, and was out the door in her car in under ten. She might not make it for the opening pitch, but if the stoplights were in her favor she'd make it to the ball field before Drew threw his last pitch of the first inning. As soon as she pulled into the ball field parking lot, she spotted her husband's hunter-green Land Rover. She pulled in next to it and got out of her car. She quickened her steps when she heard cheers and shouts of excitement coming from the stadium. She hoped they were for the Spartans. She bought her ticket and hurried through the gate just in time to see the home team leave the field.

When her cell phone rang, she glanced down at the caller ID to see it was Morgan calling. She let it go to voice mail as she put her phone in her back pocket. Even though she felt guilty, she knew she didn't have the time or the energy to listen to another of her daughter's self-made dramas. If ever there was a drama queen in this family, it was Morgan.

Jilli was searching the stands for Ian when she heard his voice in her ear as he wrapped his arms around her. "I wish you could have seen Drew pitch that inning. It was three up and three down."

Jilli turned in his arms. "I hate I missed it, but I'm here now." Taking a step back, she looked into his eyes. "He is going to pitch another inning, right? Please tell me I haven't missed his pitching."

Ian smiled down at her. "After that performance, the coach would be a fool to take him out."

Jilli sighed with relief. "Thank heavens."

"Come on. I don't want to miss another minute of this game." Ian took Jilli's hand in his and led her toward the stadium seats.

Before taking her seat, Jilli scanned the crowded stadium, looking for her mother, who was Drew's biggest fan. Her mother had been coming to his games since he was a four-year-old T-Ball player and rarely missed one. "I wonder where Mama is sitting."

"I'm sure she's sitting with some of her friends. You know how she is."

Jilli sat down. Throughout the game, she continued to search for her mother among the fans as she watched Drew pitch seven innings without the other team scoring. The final score was 9-0. Fans all around were congratulating her and Ian on another win for Drew's first season as a starting pitcher. It was shaping up to be a great season for the Ida County High School Spartans.

Jilli couldn't stop smiling as she walked back to her car. It'd been a good game. Mama would have enjoyed every minute of watching her grandson pitch. Drew and his grandmother had been close since the minute she'd brought Drew home from the hospital. There was a bond between them that hadn't been there with her mother's other grandchildren.

Jilli began to worry in earnest, and images of the terrible things that could have happened to her mother began to creep into her thoughts. By the time she arrived home, she'd convinced herself the only reason her mother would have missed her favorite grandchild's big game was because something awful had to have happened to keep her away.

She unbuckled her seat belt as she pulled her cell phone from her back pocket and called her mother's landline. She let it ring ten times. Mama only had the one phone in the kitchen, without an answering machine attached. If she were in another part of the house—Jilli kept telling her she needed to move to a smaller house since that house was way too big for her now that she'd closed down the business—it would take her several minutes to answer the call. Ending the call, Jilli frowned. She knew it'd be futile to even try to reach Mama on her cell. That phone spent most of its time in the bottom of her purse upstairs in the bedroom. Jilli decided to give it a try anyway. When it went to voice mail after the first ring, she shook her head in exasperation knowing that, once again, her mother had forgotten to charge her phone. There was only one thing left to do. Jilli pulled her seat belt back across her body and buckled it in place as she started the car. She backed out of her driveway and turned left, heading to her mother's house. She wouldn't be able to think about anything else until she saw for herself nothing terrible had happened.

CHAPTER SIX

fter ending Jake's call, Nelli remained in the kitchen chair for a good long while with her head in her hands allowing herself a heart-wrenching cry. It was rare for her to cry. It was one of the many things she didn't allow herself to do. When she'd gotten the news Nicholas had been killed, she cried not for just days, but for weeks. She'd felt she would die from the loss of the love of her life. Each day her heart had sunk deeper into the depths of sorrow and despair.

Nelli closed herself off from her family and the rest of the world after receiving the news of her husband's death. Her family did all they could to help her through those first weeks of her fresh grief. Her grandmother and brother took on the responsibility of caring for her three young daughters. Her father handled the arrangements for the funeral and contacted the Army to get all the paperwork in order so she could receive her rightful benefits. All the while, her family was in constant prayer asking for God's strength and blessings to help Nelli, the girls, and each of them through this tragedy. God did answer their prayers, but not in the way any of Nelli's family imagined.

It was Topsy who had been the answer to their prayers. In her typical fashion, she hadn't done it with gentle sympathy and understanding love. She did it with threats and shouts of the cold, hard facts she knew Nelli must face.

At first, Nelli didn't appreciate what Topsy did for her. It took her months before she could acknowledge she owed her life as well as her children's lives to Topsy. It took her even longer to admit how much she loved her for doing it. To this day, she could recall every minute of that day Topsy literally pulled her out of the bed she hadn't left in two months and threw her into the ice-cold shower; pajamas and all. As Nelli sputtered and spit out every ugly word she could think of, Topsy held her under that frigid stream of water shouting in her face.

"You don't have the right to just curl up and die! You have three little girls who just lost their father. I will not let them lose their mother too! It's not just your world that's fallen apart. It's their world too. They need to know you love them! They need to know you will not leave them alone! They are depending on you!"

Nelli tried her best to push Topsy away shouting at the top of her lungs, "I can't do it! I'm not strong enough! Leave me alone!"

Topsy was having none of it. With all her strength, she held onto Nelli as the ice-cold water poured over their bodies. "Coranelia Mae Tucker Hart, remember what the Bible tells us we are to do in times of trouble. Psalm chapter 31 verse 24 tells you to 'Be strong and take heart, all you who hope in the Lord.' It's time for you to put your hope in the Lord. He's speaking directly to you telling you to take heart and be strong."

Staring into Topsy's determined eyes, Nelli fell silent.

"My precious Nelli, you may not be strong enough by yourself, but you can find your courage, your strength, and your hope in your Lord and Savior. With His help you can get dressed! With His help you can fix those girls their breakfast! With His help you can leave your grief behind and show your daughters the strong, courageous woman you are, and who they can be one day." Topsy turned off the water whispering into Nelli's ear, "Plus, I promise, if you don't get dressed and going every day from here on out, I will throw you in this cold shower every single morning until you do!"

Nelli did what Topsy demanded of her that day and every day after. It was on that day she made a promise to never allow herself to cry tears of soul-wrenching sorrow again. She feared if those tears ever started again, they'd never end. There hadn't been another time in her life when she'd allowed those tears of sorrow to flow like they had then — until today.

Nelli got up from the kitchen chair and set it back under the table. Walking over to the kitchen counter, she tore a paper towel from the rack, blew her nose, and wiped the tears from her face. Even though her beloved Topsy had been gone from her life for years, she wished with all her heart she could tell her all about the phone call from Jake. She had no doubt her grandmother would have some Bible verse or words of wisdom to share. Since that wasn't possible, it was time to get busy and put things in order. First, she needed to locate the papers the army had sent a month after sending what remained of Nicholas's body— at least what she'd believed to be his body. She'd filed those papers away years ago and hadn't looked at them since. She needed to start her search in the filing cabinets in her office upstairs.

It wasn't until Nelli was standing at her office door that she realized it had been months since she'd been inside that room. She could remember when she'd spent more time in this office than she had in her own bed. For years it had been the busiest room in the house. That was when the house had been a bed and breakfast.

It was the business she, with the help of family, had started after Nicholas was killed. She'd known she had to do something to support herself and the girls. It was her father who'd come up with the idea of making the once grand plantation house into a bed and breakfast. After all, it had once supported a family as a boardinghouse.

With the money from Nicholas's life insurance and the death gratuity she received from the army, Nelli had added bathrooms to every bedroom, bought new beds, given a fresh coat of paint to all the rooms, and modernized the kitchen. Because her father and brothers pitched in with the renovations, there was enough money to turn the detached garage into a place for her father and Jim-Jim. Nelli and the three girls lived in the two small rooms where her father and his brothers had once lived when it'd served the family as a boardinghouse.

Once the plantation house had been transformed into a bed and breakfast, they needed to have a name for it. One evening, Nelli came across a record she remembered Topsy playing for her when she was a little girl. She put the record on the turntable. It was when she listened to the first line of the Hoagy Carmichael song she knew what the name of their bed and breakfast had to be. "Heart and Soul, I fell in love with you, heart and soul." Her heart had fallen in love with a Hart and her soul would always belong to that Hart. The house was christened the Hart & Soul Inn.

Because the house was only two miles from one of the exits on the newly constructed Interstate 16, business was good. Throughout the year travelers on their way to or from Savannah who wanted a more personal experience than they could get at a motel would book their stay at the Hart & Soul Inn. Topsy helped by taking over the kitchen. Her specialty was the old-fashioned Southern dishes she'd grown up with. Many guests booked an extra night just so they could sit down for one more meal. Her breakfasts were legendary, and no guest ever left hungry.

The business not only supported Nelli and her daughters, but also Topsy, her father, and her brother. It took all of them to make it a success. While Topsy tended to the meals, Jim-Jim and her father worked the farm and kept the grounds around the house immaculate. Nelli took care of the bookings and managed the business. It turned out she had a good head for business. As Topsy and her father aged, the girls took over their jobs. Nicola became as good a cook as Topsy, specializing in baking. Kalli found her happiness in working outside with Uncle Jim-Jim and her Papaw, making things grow, and Jilli helped Nelli run the business. Nelli recalled those days as good times when her family worked together.

Nelli opened the door to the office and stood unmoving. Her office was as she'd left it months before with nothing out of place. There were three filing cabinets lined up against the wall. She hoped she wouldn't have to go through all three to find the papers she was searching for. There had to be hundreds of file folders in each to go through.

Slapping her hands together, Nelli spoke out loud, "Well, I don't suppose those papers are going to come to me."

She blew her breath out slowly as she walked over to the closest filing cabinet. Opening the top drawer, her search began.

CHAPTER SEVEN

As Jilli drove down her mother's pecan-tree-lined driveway, she wasn't sure what she might find when she reached the house. She hoped Mama had gotten busy with some project and simply forgotten all about Drew's big ball game. After all, it was a fact her mother was getting older, and forgetfulness was usually a part of aging. She pulled her car around to the back of the house and took it as good sign when she saw her mother's 2017 Equinox parked next to her 2004 Silverado pickup truck. That meant she was most likely in the house somewhere. She'd worried she would have to drive around Ida looking for her.

Jilli parked next to the truck and headed for the back door. She knew she'd find the door unlocked. It was always unlocked. No matter how many times she and her sisters warned their mother about the dangers of not locking her doors, her doors remained unlocked.

Jilli opened the back door as she called out, "Mama! Mama!" She listened for an answer. Silence.

She walked through the house, calling out as she moved from room to room. "Mama! Mama! It's Jilli. Where are you?"

After searching the first floor without finding her mother, Jilli made her way to the stairway in the front hallway. Her chest tightened. Standing at the bottom of the stairs, she shouted as loud as she could. "Mama! Please answer me!"

"What in the world are you hollering about?"

Jilli looked up to see her mother standing at the top of the stairs with one hand on her hip and the other holding a file folder. She rushed up the stairs two at a time until she reached the top and wrapped her mother in her arms. "I've been calling and calling you. Why didn't you answer? I thought something awful had happened to you!"

"Why in the world would you jump to that conclusion?"

Jilli frowned as she stepped back. "Mama, you missed Drew's baseball game."

Her mother put her hand over her mouth. "Oh, no! I got so caught up in what I was doing. Is he upset with me?"

"Drew was so tuned into that game, I doubt he even noticed Ian and I were there."

Her mother cocked her head to one side. "How was his pitching?"

"Oh, Mama, he did great! The best he's ever done."

"That's my boy! I can't believe I missed seeing it!"

Jilli put her arm around her mother's shoulder. "It's okay. There'll be other games."

"True, others, but not that one."

"Mama, what were you so caught up in that you forgot your favorite grandson's big game?"

Her mother rolled her eyes as she shook her head back and forth. "You're not going to believe the call I got straight out of the blue this morning."

Jilli could hear the distress in her mother's voice. "What's going on, Mama? Are Kalli and Nicola okay?"

"It's a long story, Let's go to the kitchen. I'll fix us a cup of tea."

As they reached the kitchen each fell into their long-ago established routine of afternoon tea. Jilli filled the teakettle with water as her mother set out two cups from the cupboard, placed a tea bag of green tea with pomegranate—their favorite— in each cup, and set the sugar bowl on the kitchen table.

Nelli took the top from the cake stand. "You want some of this pound cake Mary Lou Stevens brought over the other day?"

"Is it good?"

"It's tolerable."

"I'll try it."

Nelli cut two pieces and placed each on a dessert plate, got out two forks, and carried everything to the table. Jilli filled the two cups with water from the teakettle and handed one cup to her mother. The two sat down at the table across from one another.

Jilli picked up her fork and took a bite of the pound cake. "You're right. It's tolerable. Now, tell me what's in that folder that's so important it kept you from your grandson's baseball game."

"It's not what's in the folder as much as it is the phone call I got that sent me on a quest to find it."

Nelli opened the folder and spread the papers out in the space between them, turning them so Jilli could read them.

Jilli frowned. "Why are you looking at these old files about Daddy's service record and his death, Mama?"

Her mother took a sip of her tea, set her cup down, and folded her hands in front of her. "I got a call today from a man who made some unbelievable claims about your Daddy."

Jilli considered her mother's statement. She reached out for her mother's folded hands. "Mama, Daddy's been dead for fifty years. How can anyone be making claims about him, believable or unbelievable?"

Nelli pulled her hands away from her daughter's. "Don't you think I know that, Jillian!"

Jilli was taken aback. It was out of character for her mother to snap at her like that. She leaned in closer, speaking in a soft tone. "I'm sorry. I do know you know that."

Nelli gave her daughter a half smile. "I'm sorry, too. It's just that. . ." She turned away.

"Mama, what is it? Please, tell me."

Her mother turned back, and Jilli was alarmed see the tears filling her dark brown eyes and running down her cheeks. Crying was out of character for her mother. She anxiously waited for her to explain to her why the call had upset her.

Her mother cleared her throat. "His name is Jake. He told me he has a letter proving your father didn't die in that helicopter crash like the army told us. He said he was taken prisoner by the Vietcong. He claims my husband, your father, was a prisoner of war. I can't stand the thought that I sat idly by mourning his death when I could have been fighting for his rescue if I'd only known."

Jilli stared wide eyed and open mouthed at her weeping mother. "That's ridiculous! Why would he make such a claim? And why is he making it now after so many years have passed?"

Her mother slapped both hands down on the table, almost knocking over her cup. "That's what I've been wondering ever since I hung up the phone. Why now?"

"Oh, Mama, it doesn't make any sense."

"I know." She scattered the papers spread out on the table. "Why would the army give me these supposed official papers confirming the death of Chief Nicholas Conrad Hart? Why weren't they aware he wasn't dead and was being held as a prisoner of war?" She reached out and gripped Jilli's hand. "And worst of all, Jilli, whose body did they send home to us? Whose body was it we cried over? And, if he didn't die in that helicopter crash, where is his body now?" She buried her face in her arms and her body shook with sobs.

Jilli's chair fell to the floor as she rushed to her brokenhearted mother's side. Taking her into her arms, she promised. "Don't you worry. I'll get the answers, Mama, even if I have to travel to Vietnam to find them."

It took Jilli several hours before she was able to calm her mother and get her to eat a bowl of tomato soup with a few saltine crackers. After eating, her mother fell into bed exhausted from the emotional upheaval of the day. Before falling asleep, she begged Jilli not to leave her alone. Jilli agreed without hesitation. She knew this was the place she needed to be. It had been frightening to see her mother, who had always been a strong and self-reliant woman, break down like she had.

After getting her mother settled and making sure she was asleep, Jilli knew she needed to let Ian know she wouldn't be home and why. She went on a search for her cell phone. After spending fifteen frustrating minutes looking, she remembered she'd gotten out of her car without it. When she pulled open the back door, a draft of cool night air hit her. She grabbed one of her mother's flannel shirts from the hook by the back door as she went out into the moonlit night alive with the hoots of a barn owl, the distant cry of coyotes, and the songs of tree frogs.

On her way to her car, she stopped to breathe in the faint fragrance of the blooms from her mother's Confederate Jasmine growing around her front porch. She slowed her steps, taking in the familiar scents and sounds of the country.

When she and Ian had first moved out to the lake, their house had been the third one to be built in the subdivision. It had felt like country living. But now, twenty years later, there were close to twenty houses surrounding the lake. As she took another deep breath, she realized how much she missed living in the country far away from the sounds and smells of a neighborhood.

Jilli spotted her phone on the passenger's seat as soon as she opened the car door. She had five text messages and two voice mails waiting. Two of the text messages and one voice mail were from Morgan. The rest were from Ian. She sat down in the driver's seat. She was ashamed that, until this moment, she hadn't given a thought to him. She hadn't even told him she was going to check on her mother when she'd driven away from the house. She hadn't given any thought to the possibility he might worry about her and where she'd gone after the game.

Sitting alone in her car, Jilli wondered why she hadn't considered Ian's feelings. Now that she thought about it, it had been a long time since she'd thought about how her actions affected him. She smiled remembering how they'd met.

When she'd first moved to Ida she was at a loss as to what to do besides work and sleep. It was her mother who came to the rescue taking her from her mundane life with an introduction to the young pediatrician who had just moved to Ida, Dr. Ian Holder Parker. When Nelli learned Ian was also a graduate of Mercer like Jilli, she saw her opportunity to get the two most eligible single people in town together. She invited Jilli and Ian to her house for dinner under the guise of talking with two high school seniors from her church who were interested in attending Mercer University. Once the two met, it was love at first sight. They were married only three short months later. Their love soon produced three children— two daughters and one son.

During the years they'd spent raising their three children and building their careers, they'd had little time left over for one another. They weren't as busy these days now that their daughters were out on their own and both of their practices were established. Yet it still seemed like they didn't have time for one another. Or could it be they just didn't take the time?

Jilli leaned her head on the steering wheel as a tear ran down her cheek. If she was being honest with herself, she had to consider the possibility she was the one who wasn't making time for Ian. She was the one who never said "no" when asked to serve on a church or community committee. She was the chair of two civic groups and president of the Ida County High School Booster Club. Plus, she was guilty of spending what free time she had taking care of her mother instead of her husband.

Jilli sat up straight, shaking those troubling thoughts out of her head. She had enough to deal with right now. She'd call Ian now and think about their relationship later, when she didn't have such pressing matters to handle.

Ian answered on the first ring. She could hear the concern mixed with a hint of irritation in his voice. "Jilli, are you okay? Where have you been? I've been worried sick!"

"I'm sorry, Ian. I'm fine. I came out to Mama's to see why she missed Drew's game." She blew out a breath. "It turned into a real drama out here, Ian."

Ian's voice immediately filled with concern. "Is your mother alright? Do you need me to come out there?"

"No, no, there's no need. I've gotten everything under control for now."

"What's going on?"

The sound of sincere worry in his voice, brought tears to Jilli's eyes. She wiped them away as she shared what her mother had told her.

"Do you think this Jake guy is telling the truth or do you think it's some kind of scam he's running on your mother?"

Jilli considered his question for a minute. "I honestly don't know, Ian, but I intend to find out more about Jake Albright and this father of his."

"Poor guy! He doesn't know what kind of hornets' nest he's walked into when Jillian Ashcroft gets involved."

Jilli laughed. "For now, all I'm going to get involved in is a bed and a good night's sleep."

"So, you're staying there tonight?"

"I promised Mama I would. She really needs me to be here, Ian."

"Then that's where you should be."

"I think before I head up to bed, I need to call Kalli and Nicola. I'm not looking forward to telling them."

"Why don't you wait until tomorrow after you've had a good night's sleep to give them the news?"

"Because I'd never hear the end of it if they found out I didn't tell them right away. You know how they react if they think they've been left out."

"You're right. It'll save you a lot of grief if you bite the bullet and call them tonight."

"Thanks. I'll call you in the morning to let you know my plans and how the night went."

"Okay. Sleep tight. Remember, I'm always here for you, and I love you."

"I count on that. I love you too."

CHAPTER EIGHT

Jilli felt unsettled after her call with Ian ended. A feeling of dread came over her at the thought of telling her two sisters about the phone call their mother had received. Even though she knew she'd eventually have to make those calls, she decided they could wait a little while longer. For now, she'd take advantage of the beauty and stillness of the clear, moonlit night. She walked to the front porch and sat on the fan-back red cedar swing her Papaw had built long ago specifically for their front porch.

As she slowly swung back and forth, Jilli closed her eyes, willing memories of her father to come to her. As usual, few came. She'd only been six years old when he'd left for Vietnam, and seven years old when his body, or at least what his family believed to be his body, had been sent home. Most of what she knew about her father she'd learned from her sisters, Topsy, Papaw, or her uncle. Surprisingly, her mother rarely spoke of him. She smiled to herself remembering some of the funny stories Uncle Jim-Jim used to talk about the adventures he and her father had together, but she'd never been sure if they were true, or tall tales he'd made up to entertain his nieces.

Opening her eyes, she looked up at the star-filled sky. If it were any other night like this, she'd say it was a peaceful night. But nothing peaceful was going on around this house tonight. Jilli knew she couldn't put off calling her sisters much longer. They needed to know what was happening with their family.

Because Kalli was her calm and more sensible sister. Jilli decided to phone her first. She tapped her foot to the ring back music on Kalli's phone as she waited for her to answer. She was thinking of what message she could leave on voice mail when she heard Kalli's breathless voice.

"Don't hang up! I'm here, Jilli!"

"What took you so long? I was about to leave you a voice mail."

"I was in the kitchen making a cup of tea, but my phone was in the living room." Kalli chuckled. "The older I get the farther apart those two rooms are!"

Jilli laughed along with her sister. Even though Kalli was only two years older, she always made it sound like it was much more.

"How did Drew do today? Mama said he was going to pitch. Wish I could have been there."

"Drew did great. I wish you could have been there too. Most of all, I wish Mama had been there."

"Mama wasn't there? That's odd. That's all she talked about yesterday when I spoke to her."

"I thought it was odd too. That's why I came out here to see why she missed Drew's game. I got worried something may have happened to her like falling down the stairs or out the back door."

"Did something happen?"

Jilli could hear the apprehension in Kalli's voice.

"Nothing physical, but something has happened." Jilli went on to tell her sister all about the phone call from Jake Albright. When Jilli finished her revelation, she silently waited for her sister's reaction.

"Well, it's a lie. The United States Army does not make reckless mistakes like telling a family their loved one is dead when he's alive and a prisoner of war no less, or sending the wrong body home to a grieving family. That man just tried to sell our sweet Mama a great big bald-faced lie."

The anger and bitterness in Kalli's voice surprised Jilli. She would have expected such a reaction from Nicola, but not from her usually calm, coolheaded oldest sister. "But Kalli, Jake Albright says he has a letter that proves Daddy was a POW of the Vietcong. Don't you think there's a chance he just might be telling the truth? Shouldn't we wait until we meet with him to see this letter before deciding if it's a lie or not?"

"Spoken like a true lawyer. No! We can't allow Mama to meet with that man. There's no telling what he could be up to, Jilli. For all we know, he could be some crazy, wacko guy who gets his kicks from getting older women to invite him into their homes and then he robs them or kills them!"

Jilli took her phone away from her ear as Kalli continued her rant. It was obvious her sister had lost control of her senses. She waited until there was silence on the other end before bringing her phone back to her ear. "Kalli, you have to calm down. You can't say any of that to Mama. She's upset enough the way it is. She doesn't need you going on and on like you're the one who's crazy and wacko. That's not going to help anyone. We need to take this one step at a time. The first thing I'm going to do is check out Jake Albright and his father. We can proceed from there."

"I'm not sure I can calm down, Jilli! This whole thing is simply wrong."

"Right or wrong, it's something we have to deal with. The most important thing we can do right now is not upset Mama any more than she already is. She's faced tough times before and gotten through them. She'll get through this too. She needs our support, Kalli, not our anger and accusations."

Jilli could hear Kalli take a deep breath. "You may be right, baby sister, Mama does need our support. Maybe I overreacted a tad."

"A tad!! Good grief, if you think that was just a tad, I'd hate to see what you thought was a huge overreaction."

"Okay! Okay! I'm calming down now."

"If this was your reaction, Kalli, I'm terrified to call Nicola to tell her. Can you imagine?"

"Listen, you've dealt with enough today. Let me be the one to tell Nicola. I can handle her."

It only took Jilli an instant to consider Kalli's suggestion. "Oh, Kalli, would you really do that for me?"

"After the way I reacted, it's the least I can do."

"You just lifted a huge burden off of me."

"Are you still at Mama's house or are you home?"

"Mama was so upset; I didn't think she should be alone. I'm going to spend the night. I don't have anything pressing tomorrow, so I'll probably spend the day with her too."

"I think that's a good idea. What do you think about me coming down tomorrow and staying for a few days? Maybe I can even persuade Nicola to come along. We could have a sleepover. We haven't had one of those in a long time."

Jilli smiled. "I think that's a great idea. I'm sure Mama would love to have all three of us here with her."

"Then I'll see y'all tomorrow. Thanks for being there for Mama, Jilli. Love you."

"I love you too, Kalli."

Jilli remained in the porch swing, thinking about all they were going to have to face in the coming days. She was organizing a mental list of what she needed to do to check out Jake's story when she saw headlights coming down the driveway. She couldn't imagine who would be coming to her mother's house at this time of night. Her heart began to pound. She was heading to go back inside when she noticed the familiar "Mercer" front plate on her husband's Land Rover.

Jilli stood at the top of the front porch steps with her hands over her heart watching as Ian got out of the car holding two insulated tumblers she recognized. "You scared me to death, Ian! What are you doing here?"

Ian smiled up at her, taking the steps two at a time and holding one of the tumblers out to her. "I thought we should have a cup of hot chocolate together like we used to do every night before kids and work made us too exhausted to do anything but fall into bed."

Jilli took the tumbler from his hand. "I can't believe you remembered. How did you know exactly what I needed tonight?"

"Because I'm your soul mate. I've always known exactly what you need. Did you forget?" Ian pulled Jilli into his arms and kissed her.

Jilli kissed him back then buried her head in his shoulder. "Maybe I did forget for a minute, but I remember now."

They sat on the swing, sipping their hot chocolate. They talked about their day without either one mentioning the phone call Jilli's mother had gotten. When their tumblers were empty, Jilli handed hers to him. "Thanks for the hot chocolate."

After setting the tumblers on the porch floor, he put his arm around Jilli. "You're very welcome."

Jilli looked into Ian's eyes, wondering when she'd stopped noticing how crystal blue they were. "We need to start back with this tradition, Ian."

Ian's mouth curled up in a smile. "Jilli, I couldn't agree more."

Jilli scooted in close to Ian, enjoying this tender moment. After several minutes of silently swinging back and forth, she felt her body relax as her eyelids closed. She jerked herself awake and sat up straight. "Oh, my! I almost fell asleep right here. I think it's time I head upstairs to bed."

Ian walked Jilli to the door where they kissed good night. As Ian headed back to his car, Jilli opened the door to her mother's house and stepped inside. Before closing the door, she turned around and called out to him, "I love you."

Ian stopped and looked back at her. He blew her a kiss. "I love you too."

Jilli smiled at Ian as she reached out with the palms of her hands to catch his kiss. As she closed the door behind her, for the first time in a long time, she could feel how loved she was by her husband.

CHAPTER NINE

After Jilli's call, Kalli's mind was racing. She returned to the kitchen and poured out her untouched, now cold, cup of tea. She refilled the teakettle with water and put it back on the stove top to heat. As she waited for the kettle to boil, she wished more than ever that Marshall was with her. He would have known exactly what to say to help her cope with the news Jilli had just shared with her. He would have held her in his arms and reassured her that all would be fine. Oh, how she missed his comforting embrace.

The whistling teakettle pulled Kalli away from her reverie. She made herself a cup of strong Earl Grey and carried it to the living room where her phone was waiting for her on the arm of the couch. She set her tea on the end table, sat down, and picked up her phone. Taking a deep calming breath, she pressed in the number for Nicola's cell phone. As soon as the phone started ringing, Kalli remembered this was the day Nicola and Alexandre were meeting with some big company about selling Sweet Hart Bakeries to them. She knew the way things went today would affect Nicola's mood and attitude. Having experienced Nicola's bad mood more times than she cared to remember, she prayed all went well today.

"Hey, Kalli."

Kalli couldn't tell from her greeting what Nicola's mood might be. "Hey, Nicola. How did it go today?"

"I can tell you Sweet Hart Bakery wasn't sold today."

Kalli rolled her eyes. There was the abrasive tone she'd feared would be in her sister's voice.

"I'm sorry."

"Well, I'm not! So, you shouldn't be either."

"Okay, then I'm not sorry."

"Well, good for you!"

Kalli couldn't help but laugh. "Oh, come on, Nicola, why are you acting like you're so upset? You and I both know you don't want to sell your bakeries to some conglomerate who doesn't give a flip about them."

Nicola was silent for such a long time, Kalli began to wonder if their connection had dropped. When her sister finally spoke again, it was as if another person had taken the phone. All bitterness had left her voice. "I'm sorry, Kalli. You're right. I sometimes forget just how well you know me. It's just that this whole business of selling frustrates me. I know Alexandre only wants what's best for us and believes selling the bakeries is the way to live our best life."

"You need to be honest with him, Nicola. Tell him how you feel about selling. Trust he'll understand."

"You're probably right. I'll think on that, but I don't have to decide anything tonight. Enough about me, tell me what's going on with you."

Kalli took a deep breath, gathering her thoughts. "Actually, there's a lot going on. That's the main reason I called. It's about Mama and. . ." She paused. "Daddy."

"Daddy? What could possibly be going on with Daddy?" Kalli could hear the skepticism in Nicola's voice.

"More than you'd ever imagine." Kalli went on to give her the details of the phone call from Jake Albright with his revelation and their mother's reaction to the news. Nicola listened without interruption until Kalli finished with her story. Where Kalli's response had been anger and declarations of deceit, Nicola's reaction was the exact opposite.

"Oh, my goodness! That's terrible, Kalli! When we thought Daddy was dead, the whole time he was alive and being held as a POW. Poor, poor Daddy."

"Well, yes, if it's true. I'm not sure we should believe this guy."

"Didn't he say he had some kind of proof?"

"He claims he has a letter he's going to offer as proof."

"Mama must be devastated."

"Jilli said she's taking it pretty hard. This whole thing has really shaken her."

"There's not a doubt in my mind it rocked Mama's world. To tell the truth, it pretty much rocks my world too. Doesn't it do the same to yours, Kalli?"

Kalli took a moment to consider Nicola's question. "I'm not convinced this Jake guy is on the up-and-up. Frankly, I flat-out don't believe him. I know the government screws things up, but it's hard for me to even consider the army got Daddy's death so wrong."

"Okay, I get that. Is this guy going to send the letter to Mama, or is he going to personally bring it to her?"

"He's going to bring it to her. I think Jilli said he's coming next week."

"That gives us some time to check his story out, and if I know our lawyer sister Jilli, she's already started."

"No doubt."

"To me, right now our main concern should be Mama and helping her get through this whole ordeal."

"That's why I think we should head on down to Ida tomorrow. We might even need to stay a few days with her."

"Good idea. Mama needs a distraction and our support. I don't have much going on right now besides my husband trying to sell the company we built together out from under me. I pretty much have a clear calendar for the rest of the week."

"You know you're not doing yourself any favors by not telling him how you feel about the sale."

"So, you say."

"I do say!"

"Okay, I'll think about how I can tell him while I'm at Mama's."

"How about I pick you up around nine in the morning?"

"Sounds good to me. Do you think I should call Mama to let her know we're coming?"

"Not tonight. Jilli said she'd helped her up to bed. We should let her rest. We can call her in the morning when we're on our way. What Mama needs tonight is our prayers."

"You're right."

"See you in the morning."

"That works for me. I'll grab some coffee and pastries from the bakery for our breakfast."

"Great! Get some rest. I think tomorrow's going to be a long day for all of us."

"No doubt. Love you."

"Love you too."

Kalli relaxed against the couch cushions and finished her lukewarm cup of Earl Grey. She considered her conversation with Nicola. Her sister's reaction hadn't been at all what she'd expected. She knew Nicola had a strong sense of justice. She always had an opinion on what she believed to be right or wrong. She should have been outraged at someone making such a claim about their father. Instead, it seemed her reaction was one of acceptance, which bothered Kalli. Was she the only daughter of Nicholas Hart who thought the claims this Jake guy had made about him were absurd?

With her phone still in her hand, Nicola headed down the hall to Alexandre's study. She lightly knocked as she pushed open the door. Her husband wasn't behind his desk as she'd expected. Instead, she found him sitting in the dark brown leather recliner in the corner, reading. He lowered his book and looked up at her over his bifocals. "What is it, *mon amour*? You look unhappy. Is it the business of the day that has upset you?"

Nicola rushed to him. She sat in his lap, put her arms around his neck, and began to cry. He set his book on the table beside his chair and wrapped his comforting arms around her. "Please, Nicolette, tell me what it is breaking your heart in pieces."

With Alexandre holding her, Nicola told him what Kalli had told her about the phone call her mother had gotten that day. By the time she finished telling him, she'd stopped crying. "Alexandre, if Mama had known Daddy wasn't dead, maybe she could have saved him and brought him home."

Alexandre patted her back. "I'm so sorry, Nicolette. I know how much you missed having a father in your life as you grew up, but I don't think your Mama could have done anything to bring him back home from a POW prison camp."

Nicola abruptly pushed away from him. "But you don't know that! It could have happened, and I could have grown up with my daddy in my life."

Alexandre gently pulled her back to him. "*Oui, pardon*, you are so right. I don't know. You could have grown up with a father."

"Oh, Alexandre, if only."

Nicola was still sitting in Alexandre's lap when his cell phone rang. He picked it up from the table beside his recliner to check the caller ID. "It's Maxwell."

Frowning, Nicola sat up. "Maxwell? Who's Maxwell?"

Returning her frown, Alexandre clicked his tongue at her. "Maxwell, the man who made the proposal about buying the bakery. The man you only halfway listened to this morning."

"Oh, that Maxwell." Nicola didn't recall ever hearing his name.

"I need to take this." Alexandre lifted her from his lap and stood. "Bonjour, Maxwell. So good of you to call."

As Alexandre carried on his conversation with Maxwell, Nicola left his study, quietly closing the door behind her. She knew her husband was irritated with her for not paying closer attention to the presentation Maxwell had given that morning. She also knew he was aware she almost always tuned out whenever business matters were being discussed. She relied on him to manage those details, but that was about to change. She needed to make her husband understand she wasn't interested in selling her business.

Nicola recognized Sweet Hart Bakery wasn't only her business. She and Alexandre were partners. She owned fifty-one percent to his forty-nine. She remembered how when they'd incorporated twenty years earlier, she protested when he insisted she be the majority partner. It hadn't made much of a difference until now. Now she had the ability to stop the sale over his advice and even over his protests.

She was ashamed of herself for thinking such thoughts. It wasn't fair to Alexandre. He'd worked hard to make their business the success it was today. He was the one who'd set the goals that led to the expansion from one store to four. Kalli was right. Nicola hadn't been totally honest with her husband. She needed to let him know exactly how she felt about selling out to a big conglomerate, but not tonight. She'd find time to sit down with him to discuss her feelings later, after she'd helped her mother deal with the unsettling phone call she'd received.

Nicola climbed the stairs to their recently renovated second-floor master bedroom. After Alexandra and André went off to college, Nicola had moved their belongings to the two guest rooms on the third floor. With the rooms on both sides of their bedroom now empty, she and Alexandre knocked down those walls and made space for a state-of-the-art 300-square-foot master bathroom with his-and-her custom designed closets on each side.

If she were going to stay with her mother for a few days until everything got sorted out, now would be a good time to pack since

Alexandre was busy. Nicola opened the double doors to her closet. As she gathered her clothes to place in her suitcase, she said a prayer asking for God's peace for her mother, her sisters, and her father's soul.

After finishing her packing, Nicola headed back downstairs. she noticed the door to Alexandre's study remained closed. She wondered if he was still on the phone with Maxwell. It'd been a good hour since she'd left him to his call. As she passed the closed door, she resisted the urge to lean against it to listen. Proud of herself for not giving in to the temptation, she continued down the hall to the kitchen. She was stressed, and when she was stressed, she baked. She was chopping the dates for the date and nut puff pastry turnover she was hoping to add to the menu of her bakeries when she heard the study door open and Alexandre's footsteps in the hall.

"Well, that was one of the most interesting conversations I've ever had," Alexandre announced as he moved in beside her and took a date from the counter.

Nicola playfully slapped away his hand. "That's for the new pastry I'm trying out."

"It's also for me to eat," Alexandre teased as he bit into the date.

Nicola smiled. "Okay, but that's one less for the pastry." She returned to her chopping.

She could feel Alexandre watching her. "Don't you want to know what made the conversation so interesting?" he finally asked.

Nicola kept chopping. "Yes, of course, tell me what made it so interesting."

Alexandre put his hand on her hand which held the knife. "Please, stop."

Nicola put the knife down on the counter and turned toward him.

Alexandre put his hands on her shoulders, looking at her with a glint of joy in his olive-green eyes. "Nicolette, they have made us an offer which makes all of our dreams come true!"

Nicola could hear the excitement in Alexandre's voice. The last thing she wanted to do was rob him of his joy, but she couldn't hide how his news filled her with a deep despair. Lowering her head, she reached up to put a hand on each of his. Her voice was barely above a whisper. "Oh, Alexandre, my darling. It's your dream, not mine."

Alexandre jerked his hands away. "What do you mean? This is what we've talked about for years!"

"You're right. We have talked about it, but I thought it was something that would happen in the distant future when we were old and tired. Not now."

Nicola watched as Alexandre's hands clenched into fists. "Why not now?"

The intensity in his voice and the disappointment in his eyes made Nicola's own fill with tears. "I'm not ready, Alexandre. I love being a part of Sweet Hart Bakery. I love how our employees and customers are like family. The business makes me happy. I'm just not ready to give all of that up."

Nicola had expected Alexandre to be frustrated and let down by her comments, but the look of anger mixed with sadness on his face wasn't at all what she'd imagined. She reached out to him. "Alexandre, please don't be mad. I'm sorry."

Alexandre stepped away from her. "I'm sorry too." The bitterness in his voice took her breath away. He glared at her for a moment before abruptly turning away. She watched in stunned silence as he walked out of the kitchen, leaving her standing there alone.

Tears ran down Nicola's cheeks. A part of her wanted to go after him to tell him she would do what he wanted, but another part of her held her where she was, unwilling to change her mind. A few minutes later, she heard his car engine rev up and the crunch of tires on the driveway as he left. They'd had fights before, but she couldn't recall a single time either one had left the house in anger. With the palm of her hands, she wiped her tears from her face. She turned back to the counter, picked up the knife, and finished making the puff pastry. Then she put it in the refrigerator and went up to bed.

CHAPTER TEN

Nelli's mind and body were exhausted by the day's events. She'd fallen into a deep sleep almost the instant Jilli closed her bedroom door. It was the distinctive sound of tires crunching on her gravel driveway that woke her. She sat up in bed with her whole body tuned to the sounds coming from outside her window. She pushed back her covers and hurried to the window. Jerking back the curtains, she saw the lights of a car as it traveled down her driveway toward her house. She glanced at the clock on her nightstand to find it was a quarter past nine. She was wondering who would be coming to see her and how quickly she could get to the door when she heard Jilli call out.

"You scared me to death, Ian! What are you doing here?"

Nelli made her way back to the bed and plopped down. She sighed. How could she have forgotten Jilli was spending the night with her? She hoped she wasn't losing her mind, but with the events of the day, it would make sense.

Never had Nelli considered for even one minute the possibility of the army getting it wrong about Nicholas dying in the helicopter crash. Now she wondered why she'd accepted without question all she'd been told. Why had it never even occurred to her that the army could have been wrong?

Of course, Nelli needed to consider there was still the possibility Jake Albright was the one who was wrong. Maybe his father made up the whole thing about his being a POW just to impress his son. Jake said he had a letter which proved Nicholas had been a POW with his father. Well, she could show him the documentation which stated her husband had died in that helicopter crash, and hers had been certified by the United States Army.

Hoping to take her mind away from thoughts of the cruelty her husband might have suffered at the hands of the Vietcong, Nelli headed into the bathroom to get a drink of water. She filled her water glass, drank down the entire contents, refilled it, and carried it back to her bedroom. After taking another sip, she placed the glass on her nightstand. She climbed back into bed and pulled the covers up to her chin. Closing her eyes, she took several deep, calming breaths. She prayed for sleep to once again envelop her and take her away from her troubling thoughts.

Nelli could hear Jilli's and Ian's voices floating up from the front porch but couldn't quite make out the words they were saying. She hoped they were getting along with one another. Over the past few months, she'd noticed how the two who'd once appeared to be so deeply in love seemed to be drifting apart. She didn't want anything to come between them that could tear down the life they'd built together. She should talk to Jilli about the importance of keeping her marriage together. Filling her mind with comforting thoughts of love and happy endings, Nelli fell asleep, but it wasn't the restful sleep she'd prayed for.

In Nelli's dream, she was running in a pasture through the fresh green grass of springtime. She could feel the cool, crisp air rushing through her hair and on her face as she ran. It occurred to her she was running like the wind, which made her laugh with the realization that it'd been an exceptionally long time since she'd run anywhere. She stopped and bent down to pick violets that were growing wild all around her feet. When she stood, she turned in circles, taking in the beauty of the day. It was then she noticed a horse galloping toward her. She knew right away it was Tucker— the black-beauty horse she'd learned to ride as a child. She clapped her hands together and jumped up and down in excitement to see her beloved Tucker was once again alive.

Tucker pulled up to a stop in front of her. Nelli reached out to rub the familiar cross-shaped white spot between his eyes. She wrapped her arms around his neck and spoke in his ear. "Where have you been, my sweet boy? I've missed you so."

Tucker whinnied as he bobbed his head up and down.

Nelli knew in that moment he wanted her to ride. She grabbed hold of his long black mane and pulled herself up onto his back. Holding on tight to his mane, she gripped his sides with her legs, clicked her tongue, and leaned forward. Tucker started off in a trot but was soon racing across the pasture. She released her hold on his mane and spread her arms out. The thrill and complete freedom she felt on her horse's back made her feel alive, more alive than she'd felt in all the years since Nicholas died.

All of a sudden Nelli was no longer on her beloved Tucker riding through the lush green pasture. Instead, she was standing alone, surrounded by a dark, murky jungle. She could feel the heat and humidity pressing in on her skin. Trees as tall as cathedrals surrounded her, and a strange white light shimmered through the vast canopy of leaves. The light seemed to be calling to her. She knew in that instant she was meant to make her way to the light.

As she began walking, Nelli looked down to see her feet were bare and the jungle floor was covered with dead, rotting leaves. With each step, her feet sank deeper into the debris. When she tried to run, the muck held her feet tighter. Despite the struggle she had to get to that light. It was a matter of life or death, but she didn't know whose death. She kept walking despite the pain and misery she felt with each step.

After what seemed like hours of walking, Nelli reached a small clearing. Although she could no longer see the white light, she felt this was where the light had been. She turned in circles, searching for some sign of the light. It was then she noticed a young man in the clearing walking toward her. As he came closer, she could see he was dressed in a shabby, threadbare army uniform. His mouth was moving. He seemed to be repeating the same thing over and over.

She called out to him. "Please, speak up. I can't hear you."

When the young man cupped his hands around his mouth, his words came to her loud and clear. "Why didn't you come help me? I shined a light so you could find me. Why didn't you come? Why did you leave me here to die?"

She could feel her heart break as she recognized the young man in the tattered uniform. It was her Nicholas. Reaching out to him, Nelli cried out, "I'm sorry! I didn't mean to leave you! They told me the light had been killed. No one told me the light still burned! I didn't know!"

Jilli smiled to herself as she thought back to the days when Ian had courted her. His surprising visit tonight gave her the same excited feeling in the pit of her stomach as those long-ago days of dating had. She stood with her back against the door, recalling times gone by, when an unexpected sound interrupted her thoughts. Something about the sound was alarming. She stepped away from the door. She stood stock still, listening, afraid to even breathe. When she didn't hear anything other than the usual night sounds, she relaxed and decided she'd imagined it, since she hadn't spent a night in this old house of her mother's in years,

Jilli was about to walk back to the kitchen to turn off the light and lock up when she heard a heartbreaking cry. She knew in an instant it was her mother. Taking two steps at a time, she rushed up the back stairs. With the cries growing stronger, she threw open her mother's door. She stood frozen as she took in the scene before her.

The light from the hallway fell on her mother's ashen, tormented face as she cried out, "I'm sorry! I would never leave you! I didn't know to look for the light! I didn't know!"

Hearing the anguish in her mother's voice frightened Jilli. She rushed to the bed and pulled her into her arms gently rocking back and forth as she whispered comforting words.

"Shh. Shh. It's okay. You're safe now. Shh."

After several minutes, the cries subsided, replaced by heavy breathing, signaling a return to restful sleep. Jilli gently placed her mother's head back on the pillow. She took a tissue from the bedside table and wiped the tears from her mother's face.

Jilli lightly kissed her forehead. "Love you, Mama. No more bad dreams."

Leaving the room, Jilli softly closed the door behind her. She went straight to her room and dropped down onto her bed. The encounter had left her shaken. She supposed her mother's nightmare must have been brought on by the troubling events of the day. Would her mother remember the dream in the morning or would the trauma erase it from her memory? She thought it best not to say anything about the nightmare. Instead, she'd wait to see if her mother brought it up.

After changing into an old pair of her pajamas she found in what had once been her chest of drawers, she washed her face and climbed into bed. She turned off the lamp, hoping sleep would come quickly. After several minutes of tossing and turning, she turned the lamp back on. Putting two pillows behind her back, she propped herself up, took her cell phone out of her purse, and began scanning her social media pages. She'd stopped to read and comment on her timeline when she noticed a post from her youngest daughter, Hazel.

The picture of Hazel made Jilli sit straight up in bed. Putting her hand to her mouth, she said, "Holy moly, Hazel! What have you done!"

Gone was Hazel's stunning shoulder-length fiery-red hair. What was left in its place was a bare-naked bald head. Hazel appeared to be sitting in a salon chair with her fallen tresses surrounding her. She was grinning from ear to ear and giving two thumbs-up. Jilli had to force her eyes away from the picture to focus on the caption under the picture she hoped would explain such a drastic action.

The title of the post was "For My Friend Raymond."

Jilli searched her brain for any reference Hazel had ever made about anyone named Raymond. She could recall none. She read on.

"Raymond was diagnosed last week with Hodgkin's Lymphoma. He's worried about losing all his hair when he starts chemo. See, Raymond, it's no big deal!"

Jilli shook her head with the realization she should have expected something like this from her passionate, impulsive middle daughter. She had to admit Hazel was showing support for what her friend was going through. She wondered if Hazel's bald head was the reason Morgan had been trying to reach her. Hazel shaving her head was something that would drive her older, level-headed, non-spontaneous sister crazy.

Jilli couldn't keep from smiling as she took one last look at Hazel's picture. Knowing the reason for her daughter's shaved head gave her a strange sense of pride. When she thought about it logically, Hazel's actions showed great courage, plus her baldness wasn't permanent. Her hair would grow back. Jilli was sure she would never be brave enough to do what her daughter had done to support her friend.

She chose a heart emoji for Hazel's post and added the word, "Beautiful!" before placing her phone back on the bedside table. She turned off the lamp and promptly fell into a deep sleep.

CHAPTER ELEVEN

Nicola hadn't been able to fall asleep. She'd been sure Alexandre would calm down after he drove around for a little while. When he was back to his reasonable self, he'd return to her. Then they would kiss and all would be forgiven. After a few hours of staring up at the ceiling, she'd concluded her husband would not be returning home anytime soon.

The suitcase she'd packed before their fight was still open on the chair, waiting for those essential last-minute items she couldn't pack until morning. She decided what she needed was a long hot shower to wash away the emotional upheaval of the day. She went into her bathroom, stripped off her nightgown, and stepped into the custom six-jet shower.

Standing in the middle of the shower, letting the spray of the steaming hot water wash over her, Nicola wondered how it happened that in a matter of hours the life she knew and the things she'd always believed could be so changed. She'd always trusted the love she and Alexandre had for one another, but for the first time ever his reaction made her question the strength of their love. After thirty-three years of marriage, could her not wanting to sell their company end their marriage? If he continued to insist they sell, could it end her love for him? She shook away the thought. There was no way she would ever allow a business decision to change her love for her husband. They'd been through tough times before. In her heart of hearts, she believed they'd get through this one as well.

Stepping out of the shower, Nicola felt better. It was as if the shower had not only cleaned her body, but also washed away those negative thoughts that had begun to creep into her mind. She loved Alexandre, and he loved her. That was the reality of the situation. The rest was just stuff they had to work through. She wrapped a towel around herself and returned to the bedroom, feeling disappointment in the pit of her stomach when she found it still empty. She'd hoped to find Alexandre sitting in his favorite chair by the window with his arms held open to welcome her onto his lap. She turned away from the empty chair.

As she let her pale blue silk nightgown fall over her head and down her body, she caught the sound of Alexandre's car. Rushing to the bedroom window, she looked out to see him getting out of his 2019 Ford Mustang Bullitt she'd given to him as a present on his sixtieth birthday.

Relief flooded through Nicola. She hurried to the empty chair to wait for him. As soon as he entered their bedroom, she'd apologize for upsetting him. She heard the beeps as he disarmed and rearmed their security system. She could hear him walking across the living room floor. She listened to the sound of his footsteps on the stairs. Holding her breath, she waited to hear him walking down the hall leading to their bedroom. Instead, she heard him continue up to the third floor. She blew out her breath in disappointment when she heard the guest bedroom door open and close. With a heavy heart, she crossed the room, got into her bed, turned off the lights, and cried herself to sleep.

❖

Nicola couldn't sleep. She'd gotten out of bed several times, determined to storm into the guest bedroom and demand that Alexandre explain his choosing not to sleep with her. Each time she got to her bedroom door, she lost her courage and returned to bed. She wasn't sure she was ready to listen to what he had to say.

As she tossed and turned, dark thoughts curled their way into her head—not only of what was going on with Alexandre, but also what Kalli had told her about the possibility of their father being a POW in a Vietcong prison camp. She'd seen documentaries of those held as prisoners who gave their accounts of the inhuman cruelty and suffering they'd endured at the hands of the Vietcong. She wondered how long her father went through hell when his whole family believed he was at peace with the Lord.

At four o'clock, Nicola got up. She couldn't stay in bed another minute with the same thoughts turning over and over in her mind. She got up and showered again. After drying off and putting on her makeup, she pulled her long ginger hair into a ponytail and secured it with a gold clip that had once held Topsy's hair on top of her head. She dressed in jeans and a kelly-green silk blouse and finished placing her essentials in her bag. She closed her suitcase, laid her hanging bag on top of it, and made her way down the stairs to the kitchen. After disarming the security system, she stepped out the back door to the carport where her Lexus was parked.

Nicola headed to the nearest Sweet Hart Bakery, only four miles away. It was not only the closest, but it was her favorite since it was the first of their four bakeries. She needed to check in with her assistant manager, Trish, to let her know she'd be out of town for a few days. She also wanted to pick up a special treat for her and Kalli to enjoy on their drive to Ida. She pulled into her reserved parking place behind the bakery and shut off the engine. She sat there for a minute, relishing the sound of the silence around her.

She knew as soon as she opened the back door to the bakery she'd be surrounded by the sounds of bustling customers and employees. This time of the morning was hectic as office workers stopped for breakfast and coffee, and meeting and event planners picked up orders for the day's events. She also knew this was the best time to get fresh-from-the-oven baked goods.

Nicola made her way to Trish's office through the flurry of the kitchen workers wishing her a "Good morning." Trish had been one of Nicola's first employees and had only been seventeen when Nicola hired her. Nicola remembered how worried she'd been about the dependability and work ethic of someone so young. But she'd soon realized she had nothing to worry about. Trish had proven herself more worthy of the job than employees twice her age. Over the years, Nicola had gradually given Trish more and more responsibilities, and now, as her assistant manager, she depended on her for planning and directing the operations of all four bakeries. Trish had never let her down.

Nicola hoped she'd find Trish at her desk. She knew there was a good chance she'd be out on the floor overseeing the staff or tending to the customers' needs or possibly at another store checking on how things were going. When she found Trish's desk chair empty, she sighed with disappointment. She sat down at the desk to write out a note explaining how she was going to Ida for a few days to check on her mother. For now, Trish didn't need to know any of the details as to her reason for going. She wrote down other pertinent information concerning the business then pinned the note to the corkboard above the desk.

With her mind on what treat to take to Kalli, Nicola stepped out of the office and bumped into Trish. Their heads collided.

Trish's hands went to her face. "I'm so sorry! My mind was on other things. I wasn't even looking where I was going."

Nicola rubbed the knot that was quickly rising on her forehead. "No, it was totally my fault. I was off in another world."

They both laughed.

Nicola pointed back to the office. "I just left you a note. I pinned it on your corkboard."

"Is anything wrong?" Trish asked as she walked into her office in search of the note.

Nicola hesitated. "No, not really wrong. I'll be gone for a few days. I need to take care of some things."

"Oh?" Trish sat down at her desk as she took the note from the corkboard and scanned it. She looked up at Nicola. "Whew! I was afraid you were going to tell me you'd sold the stores."

"Nope, not yet."

"What do you mean by that?"

Nicola blew out a breath. "If Alexandre had his way, Sweet Hart Bakeries would be sold." She waved her hands dismissively. "It's a long story that I'm not ready to share yet. Just know that for now, everything is as it has been."

"I'll take that as good news." Trish smiled up at Nicola. "So, what brings you here this fine morning?"

"Kalli's picking me up in a little while, and I wanted to get a few special treats for the ride."

Trish stood up. "Well, let's check out what we've got."

The two made their way to the front of the bakery to look through the display case. Nicola was searching for just the right sweet treat to take to Kalli when she remembered how her sister loved peanut butter. "Let's go with two Sweet Hart Reese's and Banana Croissants."

"Now that's a good choice. They're easy to eat one-handed, so she can eat and drive. Anything else?"

"How about two hot coffees, four creamers, and two packs of sugar added to that order."

Trish put together the order and handed Nicola the bag with the croissants, creamers, and sugar along with the coffees in a beverage container.

"Thanks for your help, Trish. I'll let you know when I'm on my way back."

"I hope Alexandre doesn't sell the stores while you're gone."

"Me too!"

Nicola was on her way out the back when her eyes landed on a tray of Sweet Hart Cinnamon Swirl Pancakes. Her mouth watered as she took in the aroma of the fresh baked goods. The pancakes were the best of two worlds: sweet cinnamon rolls with the classic shape and texture of pancakes. They'd quickly become one of the bakery's best sellers. She grabbed a box from the shelf and packed in eight pancakes for Mama and her sisters to enjoy for either a late-night treat or breakfast the next morning.

Taking the box, the bag, and the coffees, Nicola left the bakery. As she pulled in the driveway, she noticed Alexandre's Bullitt was gone. She'd told him she'd be leaving with Kalli this morning, which meant he didn't care to tell her goodbye. She wasn't sure what to do. He'd never acted like this before. She thought about calling him. She couldn't imagine what she could say that would make things better besides telling him she'd changed her mind about selling, which she hadn't. She decided it was better to stay silent than risk another explosion.

Nicola had just gotten out of her car when she saw Kalli's car coming down the street. She hurried into the house to grab her things. Kalli would be beyond surprised to find she didn't have to wait on her this time. At least she could make someone in her family happy today.

Even though it was only a thirty-minute drive to Nicola's house, Kalli allowed forty-five minutes of travel time just in case there was a problem with heavy traffic. Being fifteen minutes early was ideal for her since she despised being late. However, she knew her early arrival would not make her sister—who consistently ran fifteen minutes late—happy. As she parked in Nicola's driveway, she wondered just how long she'd have to wait for her sister to get ready. They had an hour and a half drive to get to their mother's house.

Kalli turned off the car's engine. She was getting out of her car when she was stopped by an amazing sight. Her younger, almost-always-late sister was coming toward her holding a beverage carrier and a bright yellow Sweet Hart Bakery bag in one hand and pulling a rolling suitcase behind her with the other, her hanging clothes draped over her arm.

"Pop the trunk."

As her fully clothed, ready-early sister approached, Kalli stared at her in disbelief.

Nicola stopped at the back of Kalli's car and stomped her foot. "Kalli, pop open the trunk already!"

Kalli leaned back in the car and hit the trunk release button. The trunk slowly opened. Nicola lifted her suitcase and placed it inside while balancing the beverage carrier. She added her hanging bag, closed the trunk, and then came around to the passenger side of the car. She opened the car door with her free hand, and got in. She placed the two coffees in the cup holders before turning toward Kalli with a smile on her face. "Surprised you, didn't I?"

Kalli stared at her in open-mouthed wonderment. "I'm in total shock. In all the fifty-seven years I've known you, this is the very first time you've ever been ready early."

Giggling, Nicola covered her mouth. "I know. I knew you'd be early, but didn't know just how early. I was determined to surprise you."

Kalli closed her car door. "Well, you succeeded. Shall we go?"

Nicola pointed forward. "Onward, sister dear!"

"I think I'll back out of the driveway to the road rather than going through your car port."

They both laughed, and as Kalli backed down the driveway, Nicola looked at her. "You don't think this will be the only time we'll laugh today, do you?"

Kalli shook her head as she pulled out onto the road. "Are you kidding? Have you ever known the four of us to not laugh when we're all together? I have no doubt that despite everything that's going on, there'll be laughter."

Nicola opened the Sweet Hart Bakery bag, took out one of the Reese's and Banana Croissants, and handed it to Kalli.

"Oh, my goodness, Nicola. That looks delicious." Kalli took the croissant and bit into it. With her mouth full, she asked, "Is there a Reese's Peanut Butter Cup in here?"

Nicola nodded as she took a bite of her own croissant. "And banana creme."

"Nicola, this is the best thing I've ever put in my mouth."

Nicola smiled at her. "I thought you'd like it. I remembered how fond you are of peanut butter. If I remember correctly, every day you made a peanut butter sandwich for your school lunch."

Kalli nodded. "I sure did, and it was my go-to meal in college."

Nicola removed her coffee from the cup holder and sipped the hot liquid as she watched the road in front of her. "I sure hope you're right about the four of us laughing together. It's just that I've been worried about how this whole situation might change us all, but mostly Mama."

Keeping her eyes on the road ahead, Kalli wrinkled her forehead as she considered Nicola's statement. "What do you mean by change Mama and us? What kind of change? You think that news will suddenly make all of us lose our sense of humor?"

Nicola rolled her eyes. "No, nothing like that. I don't know exactly how, but you have to admit there will be changes in our lives if we find out Daddy really didn't die in that helicopter crash, but was held in a POW camp to suffer all kinds of torture. Just think, Kalli—"

Kalli put up her hand up. "Stop! I'm not going there, Nicola! I think we're going to find out this Jake guy is a complete fraud, hung up on some deathbed confession his father made."

"So, you're not even going to consider the possibility the army got it wrong and this guy is telling the truth?"

"Nope, not for now." Kalli took her eyes from the road to glance over at her sister. "As a journalist, I need evidence backed by facts, not someone's assumptions."

"He says he has a letter proving it."

"We'll have to see how believable this letter of his is. Nicola, we have documentation from the army stating Daddy was killed in a helicopter crash. I can't help but believe this Jake guy is running some sort of scam."

Nicola gazed out the windshield. "What kind of scam, Kalli? Do you think he's hoping to get money from us?"

Kalli glanced at her with one eyebrow raised. "Think about it, Nicola. He might think he could get a pile of it from you if he knows you're the owner of Sweet Hart Bakery."

"Get serious! What reason would there ever be for me to give him a pile of money?

"I don't know. It's just a gut feeling I have."

"Truthfully, I don't know what to believe or who we should trust is giving us the truth. It's all very confusing to me."

Kalli finished her croissant. "Well, then, let's change the subject." She wiped her mouth with a napkin and picked up her coffee.

Staring out her window, Nicola drank her coffee without comment.

The two sisters rode in silence. Kalli noticed Nicola had barely touched her croissant. She knew her sister well enough to know something was bothering her but wasn't ready to talk about it. She also knew, try as she might, her sister wouldn't confide her feelings until she was good and ready. She'd always been stubborn like that.

Kalli hoped to break her sister's brooding silence by changing to a neutral subject. "Did I tell you Gabe has put in his request with the National Park's Service to intern at Glacier National Park this summer?"

Nicola turned to face her sister. "No! Oh, Kalli, that's so exciting."

"I know, but you do know what that means, right?"

Nicola shrugged. "That he gets to have a great summer working his dream job?"

"Well, that's probably true. I guess what I should have asked is, do you know what it means for me?"

Nicola gave Kalli a blank look as she slowly shook her head.

Kalli sighed. "It means he won't be coming home this summer."

Nicola put her hand on Kalli's shoulder. "I'm so sorry, Kalli."

"I'm sorry too." Kalli forced a smile as she glanced at her sister. "But I've decided I'm going out there for a couple of weeks after the summer semester to spend some time with him. You want to come with me?"

"I'd love to go with you. Maybe we can convince Jilli and Mama to come with us."

The prospect of the four of them going to Montana filled Kalli with excitement. "That'd be fantastic. Can you imagine the awesome time we'd have together? I know Gabe would love having all of us visit him."

Nicola chuckled. "I have no doubt we'd have a fun time, but I'm not so sure Gabe would be as thrilled to see us as we would be to see him."

Kalli laughed along with her sister. "You might be right about that."

CHAPTER TWELVE

Nelli sat straight up. Her heart pounded as her eyes darted around the room, searching for the person whose desperate voice had pulled her out of a deep sleep. In a harsh whisper, she called out to the surrounding darkness, "Who's there?"

When only silence answered her question, she leaned back against the pillows as the realization slowly came to her that the voice had been in her dream. Or had it been a nightmare? She glanced at the clock on her nightstand. It was six o'clock. She'd gotten much more than her usual seven hours of sleep, but her body felt far from rested. A lingering hopeless feeling hung over her as if she'd searched all night long for something that was just out of reach. She couldn't recall the specifics, but sensed it had something to do with Nicholas and the unsettling phone call she'd received the previous morning. It was hard to believe it'd only been yesterday morning she'd answered that disturbing call.

The weight of Jake Albright's call and a sense of impending doom held Nelli in her bed. As she sat there she remembered another time when she hadn't wanted to leave her bed. She recalled how she'd begged God to take her away from this world so she wouldn't have to face what lay ahead—widowhood with three small children. It had been Topsy who'd set her straight and made her want to live. She felt that familiar despair this very minute, but this time there was no Topsy to pull her out of bed and onto her feet. She was going to have to find the courage to face the day from within herself. She closed her eyes as she tried to remember Topsy's exact words she'd used to get her up and going.

"Nelli, remember your Bible. 'Let your hope be in the Lord: take heart and be strong; yes, let your hope be in the Lord.'"

Nelli knew she needed hope and to take heart more than ever if she was going to get through the days ahead. "Dear Lord, I know it's trusting in Your strength that will get me out of this bed and help me face all that's coming my way. I'm calling on Your power and strength."

Taking a deep breath, Nelli pulled back the covers, swung her legs over the side of the bed, and put her feet on the floor. She made her way to the bathroom. After showering, she stood in front of the mirror with only a towel wrapped around her aging body and studied her reflection.

Her once coal-black hair was now laced with white. She could see some wrinkles around her mouth and the corners of her eyes, but she didn't think there were many for a seventy-seven-year-old. She knew she had the genes from her mother and grandmother to thank for that. Her skin was a dark, leathery brown from years of working out in the sun tending to her garden and animals. Her once dark brown eyes which her mother said seemed to dance with mischief now had a watery dullness. She took in a deep breath and straightened to her full height. She grimaced remembering how, once upon a time, as the tallest girl in her class at five feet nine inches, most had looked up to her. It made her sad to know years of wear and tear on her body had worn away close to two inches.

Nelli combed through her long hair and in two quick motions flipped it up into a knot on top of her head and pinned it. It made her smile to know she wore it just like her grandmother Topsy had worn hers. She dressed in the same outfit she'd taken off the night before. Making her way to the kitchen down the back stairs, she saw through the window in the back door the sun was just beginning to peek over the horizon. The promise of another beautiful day was dawning.

Checking the time on the kitchen clock, Nelli decided there was enough time for a quick walk around the yard before Jilli came downstairs for breakfast. Just like she'd done the day before, she stepped into her knee-high black rubber boots at the back door, grabbed her baseball cap off the hook, and was out the door. Once again, she found herself walking out into the grandeur of a magnificent morning only God could create.

Nelli took in a deep breath. The morning was cooler than she'd expected. She considered going back inside to put a jacket over her flannel shirt, but hoped as the sun rose higher, the air would get warmer. She could see the bird feeder hanging off the budding dogwood tree was almost empty, so she headed to the barn out back where she stored her birdseed.

The barn had seen better days. The years of rain and baking summer sun had taken its toll. It had once kept the weather off the summer hay and sheltered animals, but now with its leaking roof and sagging boards it was draftier than a railway platform.

Nelli pulled back the barn door and shivered as she stepped out of the sun into the dark chill of the barn. The familiar scents of hay and straw and long-gone animals always took her back to the sweet memories of her childhood. This was the place of games she'd played with her brothers. This was the place she'd come to over the years for solitude. When life got too hard, this was the place she was free to indulge in fanciful thoughts of how things might have been. This was the place she needed to be today. She sat down on an old milking stool and let her thoughts take her back to days gone by.

—1968—

Nelli had her two oldest daughters in the bathtub, washing the last of the mud out of their hair and scrubbing the gritty grime off their tiny bodies. Their Uncle Jim-Jim had taken the two girls fishing at the plantation pond. She still wasn't sure what had made her agree to his plan. It could have been the thrill of having a whole afternoon where she didn't have to be the one keeping these two occupied while their youngest sister napped. Whatever it was, it was a moment of insanity. She'd known the pond was lower than normal due to the dry summer they'd had but hadn't considered what that could mean for two highly active, creative little girls and an uncle who indulged their every whim.

It turned out there had been little fishing. When Uncle Jim-Jim realized how hard it was going to be to keep hooks from puncturing little hands or other various body parts, he'd decided the girls would enjoy wading in the pond. The wading quickly turned into running in and out of the pond, creating a muddy trail, which turned into showing the girls how to make mud balls and concluded with a mud ball fight. When the three of them came through the back door and stood in her kitchen with mud oozing onto her clean floor, Nelli didn't know whether to cry or laugh. It turned out she did neither. Instead, she scolded.

"James Wallace Tucker, what in the world have you done to my daughters?"

Kalli proudly spoke up with her white teeth gleaming from her mud-splattered face. "Mama, Uncle Jim-Jim says I throw a mean mud ball."

"Me too!" chimed in Nicola.

Putting her hands on her hips, Nelli looked down at her two smiling daughters. "And who taught you to throw a mud ball?"

"Uncle Jim-Jim!" They answered in unison.

Nelli turned to her brother and said through gritted teeth, "If Uncle Jim-Jim knows what's good for him, he'd better get out of here before I throw something at him."

Jim was out the door faster than she could ever remember him moving.

Looking at her daughters, she said, "You two, get upstairs to the bathroom right now and don't wake your sister!"

Nelli emptied and filled the bathtub three times before the water stayed clean enough to finish the job. It was then Nicholas walked into the bathroom. Nelli could immediately tell by the look on his face something was bothering him. As soon as he helped her dry off the girls and get them into clean clothes, he disappeared. After she combed through their tangled wet hair and sent both to their room she went in search of her husband. She found him sitting alone in the living room, holding his head in his hands. He looked up at her as she entered the room.

"What is it, Nicholas?"

"It's not good, Nelli."

Nelli sat down beside him. She put a comforting hand on his shoulder and waited for him to continue.

Nicholas took in a breath and slowly blew it out. "I got orders today."

"Oh, no, Nicholas, are we going to have to move?"

"No." He turned to face her. "My orders are for Vietnam."

Nelli's hand flew to her mouth as tears filled her eyes. "That can't be true."

"I'm afraid it is."

"I thought they told you you're more valuable as a trainer than you would be as a pilot."

"I guess that's not how they see it anymore."

Nelli stood and began to pace back and forth. "Well then, we'll have to make them see it!"

"How do you propose we do that, Nelli!"

Nelli could hear the frustration and defeat in his voice. She stopped pacing. She sat down on the coffee table in front of him and put her hands on his knees. Leaning in close, she asked, "Are you sure there's nothing we can do?"

Nicholas ran his hand through his hair. "Orders are orders. Short of retiring from the army, there's nothing to do but follow the orders I'm given."

Nelli sat up straight. "Are you telling me you could retire?"

Nicholas's azure-blue eyes met hers. "I'm not going to retire, Nelli."

"But you could?" Nelli asked hopefully.

Nicholas hesitated. "I'm due to re-enlist in three months. Technically, I suppose if I had asked for an early separation, they might have given it to me. But I can't do that now, Nelli. When Colonel Rodgers handed me my orders for Vietnam, he asked me to re-enlist before I left. I told him I would."

Nelli stood up. Hot tears ran down her face. "You told him you would re-enlist without even talking to me? How could you even think about not discussing it with me, Nicholas?"

The look on his face gave Nelli her answer. Without waiting for him to explain, she ran out of the living room, through the kitchen, and out the back door. She wasn't sure where she was going. She only knew she wanted to be as far away from her husband and the decision he'd made without giving any consideration for her and their girls. She kept running until she found herself at the edge of the woods that met up with the plantation pond where Nicholas had placed the bench he'd made for her before Kalli was born. She threw herself down on the bench and cried until she had no tears left.

"I knew this would be where I'd find you."

Startled, Nelli jumped at the sound of Nicholas's voice.

"Why would you sneak up on me like that?"

Standing behind her, Nicholas put his arms around Nelli as he rested his chin on her head. "I wasn't sneaking up on you. You didn't hear me because you're too angry with me to even notice what's going on around you. I stood watching you for several minutes."

Nelli pushed his arms away. "You're right about one thing. I am angry with you!"

"You have every right to be angry. It was selfish and inconsiderate of me to not talk to you first. I'm sorry. Can we talk about it now?"

Nelli crossed her arms and sat back down. "What is there to talk about? I thought you already told the colonel you would re-enlist."

"I did tell him that, but I haven't actually re-enlisted yet." Nicholas stepped around the bench and sat down beside Nelli. He put an arm around her shoulder. His voice was soft and low as he asked, "What do you want?"

Nelli hesitated as she considered his question. "I don't want you to go to Vietnam."

Pulling her closer, he looked her straight in her eyes. "Okay, then I won't. I'll go in tomorrow and get the paperwork started asking for an early separation."

Nelli reached out, took his hand, and looked into his eyes. "You will?"

"Of course, I will. I'll give up my army career for you if that's what you want me to do."

Nelli raised an eyebrow. "You will?"

Nicholas clasped her hand. "I will."

Nelli put her other hand on top of his. "But is that what you want to do?"

Nicholas pulled his hands away and rested them on his knees. He took in a deep breath. "The army saved me. When I enlisted, I was a boy struggling to find my place in this world. I didn't want to be a loser like my older brother who'd been in and out of trouble. I wanted to be someone who makes a difference, who makes the world a better place."

He turned to face Nelli. "The first time I flew solo in a helicopter, I knew I was where I belonged. I'd found my place. Nelli, I love what I do. I love the army. I love serving my country." Nicholas reached out and took her hands in his again. "But I love you more than anything. If you want me to leave the army, then that's what I'll do."

When tears filled her eyes, Nelli knew she'd been wrong about not having any left. She put her arms around her husband's neck and pulled him close. "Oh, Nicholas, I don't want you to give that all up for me. I'll love you and be here for you no matter what."

Nicholas wrapped her in his arms and kissed her.

"There's only one thing I ask of you."

"Anything."

"You can't let anything happen to you over there. You have to promise you'll come back to me."

"I promise."

Using the palms of both hands, Nelli wiped away her tears. She wondered for the millionth time what her life would have been like if only Nicholas had kept his promise to come back to her. She had no doubt it would have been a better life for her and the girls. She knew how much it hurt her daughters to not have their father with them throughout their lives. She'd done the best she could. Her father, Topsy, and Uncle Jim-Jim had helped all they could, but none of them could be what the girls wanted most of all— their Daddy.

Nelli smiled imagining how proud Nicholas would be of his three girls. He'd be so impressed with Kalli's journalistic and academic accomplishments. What a kick he would have gotten out of how much Nicola looked like him with her fiery red hair and bright blue eyes. Then there was Jilli, his youngest, who he barely had a chance to get to know. Her being a successful lawyer would have him bursting with pride.

There was another, much darker scenario that edged its way into Nelli's mind. How would it have turned out if she'd stood her ground and made him leave the army? Would he have been unhappy? If leaving the army had made him unhappy, would he have blamed her? Would his blaming her have led him to not wanting to be with her? Would it have made him stop loving her? Would he have left her and the girls as he went in search of finding happiness again? Would he have turned into an angry, bitter man? Nelli shook her head. It wasn't in him to be either of those. He was a kind, loving, forgiving man. She couldn't imagine anything could have changed him that much.

Nelli was brought back to the present by the sound of the squeaky door hinge and the voice of her daughter calling out to her.

"Mama, are you in here?"

Nelli stood up so fast she knocked the milking stool over. "I'm over here."

"There you are!" Jilli smiled as she came around the corner. "I've been looking everywhere for you."

Looking away from her daughter, Nelli quickly busied herself with filling a bucket with birdseed. "I'm sorry. I saw the birdfeeder was empty, so I came down here to get some bird seed. Then I sat down for a minute, and I guess time just got away from me."

"Mama, look at me." Jilli took her by the shoulders and looked into her face. "Oh, Mama, have you been crying?"

Smiling, Nelli put her free hand on Jilli's cheek. "Come on now, sweet girl. After the news I got yesterday, don't I deserve to cry just a little?"

Jilli pulled Nelli into a hug. "You most certainly do." She patted Nell's back before releasing her. "But crying time is over for now. Kalli and Jilli are on their way, and I believe you promised me breakfast."

"Oh, I did, did I?"

"Yes, you did." Jilli hooked her arm in Nelli's and led her out of the barn. "And as hungry as I am, a homemade breakfast by the one and only Nelli Hart is not a promise I'm likely to forget."

Arm in arm, the two walked back to the house.

"I don't know what you had planned for breakfast," Jilli said as they entered the kitchen, "but your made-from-scratch biscuits with homemade sausage gravy would bless my day."

"Somehow I knew that would be exactly what you'd want for breakfast."

"And how did you know that, Mama?"

"Maybe because it's the breakfast you've asked for every morning since you were five years old."

Jilli winked at her mother. "Isn't it great how some things never change!"

"It is, Jilli. It truly is."

CHAPTER THIRTEEN

While Nelli finished cleaning up the kitchen, Jilli headed back to her house to shower and get ready for the day. She hadn't packed anything to take to her mother's house because she hadn't anticipated she'd be spending the night. In all her wild imaginings, none had come close to the actual reason her mother hadn't showed up for Drew's baseball game. She still wasn't convinced the outlandish story Jake Albright told her mother had any truth to it.

When Jilli pulled in her driveway, she reached up to press the garage door remote. As she waited for the door to open, she noticed Ian's Land Rover was still parked in its usual place. It was unusual for Ian to be home at this time of the morning. Usually, he left for his office by six. It was after eight. As the garage door closed, she wondered if he was waiting to see her before starting his day. She smiled at the thought as she opened the back door.

She found Ian sitting at the kitchen island staring at his laptop computer screen. He was frowning when he looked up as she entered the kitchen. "Have you seen this?"

"Good morning to you, too, Mr. Sunshine." Jilli went to stand behind him. "Seen what?"

Ian's usual calm voice was filled with anger as he spit out his words. "This. . .this. . . disturbing picture of your daughter's bald head!"

Jilli looked at the screen to see the same picture of a shaved-head Hazel she'd seen the night before. She nodded. "I saw it last night."

Ian turned to look at her. "You saw this picture last night and you didn't think to say anything to me about it?"

Jilli walked over to their coffee bar, poured herself a cup of coffee, and took a sip before answering. "It was late when I saw it. I figured you were already asleep. Plus, I didn't think it was a big deal."

The sound of Ian's hands slamming the kitchen island countertop made Jilli jump. "You didn't think it was a big deal our daughter purposefully made herself look like a freak?"

Jilli set her cup on the counter then pulled a paper towel from its holder, leaned over, and mopped up the coffee he'd caused her to spill. "Hazel does not look like a freak. I admit she looks different, but she's still beautiful." She stood up and looked directly at her husband. "I think what she did was brave, and I'm proud of her."

Ian stood up to his full height of six feet four inches. "You're telling me you support what Hazel has done to herself."

Jilli put her hands on her hips. "That's what I'm telling you."

Ian took a step towards her. "Then you're as crazy as she is!"

Jilli hurriedly closed the distance between them. In a soft voice, she asked, "Ian, why are you so mad about this?" She smiled up at him and placed her hand on his chest. "It's only hair. It'll grow back."

Ian pulled away from her touch as if he'd been skewered with a hot poker. "That's not the point." He grabbed his computer from the counter and stormed out of the room.

Jilli was dumbfounded by his reaction. She couldn't remember when she'd ever seen him this upset. As she turned to retrieve her coffee cup, her eye caught a movement to her left. She spun around to find Drew standing in the doorway. When her eyes met his, she could see confusion in them.

"Oh Drew, how long have you been there?"

Drew stepped into the room. "Long enough to know Dad's madder than I've ever seen him!"

Jilli took a seat at the island and patted the stool next to her. "Come sit down." When he was seated, she said, "Hazel shaved her head to support a friend who has cancer, and Dad thinks that was a crazy thing to do."

Drew blew out a breath and leaned back. "Is that it? I thought something catastrophic must have happened."

Jilli took a sip of her now cold coffee. "Well, your dad thinks something catastrophic did happen."

Drew frowned. "I don't get why that would make Dad mad. Hazel called me a couple of days ago asking me what I thought about the whole thing. I told her I thought it was a cool thing to do. In fact, I was thinking about doing the same thing to show my support for Raymond."

Jilli choked on her coffee. Between coughs, she sputtered, "Please don't do that! It could send your father right over the edge."

Drew patted her on the back. "Mom, I was kidding."

Jilli put her hand on his shoulder. "Not funny, Drew."

"It was a little bit funny."

Jilli chuckled. "Okay, I'll admit it made me laugh a little, but it wouldn't be funny to your dad."

"What wouldn't be funny to me?"

Both Jilli and Drew jumped at the sound of Ian's voice.

Jilli answered with the first thing that popped into her head. "Drew was talking about doing something crazy with his hair. I told him you wouldn't think that was funny."

"You're right about that!" Ian turned to Drew. "I don't want to hear any more about you doing something weird to your hair. You got me?"

"Yes, sir."

Ian took his car keys from the hook next to the back door. "Let's go. I'm already late for work, and I don't want you to be late for school." He turned back to Jilli. "We can finish our discussion when we get home this evening."

"Sorry, but it'll have to wait until another time. Kalli and Nicola are coming today. We'll be staying with Mama for a few days."

Shaking his head, Ian turned and left without saying another word.

Kalli and Nicola spent the next hour of their ride chitchatting about everyday life and avoiding any serious conversations. Nicola was glad Kalli didn't ask about Alexandre or anything about the selling of the bakery. She wasn't ready to talk about any of that with her sister. Although the two of them usually got along well, there were those annoying times when Kalli would spew out her I-know-better-than-you opinion as to what she should do. If Nicola disagreed or didn't do exactly what she suggested— which was almost always— Kalli would fume and fuss or, even worse, go completely silent and refuse to speak to her. The longest Kalli had gone without speaking to her was when Nicola wanted to take up the carpet in her upstairs bedrooms and have hardwood floors installed. Kalli let her know in no uncertain terms just what an idiotic move she was making.

Nicola could still recall their conversation.

With her hands on her hips, Kalli had declared in a voice louder than necessary, "Don't you realize how cold hardwood floors will be when you get out of bed in the morning? Plus, hardwood floors are not low maintenance by any stretch of the imagination. They require regular sweeping and cleaning to prevent surface damage and to keep them looking nice. And you need to clean them with expensive products that won't damage the finish, and be extra careful with water. You won't have time to take care of hardwood floors. If you want something different, have new carpet put down."

Nicola had tried to keep her voice calm. "I know all of that, Kalli, but I like the look of hardwood. It's what I want."

"Have you given any consideration to the sound? Sound bounces off hardwood floors and gets amplified, which means everything is louder— voices, the TV, musical instruments!"

Nicola fought hard to keep from laughing at the mention of musical instruments. No one had ever played a musical instrument in the bedrooms. "I can deal with loud sounds."

"Not to mention the stress hardwood puts on your joints. You know you and Alexandre aren't getting any younger. Your joints are getting older every day."

"I don't care what you say, Kalli. I'm having the carpet taken up and hardwood put down." As soon as she said the words, she knew Kalli would take offense and think Nicola didn't value her opinion.

In typical Kalli over-reaction, she had yelled, "Fine! I will NEVER step on your precious hardwood floors. You can take that to the bank!" Then Kalli had turned and stomped out of the house.

It was four months before Nicola heard from her again. Kalli never apologized for her outburst and prolonged silence. Although she had actually stepped on those hardwoods floors many times, she'd never admitted how beautiful they were.

Now Nicola heard the edge in Kalli's voice when she mentioned Jake Albright. If her sister didn't believe he was telling the truth about their father, she wouldn't be receptive to listening to anyone's view that in any way contradicted hers. The days ahead promised to be interesting.

CHAPTER FOURTEEN

When Nelli got up from the breakfast table, she put potatoes to boiling on the stove. She wanted to make her homemade potato salad to go with the chicken salad she'd made the day before. As much as her three girls loved potato salad, she knew they'd appreciate the extra effort she went to make her special recipe. While the potatoes cooked, Nelli headed upstairs to air out the bedrooms. Besides last night when Jilli slept over, it'd been a long time since anyone had slept in those rooms. She went to each of the seven bedrooms— not sure which ones they would choose to occupy— and pulled back the curtains. It was more of a struggle to open the windows than she'd anticipated. She wasn't sure if it was because the windows hadn't been opened in months, maybe even years, or if she was weaker than she wanted to admit.

After finishing the potato salad and putting it to cool in the refrigerator, Nelli went around the house making sure all was in order. When she was satisfied everything was in its place, she went out to the front porch. She was about to sit down in the swing when she noticed the familiar yellow residue covering it. Looking around the porch, she could see every surface was wearing the same yellow coat. She looked out at the budding pecan trees lining the driveway. They, along with the pine trees all around the property, were the offenders showering her front porch with pollen.

Nelli loved the beauty and newness of spring, but hated this constant battle with pollen. She hurried down the side steps, pulled the hose from its coil, turned on the spigot, and set about freeing the yellow sticky deposit from every surface. When she finished, she stood back to admire the fresh look of her front porch. She knew this task would need to be added to her daily routine for the next few weeks. She had to remember how, when she had pecans to enjoy, all this work would be worth it.

After using the towel she'd thrown over her shoulder to dry off the porch swing, Nelli sat down. She folded her arms across her chest and closed her eyes. She couldn't remember the last time all three of her daughters had been home together. All she knew for certain was it had been far too long. She wondered if the call from Jake might turn out to be a blessing after all. Shaking her head, she quickly dismissed the thought. There was no way the turmoil his phone call had caused could be any kind of blessing.

The back and forth rhythm of the swing began to lull Nelli to sleep. She'd almost drifted off when she heard the crunching sound of tires pulling off the highway onto her pecan-shell driveway. She sat up straight and opened her eyes to see Kalli's red BMW coming toward the house. She could hardly believe it when she noticed Jilli's car pulling in right behind Kalli's. A thrill went through her at having all three arriving at the same time. She could see Nicola waving to her from the passenger's side window. Nelli stood and returned her wave. Jilli and Kalli began honking their horns. As soon as their cars came to a stop, their doors flew open, and all three jumped out. With shouts of delight, they ran in to one another's arms. Nelli stood on the porch for a moment taking in the happy sight before hurrying down the steps to join her daughters in their reunion. They were all talking at the same time, making it hard to tell who was saying what.

Nelli held on to her daughters, "I can't believe y'all are here!"

Squeezing her sisters and Nelli tightly, Nicola added, "It's been way too long!"

Kalli took a step back. "Why did we wait so long to get together?"

"I believe it's y'all living such busy lives." Nelli chuckled. "That's the culprit."

Kalli hugged Nelli again. "You know what, Mama? I believe you're exactly right!"

"Oh, my!" Nelli exclaimed. "Y'all mark this day down in your calendars as the day Kalli actually said I was right about something!"

Giggling, Jilli agreed. "You're right, Mama, it is a day to remember."

Kalli pulled away again. "Okay! Okay! Enough already."

Nelli leaned over to kiss Kalli's forehead. "Kalli's right. That's enough teasing for now."

"Let's get our things out of the car and upstairs." Turning to Nelli Nicola asked, "Can I have the bedroom that looks out over the front of the house?"

"Sure, y'all can take any bedroom you want. I'll get lunch ready while you settle in." Nelli turned to leave.

"What's for lunch?" Kalli called after her.

"You'll have to wait to see."

Kalli shook her head. "I knew she was going to say that."

Nicola patted her sister on the back. "She always does."

Nicola collected her suitcase and followed her sisters into the house and up the stairs.

Jilli stopped outside the room the three sisters had once shared. "I slept in here last night." As she reached for the doorknob to open the door, she looked back at her sisters. "Do y'all want to share the room like old times? It might be fun."

Nicola looked at Jilli then at Kalli, and burst out laughing. "You've got to be kidding. It was tough enough sharing that room as teenagers. I can't even imagine it now!"

Jilli ran her hand across her forehead. "Whew! I was afraid you were going to say yes." She opened the bedroom door and went inside, leaving her sisters standing in the hallway.

Nicola pointed toward the closed door in the middle of the hallway. "You don't mind if I take the room that looks out over the porch, do you? I know it's the biggest, but it's my favorite."

Kalli forced a smile. "Go right ahead. The one at the end of the hall will suit me just fine."

Dragging her suitcase behind her, Kalli made her way to the smaller bedroom with the partially obstructed view of the backyard. She set her suitcase down, kicked off her shoes, and sat down on the bed. Even though she hadn't thought about taking the much larger bedroom with the best view, it annoyed her how Nicola assumed the bedroom would be hers. Her younger sister hadn't seemed to give the slightest consideration that she might want the larger bedroom. Kalli had grown accustomed to Nicola getting what she wanted, since that was how it'd been most of their lives. Most of the time, it didn't bother her when Nicola took what she wanted without giving any thought to what anyone else might want. However, for some reason, on this day, it did bother her.

Kalli laid back on the bed and put her arms under her head as she stared up at the ceiling trying to remember when the cycle of giving in to her sister had begun. The furthest back she could recall was the Christmas when she was six years old. She'd gotten a Betsy Wetsy doll that would wet her diaper after you fed her a bottle filled with water. Every time she changed the doll's diaper it made her feel as if Betsy Wetsy were a real baby, and she was truly her mother.

That same Christmas, Nicola had been given a Tiny Tears doll that would cry little tears after she was given a bottle. She seemed to be content with wiping away her doll's tears until Kalli made the mistake of bragging how her doll didn't just shed a few tiny wet tears, but poured out so much water she wet an entire diaper just like a real baby. From that moment on, Nicola cried for Kalli's Betsy Wetsy doll until their mother came up with a solution. The two would share their dolls with one another. Nicola was thrilled with their mother's resolution, but Kalli was devastated to have to share her very own precious baby with her sister.

The sharing solution became the pattern of Kalli's life. It expanded when Jilli grew older and began to want what her older sisters had. It went from dolls to clothes to makeup to jewelry. After a while, Kalli no longer thought of the things she was given as "mine," but rather as "ours." As she thought about it now, it was still the same for her. She was still giving in to what her sisters wanted. In the past, it'd made life much easier, less stressful. She'd accepted the life motto of "Go along to get along."

This time she wasn't sure she'd be able to go along with her sisters' or her mother's thoughts about what Jake Albright was trying to convince them was true. Her journalistic training told her to question him, not simply accept what he said because it was what the others wanted. This time would be different if they were determined to take this Jake guy at his word. This time, she was going to let them know what she thought about Jake Albright's declarations, even if it meant not getting along.

Nicola entered the bedroom she'd chosen for herself to find the room dark and gloomy, not at all as she'd remembered it to be. Tossing her overnight bag on the bed, she hurried to the tall, east-facing windows. She pulled the curtains back from the window and sunlight flooded into the room, replacing the gloominess with its radiant brightness. This was the bright, cheerful bedroom of her childhood memories.

With a smile on her lips, Nicola remembered how, when there were no guests occupying this room, it became her own secret bedroom. Late at night when she was sure her sisters were sound asleep in the tiny, cramped bedroom they shared; this was the room whose door she'd tiptoe to. This was the room whose walls she would whisper her dreams to. This was the room whose windows she would look out on a world she wished she could escape to.

Looking out those same windows now, Nicola felt a twinge of her childhood desire to escape. She thought for a minute about where she would go if she could leave right now. Maybe she'd go to an uninhabited island or to an isolated mountain cabin. She didn't know where she'd go, but she did know what she wanted to escape from. She wanted to escape from fights with Alexandre about the bakeries. She wanted to escape from the drama Jake Albright was bringing into her family's lives.

Nicola plopped down on the padded, built-in window seat and put her head in her hands. She was and always had been a determined person, never allowing anyone or anything to stop her from reaching her goals. If she had to fight for what she wanted, she fought by whatever means were necessary. She was aware of how her stubbornness and resolve often alienated others, which at times included friends and even family.

It'd never been Nicola's objective to upset anyone, but somehow, she did. She was sure her sisters often referred to her in ugly, less-than-kind words. After all, they'd been the first ones who'd gotten the brunt of her desires. She couldn't count the number of times she'd heard Kalli tell the story of how she'd had to give up some doll she got for Christmas because Nicola wanted it. Nicola didn't remember the incident. Every time she heard her sister speak of it, in Nicola's mind, it made Kalli weaker. She would have fought tooth and nail before giving up something she loved.

Jilli went into her bedroom, shut the door, and leaned against it. She would never have admitted it to her sisters, but she was disappointed they weren't going to share a bedroom like old times. A small part of her had hoped her older sisters would want to stay together. She didn't know what memories they had taken away from those years when they shared a bedroom, but the memories she held on to were ones of whispered dreams and wishes shared in the safety of their darkened room when they were supposed to be asleep. She could remember Mama coming to the door and warning them there would be severe consequences if they didn't quiet down and get to sleep. Then as soon as she walked away, no matter how hard they tried to obey, one would begin to giggle, which would start an avalanche of giggling from the other two.

As Jilli stepped away from the door, she tried to remember the last time she'd giggled. She knew she laughed and often chuckled, but she hadn't giggled in quite some time. She set her overnight bag on one of the empty beds. As she began to unpack, her mind wandered back to her days of growing up in this house as the youngest daughter of three. Many might assume that, as the youngest, she'd been the one to be spoiled. But she'd never felt spoiled if spoiled meant you got what you wanted and everyone treated you as if you were special in a precious kind of way. However, if spoiled meant you were loved, then Jilli might agree she'd been spoiled. She couldn't remember a time when she hadn't felt loved.

Jilli didn't remember much about her father, but she'd been sure of his love for her. She could remember him saying, "I love you so much, little bug. Your sweet kisses and hugs along with that smile of yours makes your Mama and me so happy. Don't you ever take them away or we'll be the saddest people in the whole wide world." She couldn't be sure he'd said those exact words to her or if she'd simply imagined he'd said them. Either way, they'd become the memory of her father she cherished most.

Once she'd finished unpacking, Jilli took out her cell phone. She needed to prepare Hazel for her father's anger concerning her new hairstyle. She selected Hazel's name and number from her contact list and held the phone to her ear as she waited for her daughter to answer. She hoped and prayed Ian hadn't called her before he calmed down.

"Hey, Mama! What's up?"

"Your father's temper, that's what."

"I take it he's heard about my hair—or lack of—and isn't happy about it."

"That's putting it rather mildly. Has he called?"

"I saw where I missed a couple of his calls while I was in class. I was standing here in the middle of the Quad deciding whether or not I should call him when you called."

"If I were you, I'd wait to make that call."

"I can't believe he's mad!" Hazel sighed. "I thought as a doctor he'd understand how hard it'll be for Raymond to not only lose all of his hair, but to go through months of cell-killing, life-sucking chemo."

Jilli blew out a long breath. "Of course, he knows, Hazel, but that's not the point. You could have given us some warning instead of us having to find out about it on FaceBook. It was shock not only for Dad, but for all of us. Plus, you know how logical your Dad is. In his mind your shaving your head in no way helps your friend survive cancer."

Hazel's voice became defensive. "So, you think what I did was stupid?"

"I didn't say that. I think what you did was brave. I totally get how you're showing your support for Raymond. But—"

Hazel interrupted, "I knew there'd be a but!"

"But a little warning would have been respectful of your father's feelings. I know you're an adult and it is your hair, but you'll always be Daddy's-little-girl to him. He's just having a hard time letting go and allowing you to make your own decisions without consulting him."

There was a long pause before Hazel spoke again. "Okay, I'll give you that. It's done, so that's that. Drew texted me to let me know he thought my slick head was polar."

"I'm guessing that means cool. I bet you didn't get the same kind of message from Morgan."

"You'd be correct." Hazel chuckled. "I don't even wanna go there."

"Me either. Do me a favor and wait a day or two until you call your Dad. I'm spending a couple of days here with Grandma and my sisters. I'll talk to him when I get back home."

"Is something wrong with Grandma?"

"No, we're just visiting."

"Okay, I'll put Dad off for a few days."

"Thanks, I appreciate it. Love you, Hazel."

"Love you too, Mama."

Jilli ended the call. She hated it when there was turmoil in her family. It gave her a headache along with a sick feeling in the pit of her stomach. How could she keep everyone—Mama, Ian, Morgan, Hazel, Drew—happy? The task was becoming more than she could handle. She dropped down on the bed. Closing her eyes, she spoke aloud the prayer she prayed every day.

"God of Grace, You make me softer, kinder, gentler, generous, forgiving, and loving. Yet I feel these gifts wearing thin. I feel my impatience rising. So, I pray today and all days for more of Your Spirit. May the grace You pour out open the door for a renewing of my mind, a restoration of my heart, and a transformation of my soul. Amen."

When she finished, she got up from the bed, revived and ready to face what lay ahead.

CHAPTER FIFTEEN

Since it was a special occasion with all three girls coming home, Nelli made the decision she would serve lunch in the dining room. She couldn't remember the last time she'd eaten a meal in the dining room. It might have been Christmas two years ago. The past few years she hadn't had all three of her daughters and their families home at the same time for Christmas. Instead, they'd come at separate times–some before Christmas and some after.

She enjoyed carrying on the Christmas traditions with each family in turn. Those traditions always brought her comfort. But after celebrating Christmas three separate times, she was worn out by the time the New Year dawned. She hoped this year all three of her daughters and their families would come for Christmas at the same time. It would be a true blessing to have her big house filled.

Nelli had just finished setting the table with her everyday china when Kalli came in the room.

"What can I do to help, Mama?"

"How about getting the drinks ready? I made lemonade."

"Fresh-squeezed lemonade?"

"Is there any other kind?" Nelli winked at her daughter.

"Actually, there is, but I guess not in this house."

Nelli put her hands on her hips. "Don't tell me you make that awful artificial stuff they claim is made from real lemons?"

Kalli kissed her mother on the top of the head as she made her way to the refrigerator to retrieve the pitcher of lemonade. "Never!"

"Never, what?" Jilli asked joining her mother and sister in the kitchen.

Kalli answered without missing a beat. "We thought you were never going to get down here to help us."

"Well, I'm here now." Jilli bowed to her sister and mockingly asked, "Oh, please tell me, Great One, what can I do to be of assistance?"

Kalli rolled her eyes. "Aren't you the funny one!"

"I thought I was the funny one!" Nicola chimed in as she entered the kitchen.

Jilli pointed a finger at her. "No, you're the funny looking one!"

Nicola punched Jilli's arm. "Take that back!"

Nelli clapped her hands together. "Now stop that and help me carry the rest of the food into the dining room."

Nicola picked up the crystal bowl with the chicken salad from the counter. "Oh, so we're being fancy-schmancy."

Nelli laughed. "Why not? I thought I'd go all out for such a special occasion with all three of my girls home at the same time."

Kalli held up the remaining bowl. "Look, y'all. She even made her famous potato salad."

After everything was placed on the table, the four sat down, bowed their heads, and clasped hands. Together they said the prayer they'd said since childhood.

"Come, Lord Jesus, be our guest. Let this food to us be blessed. Amen."

Smiling, Nelli looked from one daughter to the next. "Thank y'all for coming. Enjoy!"

For the next thirty minutes the normally silent dining room was filled with easy laughter and pleasant conversation. It wasn't until the table was cleared and Nelli brought out the dark chocolate walnut brownies and coffee that the conversation turned to what had been on each of their minds— Nelli's conversation with Jake Albright.

Kalli was the one who brought up the subject. "Mama, I think it'd really help me"—she gestured to the Nicola and Jilli— "well, all of us, to have a clearer understanding of this whole thing if you could tell us exactly what Jake Albright said on the phone to you yesterday."

Nelli took a sip of her coffee, trying to recall his exact words. "I'm not sure I can remember exactly what he said, Kalli. I can give you the gist of the conversation."

"That's fine. Just do the best you can."

Nelli set her cup back on its saucer. She folded her hands in front of her as she leaned forward. "First of all, let me start by saying he seemed like a nice young man, very polite, sympathetic, and nervous. He was trying his best not to upset me."

Kalli nodded, encouraging her mother to continue.

"The first thing that got my attention was he called me by my full name. Only telemarketers do that. I almost hung up, but something told me not to. He asked me if I was married to Chief Hart. When I said I was, he told me his father, Steven Albright, had served in Vietnam with him."

Nelli paused to look at her daughters. All three girls seemed to be hanging on her every word.

"I couldn't remember your Daddy ever mentioning that name. I know he never wrote about a Steven Albright in any of his letters. I asked him if they'd been helicopter pilots together or something like that, but then he said his father had been a prisoner of war. I was about to tell him how sorry I was to hear that when he added that Nicholas had been with his father as a POW. I told him that just wasn't true. I told him right away he was wrong because I had his death certificate given to me by the Army which clearly stated he'd died from wounds sustained in a helicopter crash."

Pausing, Nelli studied the faces of each of her daughters. She could feel compassion radiating from each one. Before continuing, she took a moment to clear her throat of the emotions threatening to overtake her voice.

"He told me the Army had lied to me, to us. Nicholas didn't die in the helicopter crash as they reported. He was taken as a prisoner of war by the Vietcong. Then he told me your father died escaping from a POW Camp, and he had a letter to prove it."

Nelli couldn't hold back her feelings any longer. She put her head in her hands and began to cry. Jilli was at her mama's side before the other two had a chance to react.

"Oh, Mama, it's going to be okay." Jilli said as she bent down beside her and wrapped her arms around her.

Nicola's eyes filled with tears as she reached out to put a comforting hand on her Mama's shoulder. "Jilli's right. We're all here for you, Mama. We'll get through this together."

Kalli sat back in her chair and folded her arms. "I don't believe him. I think he's feeding you a bunch of bull!"

Nelli sat up wiping the tears from her face to stare at her daughter.

Nicola slapped her hand down on the table. "You've got to be kidding me, Kalli! That's your reaction! You are such a—"

Nelli held up her hand, interrupting her middle daughter. "Wait a minute, Nicola." Looking over at Kalli, she said, "Tell me your thoughts on why you don't believe him."

Kalli leaned toward her mother. Putting up her index finger, she began her explanation, "First of all, you have an official certificate of Dad's death from the Army."

Holding up two fingers, she continued, "Second of all, it doesn't make sense that this Steven Albright stayed silent for over fifty years and waited until he's on his death bed to tell his son to contact us."

Holding up a third finger, she added, "And third of all, we know nothing about this Jake Albright who wants to come to your house to show you some sort of letter that's supposed to legitimize his claims."

Kalli leaned back in her chair and crossed her arms over her chest. "I believe his wanting to come here is part of his scam. I think he's up to something, like convincing you to give him money to go to Vietnam to supposedly retrieve Dad's body. He'll take the money, and we'll never see him again."

Nelli covered her mouth in shock. "Oh, Kalli, why are you so cynical?"

Nicola didn't wait for Kalli to answer. "She's a journalist, Mama. She doesn't trust anyone. She believes everyone has an ulterior motive."

Kalli pointed her finger at Nicola. "And I'm right ninety-nine percent of the time."

Jilli stood up and walked over to put her hand on Kalli's shoulder. "You may be right, Kalli, but we need to approach this systematically before jumping to conclusions. Let's start by finding out what we can about Jake Albright. We also need to contact the Army to check out Steven Albright's service record to verify he was, in fact, a prisoner of war in Vietnam."

"And we can find out if they're aware a scam is being used to get money out of other military widows," Kalli added.

"You're both right," Nicola said. "The good thing is we have time to verify and get the facts before Mama has to meet with Jake Albright."

Nelli gazed at her daughters through shining eyes. "I thank God you three are here to help me work through this whole thing. I love you all so very much."

As soon as the dishes were cleared away from the dining room and the kitchen was put back in order, Jilli was at her mother's desk making a list. That was how she started all her big projects. Things always seemed overwhelming to her until she was able to put things in order. After looking over her list, she decided the best place to start was to arrange for a background check on both Steven and Jake Albright. It was possible a thorough background check might take several days or even a week. Since they were to meet with Jake in only a few days, she needed to get that started as soon as possible. She picked up her cell and punched in her law office number.

"Hart Law Office, Sade speaking. How may help you?"

"Hey, Sade, it's Jilli."

"Good grief, Mrs. Parker, I didn't even know it was you calling. I didn't think to look at the caller ID before I picked up the phone. Are you still at your Mama's?"

Sade Price had been the first person Jilli had hired after she purchased the law firm from Mr. Harrison. Jilli believed hiring Sade, who'd just graduated high school at the time, had been one of her better decisions. She rarely missed a day of work, and Jilli couldn't remember a day when she didn't have a smile on her face. The only criticism she had about her secretary was how much she liked to hear herself talk. She could make a narrative about a one-minute encounter with a person into a thirty-minute story.

"Yes, I'm still here at Mama's. Kalli and Nicola got here a little before noon."

"That's so nice y'all are together. I love it when my whole family gets together. We have the most fun and—"

Jilli interrupted, "That's nice. Now, listen, Sade, I need to get a background check on a couple of people. Didn't we use Marv somebody-or-other from over in Walbridge that last time we had to run a background check?"

"That was Marv Hammond, but I don't think he's in business anymore. I heard he shut down his PI business and moved to Florida to be near family. I think he has a brother and sister who live down there."

Jilli blew out a breath. "That's disappointing. He was good. Do we know of any other private investigators around this area?"

"Well, it's funny you would ask me about that today. Yesterday I wouldn't have had an answer for you, but today I do. This gentleman— a rather good-looking one if I do say so myself— stopped by the office late yesterday afternoon. He said he used to live here in

Ida, but moved away to Augusta years ago to seek his fortune. When he didn't find his fortune there, he decided to come on back home."

"And that helps us with a private investigator how?"

"Oh, my goodness, I forgot to mention the most important thing about his visit. He's a private investigator and setting up shop right here in Ida. He stopped by to give me his card in case we ever find ourselves in need of his services."

"You say he's from Ida originally?"

"That's what he said."

"What's his name, Sade?"

"Just a minute. Let me find his card. I put it away in a special place, but for the life of me I can't remember where that might be."

Jilli tapped her pencil on the desk while she waited for Sade to find the card.

"Oh, here it is. His name is Aaron Bailer."

Jilli dropped her pencil. "Say that name again."

"Aaron Bailer."

"You've got to be kidding me. Aaron Bailer? Are you telling me Aaron Bailer is a private investigator right here in Ida?"

"That's the name on the card. Do you know him?"

"I did know him." The memory came flooding back to her of sitting on the steps outside Ida County High School when Aaron Bailer changed her life by inviting her to join the ICHS Debate Team. Jilli picked up her pencil. "Give me his number."

When Jilli announced she was headed to their mother's office, Kalli offered to get in touch with a contact she'd made at the Pentagon for a freelance article she'd written. Although it'd been over a year since she'd spoken with Colonel Whithew Badger, she was confident he'd remember her since he'd asked her out on a date when he'd learned she was a widow. Professional ethics necessitated she decline his offer, but she'd been tempted. She was pleased when she found she hadn't deleted his private number from her phone contacts.

Wanting privacy, Kalli stepped out to the front porch as she punched in the colonel's number. She put her cell phone to her ear and waited for him to answer. It didn't take long before she heard his gruff, no-nonsense voice.

"Colonel Badger here."

"Colonel Badger, this is Kalli Abbott. I'm not sure if you remember me or not, but I interviewed you about a year ago for the *Atlanta Journal-Constitution* for my article about women serving in the military."

"Of course, I remember you, Dr. Abbott. If I remember correctly, that was a professionally written article."

"Thank you, sir, but please call me Kalli."

The colonel's voice took on a softer tone. "Okay, then I'd be pleased if you would call me Whit. How are you, Kalli?"

"I'm doing fine, sir, uh, Whit. How about you?"

"I'm fine as well. To what do I owe the pleasure of your phone call today, Kalli? Are you writing another article?"

Kalli suddenly realized she hadn't put as much planning as she should have into what she wanted to ask him. She closed her eyes and focused on how to phrase her request. "No, Whit, this is on a more personal note. I believe I told you how I lost my father in Vietnam."

"Yes, I do recall you mentioning something about his being killed in a plane crash."

"Yes, it was a helicopter crash. He was the pilot, and his entire crew was killed." Kalli paused for a moment before continuing. "At least the Army told us that was how he died."

"I'm not sure what you mean. It sounds as if you're questioning whether the Army gave your family an accurate accounting of your father's death."

"Actually, it's come into question, Whit. That's why I've called you."

"Please continue."

"Yesterday my mother got a phone call from a man who says he has a letter his father wrote on his deathbed. In this letter he makes the claim my father didn't die in a helicopter crash as we'd been told. Instead, he was taken prisoner by the Vietcong and later died trying to escape from a POW Camp."

Kalli's story was met with silence.

Resolute, Kalli continued. "I think he's made up this story as part of some scam to take advantage of my mother, but what he told her does give me pause. I have to admit it's put some doubt in my mind as to what the Army told us all those years ago."

"And you've called to ask me to check out his story against the one your family was given by the Army?"

Kalli blew out the breath she hadn't even realized she'd been holding. "Yes, or give me a name of who I need to contact to help us clear this up."

"I'll see what I can do. Let me get some information from you." Whit's voice was all business. "I need your father's full name, his rank, his service number if you have it, and the date of his death, or rather, supposed death. It would help if you could get a copy of his death certificate to me."

"I'll get all of that to you, Whit, as soon as I can." She paused. "Thank you so very much, Whit. I can't tell you how much your willingness to help means to me and my family."

"I want to get to the bottom of this, Kalli. If this guy who called your mother is running a scam, the Army needs to be aware. If it turns out it is a scam, it just might be more common than we know. And if the Army declared a soldier dead when he was still alive and could have been rescued, then that's a travesty as well."

"Once again, I can't thank you enough for offering to help us with this, Whit."

"I'm glad I can be of help, Kalli. Please assure your mother we'll get to the bottom of all this."

Before ending the call, Whit gave Kalli his email address so she could send the information he requested.

Kalli put her phone in the back pocket of her jeans and sat down on the front porch swing. She was so deep in thought about her conversation with Whit she didn't notice Nicola had joined her on the porch until she sat down next to her on the swing.

Nicola put her hand over Kalli's "How did it go with your Pentagon contact?"

"It went well." Kalli looked over at her sister. "Actually, I think it went great. I have to send him some information about Dad, then he'll start investigating Jake Albright's claims."

Nicola patted Kalli's hand. "That's good to hear."

Glancing around the porch, Kalli asked, "Where's Mama? I need to get that information about Dad from her."

"She went upstairs to her bedroom. She said she needed a little nap. I don't think she got much sleep last night."

"I bet she won't be sleeping much until we clear this whole thing up."

Nicola nodded in agreement.

"Do you know what Jilli has found out?"

"I haven't seen her since lunch."

Kalli turned toward the sound of the front porch door opening and watched as Jilli joined them.

"What are y'all up to?" Jilli asked.

Kalli stopped the swing for Jilli to sit. "A person I know at the Pentagon has offered to help us find out who's telling the truth."

"That's good."

"What about you? Have you found out anything about Jake and his father?"

"Not yet, but I've got the name of a private investigator I'm going to contact to help us with that." Jilli clapped her hands together. "And you're not going to believe who it is."

"Who is it?" Nicola asked.

"Aaron Bailer!"

"Aaron Bailer?" Kalli and Nicola said at the exact same time.

"Yep. Sade said he stopped by yesterday to give her his card. Said he's moved back after living in Augusta for a several years to start his own business as a private investigator."

"The thing I remember most about Aaron Bailer," Kalli said as she leaned back, "was how good looking he was. I think every girl in the whole school was in love with him."

"Well, I sure wasn't," Nicola said. "I thought he was arrogant and full of himself."

Kalli chuckled. "That's because he's the only boy in school who never gave you the attention you thought you deserved."

"And that's because Nicola only had eyes for Tony Meeks." Jilli fluttered her eyelashes at Nicola.

"Oh, my!" Nicola put her hands to her cheeks. "I haven't thought about Tony in years and years."

Putting a finger to her lips, Kalli said, "Hmm, if I remember right, you two were pretty crazy about each other. There was a time when you thought he was the one you'd end up marrying."

"No way I ever thought about marrying Tony!" Nicola said shaking her head.

"Yes, way! You wrote Nicola Mae Meeks all over your notebooks," Jilli said laughing.

Nicola rolled her eyes at Jilli. "I guess I do remember thinking I was crazy in love with Tony."

"Okay, enough about Tony." Kalli stopped the swing and leaned up to get her sisters' attention. "Getting back to Aaron Bailer, handsome or not, I just hope he can find out what we need to know about Jake and his father."

"That's what I'm going to hire him to do," Jilli said as she started the swing in motion once again.

The three sat in companionable silence swinging back and forth contemplating the events of the past few days.

Kalli's voice broke the silence. "I'm not sure what's going to happen or what we're going to find out over the next few days. But I do know I'm glad we're here together to help Mama through it all."

CHAPTER SIXTEEN

Entering her bedroom, Nelli was welcomed by a soft, warm breeze from the open windows. She kicked off her shoes, sat down on her bed, and breathed in the fresh air. In one fluid move, she lifted her quilt from the end of her bed and wrapped it around her as she laid her tired body down.

As she lay there, Nelli's mind went back to the lunch time conversation with her daughters. She grimaced. It had all been so pleasant until she'd let her emotions get the best of her which had upset her daughters. She hadn't meant for that to happen. She was usually so good at keeping her emotions in check. It was obvious to Nelli this whole thing with Jake Albright was causing her to lose control. The thought now came to her that she may have been wrong to involve her daughters.

What bothered Nelli most of all was knowing how much her crying must have upset Jilli. She was Nelli's sensitive child. When Jilli was put into her arms the day she was born, Nelli could hardly believe she was hers. Kalli had been born with hair as black as coal just like her own. Nicola had been born with fiery red hair just like her father's. This daughter, at first glance, appeared to have been born without hair, but upon closer inspection soft, silvery tufts of hair could be seen covering her head. There hadn't been a fair-haired member of their family in three generations, until now.

As Jilli began to grow, it became evident to Nelli just how different she was from her two older sisters in more ways than her hair color. Both Kalli and Nicola were healthy, active children who loved to run and play outside from dawn to dusk. As a small child, Jilli was plagued with allergies which left her weak and unable to leave the house. As she got older and stronger, she grew out of her allergies, but continued to confine herself to the house. She became Nelli's constant shadow. Wherever she went, Jilli went. Whatever she was doing, Jilli wanted to do or at least try to do.

At first, Nelli worried something was wrong with Jilli because she never seemed to want to venture outside the house. It was such a drastic change from her sisters. But as Jilli grew older, it became obvious to Nelli she found pleasure in being with her and helping her in any way she could, including making sure she never did anything to upset her.

Pushing thoughts of Jilli and Jake Albright's troubling news out of her head, Nelli fell asleep.

Nelli couldn't believe how quickly her fifteen-minute nap ended. She got out of bed and stopped by her bathroom to splash some water on her face before going down the back stairs to the kitchen. When she got to the kitchen, she noticed the large cast iron skillet that had once been her mother's filled with frying chicken on one of the burners. She decided Nicola must be preparing their evening meal. But fried chicken was a strange thing for Nicola to fix since neither of her sisters would eat anything fried.

She walked through the kitchen and out the back door, looking for her middle daughter to find out why she had left the fried chicken unattended. When she stepped off the porch's bottom step onto the cool, damp grass, she was surprised to find she hadn't put on her shoes after getting up from her nap. She couldn't remember when the last time was she'd walked out into her backyard with bare feet. She started to go back in the house to get her shoes, but decided she liked the feeling of being barefoot. She had happy memories of how as a child she'd run around with bare feet most of the summer and how much she loved the freedom of it. Feeling carefree once again, she took off running.

Nelli came to a dead stop when she came upon the wooden cabin her grandmother Topsy had once lived in instead of her garage in the backyard. The longer she stared at the wooden structure, the more she was convinced it was the same wooden cabin that had been torn down over twenty years ago after Topsy passed away. Filled with confusion and apprehension, she made her way to the familiar front door. With only a light tap on the door, it swung open. She stood frozen by the scene before her.

There was Topsy, sitting in her favorite rocking chair, engrossed in the book she held in her hand. When she looked up to see Nelli, she closed her book and took off her reading glasses. After setting her book and glasses on the side table, she held out her arms to her granddaughter.

"Oh, my sweet Nelli Belle, I've been waiting for you."

Nelli rushed into her grandmother's open arms. Burying her face in her shoulder, she began to cry.

Topsy began rocking back and forth as she patted Nelli's back. "Now, now, my little one, you're safe with me. Hush, there's nothing to cry about."

Nelli wrapped her arms around Topsy's neck. "Oh Topsy, I'm so glad to be here with you. I've missed you so."

"Why, child, I've been here for you the whole time. You just had to want to find me."

Nelli pulled away to look in her grandmother's face. "What do you mean, Topsy?"

"I know you've been having a hard time since that man told you all he did about Nicholas. I've wanted to help you through this troubled time, but you haven't called on the one who can really help you even one time."

"Do you mean Daddy?"

"No, girl! I shouldn't have to tell you who you need to be calling on to get through this hard time."

"I don't know who you mean."

"Well, I can't tell you. You have to find out for yourself."

"Oh, please just tell me, Topsy! Who's the someone who can help me sort all of this out?"

Topsy shook her head. "No, it's all up to you. Now, you need to get up from my lap and go on back to the house. I can smell that fried chicken your Mama is cooking for supper tonight."

Nelli didn't want to leave the comfort of her grandmother's lap, but when Topsy abruptly stood, Nelli fell to the floor.

Nelli woke with a start. Her eyes frantically darted around the room. It took several minutes before she understood she was in her own bedroom at her home and being with Topsy had been a dream. She pulled the quilt up to her chin as she thought back on her dream. It had felt so real. It was as if she'd truly spent the afternoon visiting with her grandmother. Sitting there in Topsy's lap, with her arms wrapped around her neck, she'd felt at peace. Turning toward her bedroom window, she curled her knees up to her chest and closed her eyes. She wondered if she could make herself fall back to sleep and reclaim the feeling.

After several minutes, she recognized the futility of trying to recapture her dream. She tossed back the quilt, sat up, and slipped her feet into her shoes. She chuckled to herself remembering how her shoes had been the one thing she'd forgotten to put on in her dream. She sat on the edge of her bed considering the reasons why she had returned to her childhood in her dream. What had made her conjure up Topsy? Had she wanted to go back to the innocence of being a child? Was she looking for comfort? Maybe there was no reason at all for the dream, and it was just a senseless wandering of her tired mind.

Nelli made her way to the bathroom where she washed her face and brushed her hair. After studying her reflection in the mirror, she decided she needed to brighten up her face. Searching through her makeup drawer, she found a tube of lipstick—something she rarely wore. Topsy had always told her a woman wasn't presentable until she'd put on her lipstick. After covering her lips, she smacked them together and smiled, knowing her grandmother would be pleased she'd taken the time to look "presentable."

As Nelli stepped out of her bedroom and made her way down the hall, she had an uneasy feeling she'd left something important behind. She turned and walked back to her bedroom. She glanced around the room. Everything seemed to be in its place. What had called her back? She closed her eyes, blocking out the world around her. It was then she heard her Topsy's words as clearly as if she were standing right there beside her.

We know you've been having a hard time since that man told you all he did about Nicholas. I've wanted to help you through this troubled time, but you haven't called on the one who can really help you even one time.

Nelli now knew who her grandmother was talking about. She knew who it was she needed to call on this very minute. She stood in the door of her bedroom and bowed her head as she folded her hands. She spoke her prayer out loud.

"Blessed Father, You know every decision I need to make and every challenge I face. Please, Lord, forgive me for the times I try to figure this life out on my own. I need You. I need Your Holy Spirit to give me strength, wisdom, and direction. In Jesus' name I pray, Amen."

CHAPTER SEVENTEEN

Nelli went down the back stairs after her nap and straight into the kitchen. She glanced at the stove almost expecting to see her mother's old cast iron skillet on a burner filled with frying chicken. Shaking the vision from her head, she walked to the sink to fill the teakettle with water. After setting it on the stove to heat, she went in search of her daughters. They weren't in the house, so she headed to the front porch where she found them sitting on the front porch swing deep in conversation.

"I've looked all over the house for y'all," Nelli called out as she opened the door. Kalli scooted over and patted the spot between her and Nicola. "Come join us, Mama. This swing is big enough to hold all of us."

Nicola put her arm around Nelli as she sat down. "How was your nap?"

Nelli hadn't decided if she would tell them about her dream or not. It might be something she'd share later. She patted Nicola's leg. "Actually, it was a good nap. It was exactly what I needed."

"Glad to hear that," Nicola said. She rested her head on Nelli's shoulder.

Jilli leaned forward. "We've been busy while you were resting. I think I've found a private investigator to check out Jake and his father."

Kalli quickly added, "And I was able to talk to my contact at the Pentagon who promises to check out Jake's claims. I'm confident he'll be able to verify Daddy was killed in that helicopter crash as reported."

"It does sound like y'all have gotten the ball rolling on this whole investigation thing." Looking to each of her daughters, Nelli added, "I couldn't ask for a better team to help with this problem. I can't thank y'all enough. It means a great deal to me to have each of you here with me."

Kalli patted Nelli's shoulder. "We're glad we can help, Mama."

Jilli put her foot out to stop the forward motion of the swing. Turning her head from side to side, she asked, "What is that noise?"

Nicola leaned forward to listen. "It sounds like some sort of whistle."

Nelli slapped Nicola's and Kalli's legs as she jumped out of the swing. "Oh, my goodness. That's the teakettle I put on before I came out here." She paused to look back at her daughters and asked in her best British accent, "How about a spot of tea?"

All three girls laughed as they rose as one from their places on the swing to follow their mother into the house. Soon they were all settled at the kitchen table, each with a cup of Earl Grey tea.

Nelli took her seat at the end of the table. She looked at her daughters who were seated before her. "It seems we've spent most of our time together talking about the past since y'all arrived. Let's talk about the present. Tell me what's going on in your lives right now."

Jilli blew on her hot tea. "Well, I guess I should tell y'all what Hazel has done to herself, which, I should add, has greatly upset her father."

Kalli set down her cup and turned to her sister. "Oh, my, that sounds ominous."

Jilli glanced around the table before blurting out, "She shaved her head."

"Shaved her head!" Nicola put her hands to her head, "Not all of her beautiful red hair?"

"Yes, ma'am. Every last strand snipped and shaved off, gone."

"What in the world made her do such a thing?" Nelli asked. "I know my granddaughter well enough to know she didn't just do it on a whim or a dare."

"You're right about that, Mama." Jilli took her cup in both hands and sipped her tea. "She did it to show her support for a friend who has Hodgkin's Lymphoma and starts chemo this week."

"Good for Hazel," Nicola said taking her hands from her head. "That took a great deal of courage. I have to admire her for that. I sure wouldn't be brave enough to shave my head."

"I agree with Nicola. She showed both bravery and friendship. You don't seem to be upset with her, so why is Ian so upset?" Kalli asked.

"I have to admit, I was shocked when I first saw her picture on FaceBook, but then I realized, it's hair. It'll grow back." Jilli shook her head. "I'm not sure I know the answer as to why Ian is so upset. I stopped by the house this morning to get some things to spend the night here, and he'd just found out about it."

"Maybe when he has time to adjust to the whole thing, he won't be so mad," Nelli offered.

"I'm not so sure. If I had to guess, I would say he was mad because she did it without talking to him about it first. You know how close the two of them have been, rather, were, before she went off to college. I would guess it's his feelings that are hurt most of all."

Smiling, Nelli put her hand over Jilli's. "It's a hard thing when your children grow away from you as they grow up. Give Ian some time. He'll come around."

Nicola pulled her phone from her back pocket. "I don't know about y'all, but I just have to see a picture of my bald niece before I can believe it. You say she put her picture on FaceBook?"

Before she'd even finished talking, Nicola had pulled up the picture Hazel had posted of her naked head. She began to giggle as she looked at the picture. "Oh, my, Jilli! That is shocking!"

Nelli held out her hand. "Let me see." She took Nicola's phone and stared at the picture of her granddaughter. She immediately put a hand over her mouth to stifle a laugh.

Kalli grabbed the phone from Nelli's hand. Unlike Nelli, she couldn't suppress her laugh. As soon as she started laughing, Nelli and Nicola joined in. Before long, the three were in hysterics. Tears were flowing down their cheeks. Nelli's sides ached. The harder she tried to stop, the more she laughed.

Still laughing, Nelli got up from the table. "Y'all are going to make me wet my pants!" She hurried off in a fast walk toward the bathroom.

After cleaning up the kitchen from their afternoon tea, each sister drifted away looking for some alone time. Nicola headed upstairs to put on the boots she'd packed in hopes she'd find some time to walk through the woods and down to the pond. Since she'd arrived, the argument she and Alexandre had the night before had been on her mind. She hoped the long walk would help her sort out her feelings. After putting on her boots, she went down the back stairs and headed out into the warm Georgia afternoon. She stopped to breathe in the fresh air. Spring was her favorite season and one of the main reasons she wanted to stay in the South.

Not wanting to walk through the woods by herself, Nicola whistled for Blue. Blue was a Labrador and Border Collie mix. Blue didn't exactly belong to her mama, but he'd made her house his home during the day. Each evening, when his true owner passed by on his way home from work, he'd honk twice, signaling Blue it was time to come back to his house. For the past ten years, the plan had worked out well for all involved. Each day, Blue lived and ate at her mama's house. Each evening he left to sleep and eat at his owner's house. The arrangement might seem strange to some, but to Blue, who didn't like to be alone, it was the best of both worlds.

Just as Nicola started on her way to the pond with Blue by her side, she heard the creak of the back door opening. She turned and saw Kalli come hurrying down the steps toward her holding up her hand.

"Wait for me! I want to go with you."

Trying not to show her disappointment, Nicola waited for Kalli to catch up. "I thought you were staying with Mama. You didn't say anything about wanting to go for a walk."

"I decided I wanted some fresh air."

Looking down at Kalli's feet, Nichola frowned. "I'm going to the plantation pond. It might be muddy. Those pretty white tennis shoes will be ruined if it is."

Kalli smiled. "I'll take my chances."

Understanding her sister was determined to join her, Nicola shrugged. "Let's go then."

As they walked Kalli chatted about the beauty of the flowering dogwood trees and purple irises along the way. Nicola paid little attention to what her sister was saying. Her mind was busy recalling the conversations and ensuing events of the previous evening. Now that she thought about it, she had to admit that Alexandre made some appealing points to selling the business. First, there was the money to be made from the sale. But she argued to herself, it wasn't like they needed more money. Second, the extra time she'd have. But she couldn't imagine how she would fill her days without tending to her bakeries.

When they reached the plantation pond, Kalli sat down on the bench. "I almost forgot how peaceful and quiet it is here."

Nicola sighed. "I know what you mean. I've always been drawn to this spot. When I was young it was the place I came to work out life's problems." She stared out over the clear, calm water, noticing the mirror reflections of the trees surrounding it.

She continued without taking her eyes off the pond. "This is the place where I decided to take the tennis scholarship Merritt Atlantic College offered instead of going to the University of Georgia with my friends."

She picked up a couple of smooth rocks on the ground and began skipping them across the pond's still surface. Her skipping skills were rusty. Three skips were the most she was able accomplish. She remembered a time when she could get at least five skips across the pond with little effort.

She sat down on the bench next to Kalli. "I can only imagine what my life might have been like if I'd gone to the University instead of to France with Merritt's tennis team. I probably would have married a Georgia boy instead of my handsome Frenchman. I doubt I'd have started a bakery. Most likely, I'd have been a teacher like I planned."

Kalli chuckled at the idea. "I'm sorry, but I just can't see you as a teacher. You don't have the patience for it."

"You're right about that. Lucky kids I didn't!"

They both laughed.

"You chose your career wisely when you started your bakery," Kalli said. "I remember you standing on that wooden stool next to Topsy with a dish towel tied around your waist and that red hair of yours pulled back in a ponytail. Topsy rolled out the dough and you cut it into biscuits with a glass. Then Topsy turned the whole job over to you. You've always made the best biscuits. To this day, I couldn't make an edible biscuit if my life depended on it!"

Nicola patted Kalli's knee. "Well, thanks. But right now, I'm wishing I'd chosen a different path for my life."

Kalli put her hand over Nicola's. "What's going on, Nicola? Do you want to talk about it?"

Nicola blew out a long breath. "Alexandre and I had a fight, a big, explosive fight, over selling the bakeries. I took your advice and told him I was against selling. He didn't take the news well."

"Oh, Nicola, I'm so sorry. I thought telling him how you felt about it would be the right thing to do."

"I agree. I still think it was the right thing to do."

"Help me understand why you're so against selling?"

Nicola thought for a moment before answering. "I couldn't believe the number of bakeries there were in Paris. It seemed as if there was one on every corner. I still remember the first French bakery Alexandre took me to on our second morning together. The name of the bakery was Fait Maison, which translated to English means 'homemade.' I'd never known anything like it in Georgia. It was a charming, alluring place filled with crunchy baguettes, esoteric breads, and decadent pastries. I went from one glass case to the next, unable to decide what to buy for my breakfast. Finally, Alexandre decided for me. We took our pastries and espressos outside."

Her heart rate picked up with excitement at the memory. "We sat down and Alexandre handed me a pastry I'd never seen before. He explained it was a Viennoiseries. Oh, Kali, when I put that flaky, delicate pastry in my mouth, I'd never tasted anything so wonderful." She smiled remembering how she'd sent Alexandre back inside to get two more. "That was the day I fell in love with French bakeries."

"You're making me hungry," Kalli said, licking her lips. "Go on."

Nicola continued. "After I decided to stay in France I knew I had to find a job. I didn't have to think long to know where I wanted to work. I went straight to Fait Maison to apply. Within a week, I was hired to work the front counter. Within six months, I was sent to their bakery house where the mixing and baking took place to help with cleaning up. After another six months I was assisting with the baking. During my time at Fait Maison, I got to know the owners, Madame and Monsieur Bourdon, well. Monsieur Bourdon was the pastry chef. He elevated me to an apprentice to teach me the fine art of creating French breads and pastries. Those hard, long days of mixing, kneading, and working in the heat from the hot ovens were tough, but well worth it. It's because of Monsieur Bourdon being such a taskmaster that I was able to make my own bakeries a success."

Kalli put her hand to her chest. "I can't believe you've never told me the story of how you learned to make your pastries. I've always wondered."

"Now you know." Nicola frowned. "But there's not a happy ending to this story. Sadly, the Fiat Maison had to close. Even though their bakery had the seal of authenticity, depot stores were getting most of the bakery business. Depots are shops that merely sell bread and pastries. They don't make them from scratch at the bakery, but buy industrially made frozen product to bake and sell. Their way of distributing their bakery products cuts costs and they can sell for less. I've never understood how or why the people began to think only of the cost and stopped caring about the taste."

"So, if I go to France today, I might not find an authentic French bakery like I've read about in books?"

"That's right. That's why I'm so against selling out. It frightens me to think of my stores becoming depots. I want Sweet Hart Bakeries to remain authentic. I could read between the lines of what that salesman from the conglomerate was saying. Their plan is to industrialize the process at one central location. They'll make everything there, then every morning they'll deliver those goods to each store. How can I let such a thing happen to the bakeries I've given my life's blood, sweat, and tears to create?"

Nicola stood up and began to pace. "It's not just selling out to a conglomerate that's upsetting me. It's knowing how much Alexandre wants me to sell. Last night he made his feelings clear. He also made it crystal clear he doesn't much care what I think."

Tears began to roll down Nicola's cheeks. "In all the years we've been married and through all the fights we've had, I've never known him to be so angry with me that he'd choose to sleep in another room rather than be with me."

She stopped pacing and wiped at her tears as a disturbing thought came to her. "Do you think there could be something else going on that I don't know about? Could it be he wanted a reason to be mad at me?" A more frightening thought swept into her mind. "Do you think Alexandre is looking for a reason to leave me?"

Kalli stood and grabbed Nicola's shoulders. "That's crazy talk, Nicola! Alexandre loves you, and you know he does. Don't make this any bigger than it is. It was a fight. You both got mad. That's it. Nothing more."

Nicola turned her tear-filled eyes toward Kalli. "I hope and pray you're right."

"You two are too much in love to let something like this come between you. I'm sure as soon as you both have some time to calm down, the two of you will work it out."

Kalli pulled Nicola into her arms and held her until she stopped crying.

Taking a step back, Nicola wiped the tears from her face with her sleeve. "Thank you, Kalli, for your help. Please don't say anything to Mama about this. She's got enough to deal with. I don't want to add my problems to hers."

"I won't say a word. But when this whole thing with Jake Albright is over, I think you need to tell her what's going on with you and Alexandre."

Nicola took Kalli's hand in hers and gave it a squeeze. "I promise I will."

CHAPTER EIGHTEEN

After tea, Jilli went up to her bedroom to get her phone and the notebook she'd written down Aaron Bailer's number in. She sat down on the edge of the bed, punched in his number, and waited for him to answer.

A young Southern female voice answered. "Good afternoon. Ida Legal Investigations, Audrey speaking."

"Good afternoon, Audrey. I'm Jillian Parker of Hart Law Firm here in Ida. My secretary told me Mr. Bailer stopped by our offices today with his card. I need to speak with him about his services. Is he available?"

"Yes, ma'am. I'll put you right through."

Jilli tapped her pencil against her notebook as she waited. It was several minutes before she heard Aaron Bailer's voice in her ear.

"This is Aaron Bailer. How may I be of service to you, Ms. Parker?"

Jilli hesitated for a moment deciding if she wanted to make this call strictly professional or more personal. She decided to go with personal since her call was of a personal matter. "Aaron, this is Jilli Hart. I don't know if you remember me or not, but we were on the Ida County High School Debate Team together."

Aaron hesitated for a moment. "I can't believe this! Of course, I remember you, Jilli! Oh my, I can't believe this is the one and only feisty little Jilli Hart. In fact, if I remember correctly, I'm the one who recruited you for the debate team."

Jilli chuckled. "Yes, you did. I don't know if I ever told you this or not, but your invitation to join the debate team changed my life."

Aaron's voice took on a serious tone. "In a good way, I hope."

"Definitely in a good way. I loved being on the debate team. In fact, it was the main motivation for my becoming a lawyer."

"No, kidding! That's great to hear, Jilli."

"Yes, in fact I have my own law firm right here in Ida. I took the firm over from Mr. Harrison when he retired. My secretary told me you stopped by to introduce yourself and gave her your card. That's why I'm calling you. I find I need a private investigator."

"Hart Law Firm, right? I just put that together right now. When Aubrey said Jillian Parker was on the phone, it threw me off."

"I understand. I started practicing law here before I married, so when I took over the law firm, I used my maiden name since most people around here recognized the name Hart. That's why I used Hart instead of Parker." Jilli had no idea why she felt the need to explain the name of her law firm to Aaron. She stopped talking.

"Okay, then, Jilli Hart Parker, how may I be of service?"

Jilli cleared her throat. "I don't know if you are aware of this or not, but my father was killed in a helicopter crash in Vietnam when I was very young."

"I think everyone in town knew the Hart girls grew up without a father, but I wasn't aware he was killed in a helicopter in Vietnam."

"Well, that's actually the problem. We grew up believing he'd died in a helicopter crash, but now we're not sure."

For the next five minutes, Jilli filled Aaron in on what her family had been told by the Army, then the phone call from Jake Albright with his disturbing declarations, and all that had transpired since.

When Jilli finished telling her story, she was silent as she waited for Aaron's reaction. "That's a great deal for a family to deal with, Jilli."

"You're right about that. We're supposed to meet with this Jake Albright next week. I want to hire you to do a full background check on both Jake and his father, Steven. I want to know everything I can about the two before our meeting."

"You say your family is meeting with him next week? What day?"

"The 29th."

"That's Tuesday."

"I know it's short notice."

"I'm not sure how thorough my investigation can be given the narrow time frame. It all depends on how much information there is out there on the two of them. However, I should be able to get the basics by then."

"The basics will help. Right now, we don't know anything about this guy or his father."

"I'll do what I can, Jilli."

"I appreciate that, Aaron. Send your contract and a list of what you need from me to get started to my office. I'll have it back to you within the hour along with your retainer."

"Thank you, Jilli."

"No, thank you, Aaron."

As Jilli ended the call, she prayed Aaron would be able to help her family have a clearer understanding of the men they were dealing with.

She sat on the bed for a few minutes more thinking back to her time as a member of the Ida County High School Debate Team. If her children had known her back then, they'd have called her a nerd or whatever the slang word was these days for a studious person lacking in social skills. Whatever the name, she had fun being a part of the debate team. She'd learned a great deal about researching and preparing for a debate from Aaron. He'd been a good mentor. His choosing to be a PI surprised her. She'd have thought he'd go into law or politics. She hoped he was as good at his job now as he had been as team captain back in high school.

Jilli glanced at the clock on the bedside table. If she was going to get the information Aaron wanted from her back to him in an hour, she needed to get moving. She went to the bathroom, brushed her teeth, and combed her hair. As she was putting on some lipstick, she wondered what Aaron would think of her now she was in her fifties. She sure wasn't the feisty teenager he'd known in high school. She smiled to herself when she thought about seeing him again. After all, he'd been her first crush.

Jilli hurried down the back stairs to the kitchen where she found her mother sitting at the kitchen table. The top of the table was completely covered with papers. She was so engrossed in what she was doing, she didn't look up when Jilli entered the room.

Jilli put her hand on her mama's shoulder. "What are you doing?"

Her mother reached up to put her hand over Jilli's. "Oh, hey, honey. These are the papers the Army sent me after your Daddy died. I also pulled out the newspaper articles, letters of condolences, as well as some random things I thought might be of interest. I thought it'd be a good idea to get everything out so y'all are aware of the facts of the case. After all, y'all were just little girls when he died."

"I think that's a smart thing to do, Mama." Jilli looked around. "Where are Kalli and Nicola?"

"I think they took a walk. I'm sure they'll be back soon." Nelli smiled at her daughter as she spread her hands across the table. "Why don't you sit down and take a look?"

"I'd love to, Mama, but right now I have to go to my office." Jilli leaned over to kiss Mama's cheek. "I've hired a private investigator. He's going to do a background check on Jake and his father. I have to go to the office to get some things he needs to get started."

Nelli bit her lip as she looked up at Jilli. "Do you think he'll need any of these papers to get started?"

"No, Mama. He's doing a background check. I don't think any of that would help him. I'll be back by supper."

Jilli went out the back door. As she started her car, she noticed Kalli and Nicola coming from the direction of the pond. Jilli let her window down to call out to her sisters. "Where have y'all been?"

As they got closer, she could see Nicola's eyes were red. She turned off the car's engine, opened her door, and hurried toward her sister. "Nicola, is everything okay?"

Nicola waved her hands in front of her face. "I'm fine. Just allergies. Guess I got a little too much of this fresh country air. Where are you going?"

"I've hired Aaron Bailer to check into Jake and his dad. I'm headed to my office to get what he needs to get started on his investigation. Mama's in the kitchen. She wants us all to go through some papers she's pulled out. Y'all go ahead. I'll be back by suppertime."

"Okay, then. See you when you get back," Nicola said.

Jilli walked back to her car, not totally convinced Nicola was simply suffering from allergies. As she drove down the pecan-lined driveway, she wondered why her sister always wanted everyone to believe her life was perfect. In Jilli's experience the harder someone worked to make you believe their life was perfect, the more likely it was the exact opposite was true. She hoped she was wrong about Nicola.

Jilli gave Sade a call on the way to the office. "Hey, Sade, I wanted to let you know that I've hired Aaron Bailer to investigate a private matter. He's supposed to be sending over a contract along with a list of the information he'll need to get started."

"Yes, ma'am. It was delivered a few minutes ago."

"Well, that was fast. I'll be there in five."

"Before you hang up, I thought I should let you know Morgan called. She said she's tried to reach you for two days, but hasn't had any luck. She stressed how much she really needs to talk to you. Her exact words were, 'Tell Mama it's important.'"

"I'm sure it has something to do with her sister. Thanks, Sade."

As Jilli ended the call, an uneasy feeling came over her about her oldest child. She'd assumed Morgan was upset with Hazel's actions, but now considered there might be something else her daughter wanted to talk to her about. When Morgan was in high school and college, she'd shared her life freely with her mother. However, that changed once she graduated from nursing school and moved to Wilmington, North Carolina. She'd taken a job there as a nurse in the Cardiac Care Unit at New Hanover Regional Medical Center. These days, she rarely bothered to come home for a visit. Jilli made a mental note to give her a call as soon as she finished her business at the office.

Jilli pulled her car into her reserved parking place in front of Hart Law Firm and hurried into the office. Sade looked up as Jilli entered. "That was fast."

"I was only at my mama's house, Sade. It isn't that far."

Sade handed Jilli a manila envelope. "Here's everything Audrey brought over from Mr. Bailer."

Jilli took the envelope as she headed to her office. "Thanks, Sade." She turned back before going into her office. "Would you please get Morgan on the phone for me?"

Jilli shut her office door and went to her desk to fill out the contract and put together the information Aaron would need to get the background checks of Jake Albright and his father. She was writing out the retainer check when the desk phone rang. Jilli picked up, expecting Morgan would be on the line.

It was Sade. "You have a phone call, but it's not Morgan. It's Dr. Parker."

"Ian's calling?" The last thing she wanted to do was continue their fight from this morning. Jilli blew out a breath in frustration. "Tell him I'm busy, and I'll call him back when I'm free."

Jilli resealed the envelope with the requested information and her personal check. When she stepped out of her office to hand the envelope to Sade, she found her on the phone.

Sade looked at Jilli and shrugged her shoulders. "Yes, sir, Mrs. Parker is here, but she says she'll return your call as soon as she can."

Sade put her hand over the phone. "Mr. Parker says he needs to talk to you. It's important."

Jilli handed Sade the envelope. "Please get this to Mr. Bailer's office ASAP." With a sigh, she added, "Okay. Go ahead and put him through to my office."

Sade took the envelope. "Dr. Parker, I'm sorry for the delay. Please hold while I transfer your call."

Jilli went back into her office and closed the door. She walked behind her desk and picked up the phone as she sat down in her chair. "Ian, what's so important it can't wait?"

"Well, hello to you too!"

Jilli realized her voice had betrayed her true feelings. Being irritated because he was calling her was unfair to him. After all, he could be calling to apologize. "I'm sorry, it's been a busy afternoon. Let me start over." She cleared her throat. "Hello, Ian, how's your day?"

"That's much better. Truthfully, my day hasn't been all that good. I had a fight with my wife this morning, which set the wrong tone for my day."

"I'm sorry to hear that."

"I decided if I wanted my day to improve, I needed to apologize to my wife. I may have overreacted just a smidge and blown the situation out of proportion."

A grin spread across Jilli's face as she leaned back in her chair. "I'm quite sure your wife would be most receptive to an apology."

"I'm sorry, Jilli. Something just snapped inside me when I saw that picture of Hazel, and I just went. . . stupid."

"You'll get no argument from me."

"I was wrong to react the way I did. I offer my sincere apology, my love."

Jilli knew it wasn't easy for Ian to concede he was wrong. In fact, in all the years she'd known him, she could probably count on one hand the number of times he'd admitted he'd done anything wrong. "And I sincerely accept your apology, my love."

"And you're going to be very proud of me."

"I already am."

"No, I mean really proud of something I've done."

"Do tell."

"I called Hazel."

Jilli's body tensed. "Oh, Ian, please tell me you were kind."

"Okay, I was kind. I told her I was proud of her for supporting her friend during a difficult time in his life."

Jilli felt her muscles relax. "I can't tell you how happy that makes me."

"We had a good talk and not just about shaving her head."

"Thank you for talking to her, Ian."

"Now, tell me how things are going with your mama and sisters?"

"Things are good. I've hired a private investigator to do a background check on Jake Albright and his father. Kalli has contacted the Army to have them check on things. And, when I left the house, Mama, Kalli, and Nicola were getting ready to go through a bunch of documents."

"I'm glad to hear everything is moving along. I hope y'all can get this cleared up. Do you want me to say anything to the kids about any of this or should I hold off until y'all have things settled?"

Jilli took a moment to consider before answering. "Let's wait until at least next Tuesday. I'll know more after we meet with Jake Albright."

"Okay, I'll wait."

"Remember, you and Drew are batching it tonight. There's a frozen lasagna in the freezer if you want to fix that for supper."

"I think we'll pass. We're eating out tonight. Just a couple of guys on the town."

Jilli laughed. "Well, you two have fun."

"We will. You have a good time with your mama and sisters. Love you."

"I love you."

Jilli hung up and turned her chair toward the window. Looking out on downtown Ida, she silently prayed. *Thank you, Lord, for blessing me with a loving husband.*

CHAPTER NINETEEN

At the sound of footsteps, Nelli looked up to see Kalli and Nicola coming through the back door. They walked over to the table to look at the papers.

Nicola said, "Jilli mentioned you were in here going through a bunch of papers. Wow! I didn't know there was this much stuff from when Dad was killed."

"I didn't either." Nelli pulled back the empty chair next to her and patted it with her hand. "Why don't y'all come help me sort through them?"

Nicola sat down in the chair. "What exactly are we looking for?"

"Guess the first thing I want you to look for are discrepancies in the papers I received from the Army. By reading all of this, y'all can get a better understanding of what happened and the order of events."

"Looks to me like you've pretty well got it sorted out, Mama," Kalli said as she took a seat across the table from the two.

Nelli pointed to the piles of papers. "I've stacked them by dates. Pick a pile and start through it."

Throughout the afternoon and into the evening, the three of them went through every piece of paper the Army had sent as well as clippings about Nicholas's helicopter crash in several of the local and surrounding cities' newspapers. Nelli realized she'd never shown them to her daughters. Now she wondered why she'd kept all of this filed away over the past fifty years instead of sharing it with her daughters. Had she wanted to keep it all for herself or had she wanted to spare them the heartache of it all?

When they finished, they all agreed these papers confirmed the Army's official version of how Nicholas Conrad Hart had been killed. Nicholas had flown into enemy territory during battle to retrieve wounded soldiers. His helicopter had taken on enemy fire and crashed in the dense jungle.

Kalli sighed. "Mama, after looking through all of these papers, I'm convinced more than ever Jake Albright is running some sort of scam."

Resting her elbows on the table, Nicola leaned in and folded her hands together. "I'm not totally convinced."

Kalli pushed back from the table. "You've got to be kidding me!"

Nicola looked at Nelli. "Tell me why you didn't have them open Daddy's casket?"

Unable to meet Nicola's eyes, Nelli stared down at the table. She'd hoped she'd never be asked that question. She remembered how her father had begged her to look in the casket. He'd told her Nicholas' death wouldn't be real to her until she saw what remained of his dead body. But he hadn't understood why that was the reason she wouldn't look.

A shuddering sigh escaped Nelli as she looked up. "I was afraid if I saw what remained of his dead body, I'd lose all hope and die."

Nicola leaned over and wrapped Nelli in her arms. "I'm so sorry, Mama."

"It's okay," Nelli said patting Nicola's cheek. "Right now, I wish I'd let someone look. Maybe then we wouldn't be in this mess."

Kalli reached out and took Nelli's hand. "Mama, you know what they say about hindsight?"

Nelli and Nicola answered together. "It's always twenty-twenty."

"It's true," Kalli agreed. "However, you need to find peace with the decision you made back then."

Nelli smiled at Kalli. "You're right, and I can assure you that sharing the past with you two today has brought me closer to that peace."

Jilli stumbled through the back door, her arms loaded down with the groceries Nicola had asked her to pick up on her way home. Neither Kalli nor Nicola took notice. The two were busy rushing around the kitchen putting the finishing touches on supper.

"Hello! I could use some help here."

Nicola was the first to come to her rescue. She took two bags from Jilli's arms. "Sorry. I didn't hear your car in the driveway."

Kalli followed behind Nicola and relieved Jilli of two more bags. "You should have called. We would've met you at the car."

Jilli shook her arms to get the circulation going again. "I thought I could get it all without asking for help."

"Typical Jilli," Kalli said under her breath.

Jilli set the remaining bag on the kitchen counter. She turned to confront her oldest sister. "I heard that, Kalli. What are you talking about?"

Nicola stepped between them. "She didn't mean anything. Come on. Let's get all of this put away and supper on the table."

Jilli looked around the kitchen. "Where's Mama?"

Kalli began transferring the eggs from their carton to the tray in the refrigerator. "I thought she might be upset after looking through all those papers. It was obvious they'd brought up some bad memories. So,

I asked if she could find some wildflowers to make a centerpiece for the dining room table. I thought the fresh air would do her good."

Jilli smiled. "I'm sure it will."

After the three finished putting away the groceries, Kalli said, "You two set the table. Now that we have everything we need; I'll finish up in here."

Nicola and Jilli looked at one another then back at their sister. Together they bowed and said, "Yes, Your Majesty." Breaking down in laughter, the two fell on one another.

Kalli put her hands on her waist. "Ha! Ha! You two are just so funny!"

Still laughing, Jilli managed to ask, "Who died and made you queen?"

Kalli answered, "No one had to die. I've always been the queen."

Kalli's statement threw Nicola and Jilli into another fit of laughter. At that moment, Nelli walked in the kitchen from the front of the house holding a bouquet of red, pink, and purple wildflowers.

"What's going on here?" Nelli asked.

Jilli was the first to regain her composure. She pointed her finger at Kalli. "She thinks she's the queen, and we're supposed to obey her!"

Looking at Kalli, Nelli raised one eyebrow. "You're the queen?" She put her hand on her chest. "I thought I was the queen!"

Open-mouthed, Kalli stared at her mother. Then she began to laugh. Soon all four were doubled over in laughter.

When they finally got themselves under control, Nelli held out her bouquet of wildflowers. "Let me get these in water before they wilt. I'll leave it up to the three of you to get supper on the table." She headed to the front hall closet to retrieve one of her many crystal vases.

Nicola set the dining room table with Mama's everyday china as Jilli went behind her placing the silverware and napkins. The two went back in the kitchen to help Kalli carry their supper of chicken-and-wild-rice casserole, citrus salad with honey-orange vinaigrette, and croissants from Sweet Hart Bakery to the table. When Nelli set the vase of beautifully arranged wildflowers as the centerpiece. Jilli smiled. She could see all was perfectly in place for a special meal for the Hart family.

Bowing her head, Mama prayed, "Dear Lord, thank You for the blessing of having all three of my daughters at my table this night. We thank You for the many memories we've shared at this table. We thank You for the many suppers we've eaten here together. We ask You for Your blessing on this meal we're sharing this very night. In Jesus' name, Amen."

Kalli spooned out a helping of the casserole on her plate. "We sure have shared some great memories at this table. Do y'all remember that guest we had with a long mustache that he curled up on each end?"

Nicola pointed to her upper lip. "The guy who used to take out his little comb, then proceed to comb his disgusting Fu Manchu mustache at the table right over the food? Yuck!"

Jilli didn't know what they were talking about. She stared blankly at her sisters. "I don't remember anyone like that."

Ignoring Jilli, Nelli chuckled. "I remember him. He was a guest several times throughout the years. What was it Jilli called him?"

Nicola and Kalli stared down at their plates, apparently searching their memories.

Kalli looked up and snapped her fingers. "Spaghetti Face!"

"That's right. She thought he had spaghetti on his face," Nelli said as Kalli and Nicola nodded in agreement.

Jilli frowned. "I don't remember. . .."

Nicola, who seemed to not hear Jilli, began talking. "Oh, I've got one. Remember that groping, tongue-kissing couple who told us they were on their honeymoon, and then her husband showed up in the middle of the night?"

"Oh, do I!" Nelli said, raising an eyebrow. "They stayed almost a whole week. When her husband ran up those stairs and jerked her out of bed, I thought he was going to kill her or the man she was with."

Kalli covered her ears. "What I remember about that was the shouting and screaming. Nicola and I were scared to death. We ran into your room and hid in the back of the closet."

Jilli narrowed her eyes at Kalli. "Where was I?"

Kalli took a moment to consider her question. "Come to think of it, I don't remember where you were. You probably slept through the whole thing." She turned to Nicola. "Do you remember where Jilli was?"

Nicola cocked her head to one side. "I don't. That's weird we wouldn't have grabbed her up and taken her with us. Guess we forgot she was there."

Jilli crossed her arms as she sat back against her chair. "Well, that doesn't surprise me."

"Oh, the adventures we've had running a bed and breakfast," Nelli continued without reacting to Jilli's statement. "If I remember correctly, they left without paying. I was so glad to see them leave; I didn't even try to collect. Your Uncle Jim-Jim wanted me to call the police on them, but I never did."

Kalli clapped her hands together. "That reminds me of the strange little bald-headed man who tried to leave in the middle of the night without paying."

"I remember him." Nicola pointed at Kalli with her fork. "Wasn't he the guy who wore the green bow ties that bobbed up and down when he talked?"

"Mr. Pearlman," Nelli said, shaking her head. "He was a strange one. When he called to make a reservation, he specifically asked to be given the front room over the porch. The room you're in." She pointed to Nicola. "He said he'd seen a picture of the Hart & Soul Inn on the front of our brochure and, as a writer, thought the view from that room would be inspiring."

Nelli chuckled. "Turned out what he was inspired to do was go out his window onto the roof of the porch, down the trellis, and leave without paying. His plan failed when he fell off the trellis and landed on his backside in the rosebushes. He woke up the whole house with his cries of pain. Then he had the audacity to file a personal injury lawsuit against us. All he hurt in his fall was his dignity."

Kalli and Nicola shook with laughter as they recalled the incident.

Jilli spoke through clenched teeth. "I don't remember any of that. Where was I when all these things happened? Did y'all have me locked away somewhere?"

Nelli put a hand on her shoulder. "Darling girl, you were right here. I promise we never locked you away. Maybe you were just too young to remember."

Jilli sighed heavily. "Mama, I'm only two years younger than Kalli, and a year younger than Nicola."

Grinning, Kalli leaned in toward Jilli. "I know something I bet you'll remember."

Jilli looked at her. "What?"

"Remember the year we all got roller skates for Christmas?"

Jilli nodded. "I think I was seven. I think you taught me how to skate."

"That sounds about right. We were skating back and forth on the front porch. which was okay, but it got a little boring. So, Nicola came up with a brilliant idea."

Jilli gasped. "Oh, yeah, I remember this part." She turned to Nicola. "You decided it would be lots of fun to go out back and skate down that huge dirt hill Uncle Jim-Jim made when he dug out that drainage ditch. And who did you both convince to try it first?"

Nicola put her hands to her mouth. "I'd totally forgotten about that."

Jilli narrowed her eyes at her sister. "You're telling me you totally forgot I broke my arm when I fell head over heels all the way down the hill?"

Nicola grinned. "I'm sorry, but you need to remember I did pick you up and carry you all the way back home."

"I do remember, and..." Frowning, Jilli turned back to Kalli. "I remember you're the one who just stood there laughing."

Kalli shrugged. "What can I say? I thought it was funny. In fact, I'd bet a million dollars if we had a video of it and you watched it today, you'd laugh too." She bowed toward her. "You're welcome for the memory."

"Speaking of memories." Jilli glanced around the table. "How about the time I slashed my foot open when I stepped on the broken chicken bone Kalli threw out in the yard because she didn't want to walk the bones all the way out to the garbage can like she was told? It was just one more time Kalli hurt me."

Kalli almost choked on the bite she'd just taken. "That is such a lie!"

Jilli turned to her mother. "Isn't it true, Mama? Kalli threw those chicken bones out the back door, and I stepped on one with my bare foot. The gash was about this long." She held up her hands about five inches apart. "I still have a scar."

Nelli tapped her fingers on her temple. "I'm not sure I do remember that incident, Jilli. Did you have to have stitches?"

"Mama, you have to remember. There was a trail of blood from the yard all the way to the kitchen from where Uncle Jim-Jim carried me to the sink. Blood was gushing out everywhere. He washed it off and said he thought it needed to be stitched up. You sat at the kitchen table with your head between your knees because you thought you were going to faint from seeing all of that blood pouring out of my foot."

Frowning, Nelli slowly shook her head. "For the life of me, I can't remember that happening."

"That's because it didn't happen," Kalli sneered. "You got a little cut on your foot, and you made up a whole story about it being a chicken bone I threw out."

Jilli glared at Kalli. "I did not make it up, and it wasn't a little cut. It was a gash, a long one."

Nelli stood and began to clear the table. "Okay, okay. Enough with the memories. Let's put all of that aside. I believe Nicola has a treat for us with a new dessert straight from her Sweet Hart Bakery.

Jilli, would you please make the coffee while Kalli and I clear off this table."

Jilli pushed back her chair and stood. "Fine, Mama, I'll put it aside for now, but I know I'm right."

"That's because you always think you're right, Jilli," Kalli called back over her shoulder as she carried the stack of plates from the dining room.

Jilli stomped her foot at her sister.

Nicola came up beside Jilli. Putting an arm around her shoulder, she whispered in her ear. "Just let it go. Remember we're here for Mama, to give her support. Fighting is not what she needs from any of us."

Jilli leaned her head on Nicola's shoulder. "You're right. Thanks for reminding me." Softening the tone of her voice, she called out, "I'll fix the coffee, Mama."

The two sisters smiled at one another.

Nelli called back. "Great. When it's ready, take it to the living room. We'll have our dessert in there tonight."

Nicola squeezed Jilli's shoulder. "Wait until you taste these Sweet Hart Cinnamon Swirl Pancakes I brought. You'll think you died and went to heaven."

CHAPTER TWENTY

After setting her empty plate on the coffee table, Kalli leaned back in her chair. "Whew! I cannot believe I ate two of those. Nicola, tell me one more time what those were called. I want to make sure I remember the name so I can order them for the next book club meeting I host."

Nicola chuckled as she picked up Kalli's plate. "I'm glad you liked them. They're one of our newest desserts. We call them Cinnamon Swirl Pancakes."

Jilli handed Nicola her empty plate. "Well, whatever you call them, after that first bite, it was just like you said. I thought I'd died and gone to heaven."

"I told you."

"To me they're too rich to be called something as simple as a pancake," Nelli said as she added her plate to Nicola's gathered stack.

"Well, to tell the truth, I wanted to call it a galette, which is French for a flat round cake, but I was outvoted by my store managers and Alexandre. They said it was too fancy a name and people would relate more to pancake. So, that's the name I'm stuck with."

"How is Alexandre?" Nelli asked. "He hasn't been down here in quite some time. Why don't you invite him to join you for the weekend, Nicola?"

On her way to the kitchen with the plates and utensils, Nicola stopped abruptly, surprised by her mother's suggestion. She wondered what had made her make such a proposal. She turned back. "I thought this was a mother-daughter weekend."

Jilli smiled up at Nicola as she put her hands together in a plea. "Oh, Nicola, please do! I could invite Ian to come over. It'd be fun to have them both here with us."

Nicola continued to the kitchen without responding. She set the plates down beside the sink and began rinsing them before placing them in the dishwasher. She was hoping she wouldn't have to mention the possibility of the sale of her bakeries or the fight with her husband to her mother or younger sister. It wasn't something she wanted to burden them with right now. They had enough to deal with without bringing her problems into the mix. She'd only confided in Kalli because she'd needed to talk to someone about it. She sighed, hoping she could find a way to explain it all to them.

Nicola poured herself another cup of coffee. She picked up her mug and the half-full pot and returned to the living room. "Anyone want more coffee?"

From the sympathetic looks on her mother's and Jilli's faces, it was obvious Nicola wouldn't need to explain anything. With a scowl on her face, she turned to her oldest sister. "Kalli! What did you tell them?"

Jilli jumped up from where she was sitting on the floor, took the coffeepot from Nicola's hands, and set it down on a coaster on the end table. She wrapped her arms around Nicola. "Oh, Nicola, I'm so sorry. I had no idea you were going through all of that. I could tell something was wrong when I saw you this afternoon. I thought it was about Dad. I had no idea of the troubles you've had on your heart."

Nicola hugged her sister back. "I'm okay. Really. Kalli shouldn't have said anything." She narrowed her eyes at Kalli. "Right, Big Sister?"

Kalli shrugged her shoulders. "I thought someone should tell them." She leaned forward to pick up the coffeepot, filled her cup, and took a sip. "I was only trying to help."

Nicola wasn't surprised how casually Kalli had betrayed her trust without seeming to have any regrets.

"I'm sorry you're going through such a difficult time," Nelli said. "I just wish you'd have trusted me enough to share what was going on in your life."

There it was. Nicola knew the words would come out at some point. It was how Mama used guilt on her daughters. First, she would acknowledge you were going through a hard time. Then she would hit you with the guilt. Even to this day, the two-punch worked to make Nicola feel she'd disappointed her mother yet again.

Nicola turned from Jilli and held out her hand. "I'm sorry, Mama. It was just so complicated. I'm still working through it in my own mind."

Nelli leaned forward and took Nicola's hand. "It's okay. I understand."

Nicola sat down beside her. "It all boils down to Alexandre wants to sell the bakeries, and I don't. He wants to retire, and I don't. He wants to go to France to live, and I don't. I just wish either André or Alexandra wanted to take over the Sweet Hart Bakery stores. If one of them did, it'd be so much easier for me to give it all up. But right now I love being a part of this business. It's been my passion for most of my life."

Nelli patted Nicola on the back. "I'll be praying for you both. I believe it'd help both you and Alexandre if you would ask God for His help in resolving this conflict you're having."

Kalli asked, "By the way, what is it Alexandra and André want to do? I know they're both in college. Do they have careers in mind, or are they just going to be professional students?"

Nicola wasn't sure if Kalli meant to sound condescending about her children or was simply trying to take the conversation in a different direction away from the problems she and Alexandre were having. "We were beginning to think Alexandra might be going for professional student, but it looks like she'll finish her master's degree at Berkeley in microbiology this spring. She's fielding job offers from several hospitals. I'm hoping she'll go with Mayo in Jacksonville, but who knows for sure. Then André's still at Northwestern majoring in political science. He's still got another year to go."

Kalli chuckled. "Does he still talk about being president one day?"

Nicola nodded. "He's said he wants to be president since he was three years old. Who knows?"

"I do!" Jilli said, raising her hand. "That boy has charisma. If not president, he'll be the man behind the president."

Nelli chuckled. "I'm proud of both of them, as well as all of my grandchildren. I pray every day for each of them to be blessed with a happy life."

Jilli kissed her fingers and pointed to heaven. "From your mouth to God's ears. I worry about my middle child sometimes."

"She'll be fine," Kalli said, picking up her cup. "I think we've all raised a pretty great bunch of kids."

Nelli rose to her feet. "I agree with you there. Now, I'm heading to bed before I'm too tired to walk up the stairs." She kissed Kalli and Jilli on the cheek and said, "Good night to each of you. I love you all."

Nicola stood for a good night hug. Her Mama walked to her, took hold of her shoulders, and looked straight into her eyes. "Don't forget to say your prayers tonight. Prayer is a powerful thing." Nicola felt tears come to her eyes, and she could only nod before her Mama turned and headed up the back stairs to bed.

The next day was a perfect Georgia spring day. The leaves on the trees were a vivid green and the grass felt soft and lush. The warming sun was shining bright in the cloudless blue sky. It was a day when the heavenly, intense scent of the Confederate Jasmine in bloom announced spring had arrived in Georgia.

Nicola and Jilli spent the morning raking the dead winter leaves from the yard and carting them away to the composting bin behind the barn. While they were busy with that chore, Kalli and Nelli headed to Ida to Grandma's Garden Shop to buy baskets of ferns to hang on the front porch, geraniums, and other various plants to fill the planters set at each column, and seedlings for the vegetable garden. All three girls had tried to talk their mother out of planting a vegetable garden this year, but Nelli wouldn't hear of it. She loved the fresh vegetables it provided and enjoyed canning and freezing the extra produce for the winter months. She'd made it clear to her daughters it was what she liked to do, and she planned to keep doing it until they put her in the grave.

After a lunch of leftover chicken and potato salad, all four got busy with hanging the ferns every twelve inches around the front porch. It took hours to empty the six huge planters then refill them with compost and soil topped off with an exact amount of fertilizer. Nelli oversaw the work of her daughters to make sure each plant was set in the planters correctly, not too shallow nor too deep.

She was determined to attach the plow to her small tractor to prepare the soil for her garden. After two failed attempts, her daughters were able to talk her into hiring someone to prepare the soil for her. Jilli promised she, Ian, and Drew would help her plant her garden.

It was well after seven o'clock before the four finished with their day's work. They were covered in dirt and their bodies were tired, but Nelli felt a sense of deep satisfaction and pride in all they'd accomplished. After they'd each showered, they sat down to a light supper of tomato soup and grilled cheese. As the girls made their way up the stairs, they expressed their hopes of sleeping late the next morning.

Nelli was the last up the stairs. By the time she walked past her daughters' rooms, their doors were closed. She stood in the hall outside their rooms and said loudly, "Good night, my hardworking girls. Sleep tight. Don't forget we have church in the morning. I'll get y'all up around seven."

As Nelli walked away, she could have sworn she heard a groan behind each of the closed doors. She made her way to her own bedroom with a smile on her face. It would be the first time in years she'd have all three daughters sitting with her on her church pew.

CHAPTER TWENTY-ONE

True to her word, Nelli roused her daughters at seven a.m. the way she'd waked them up when they were living at home. She played—rather, banged out—a hymn on the piano as she sang along. Her hymn of choice had usually been "Power In The Blood," but today since she was filled with joy she chose "Joyful, Joyful, We Adore Thee." She was starting the third verse before she heard sounds coming from the second floor. She was halfway through the fourth verse when she saw Nicola—who obviously hadn't taken the time to run a brush through her hair or put on a robe— making her way down the steps.

Nicola made it to the bottom step before she spoke. "Mama, what have I done to you to make you want to torture me like this?"

Smiling at her daughter, Nelli shook her head and put her left hand to her ear. "Sorry, I can't hear you."

Nicola took two steps closer and with her hands over her ears shouted, "Please, Mama!"

Keeping the smile on her face, Nelli sang out with the tune she was playing, "There's French toast and bacon in the kitchen. I'll be there as soon as the other two show their faces."

Rolling her eyes, Nicola turned her back on Nelli and headed to the kitchen.

Nelli was repeating the first verse of the hymn when Jilli came down the stairs— in her robe and with her hair brushed— smiling and singing along. Still singing, she sat down on the piano bench next to Nelli. The two of them looked toward the staircase when they heard Kalli's high heels clicking on the steps. They saw she was dressed, her hair styled, and she was wearing makeup. A deep frown was set on her face.

Kalli stopped at the bottom of the steps and put her hands on her waist. "Enough is enough, Mama! We all got the message!"

Nelli stopped. "Good! That's all I wanted." She got up from the piano bench. "I made breakfast. Let's eat!"

Jilli got up from the bench, and followed Nelli into the kitchen. She called back over her shoulder to Kalli, "Are you coming?"

Kalli sighed. "I suppose so."

Nicola was sitting at the kitchen table with a plate piled with French toast and another plate with bacon. She took a huge bite of her French toast. "Mama, this is some of the best French toast I've ever eaten. It's not like what you used to make when we were growing up. What's your secret? Is it the batter?"

"Good grief, Nicola, don't talk with your mouth full. Haven't you learned any manners?" Kalli put three pieces of French toast on her plate.

Nicola stuck her tongue out at her sister. Kalli replied by sticking her tongue out.

"Real classy, you two," Jilli said as she sat down next to Nicola.

Nelli shook her head. "Some things just never change."

"What do you mean, Mama?" Jilli asked.

Nelli pointed at each girl in turn. "I'm talking about the three of you. Y'all are talking to each other just like you did when you were teenagers living under this roof."

Nicola's eyes narrowed on Kalli. "It's not my fault. She's the one who started it."

Kalli smirked. "You're so right, Mama, just like old times. Nicola always has to put the blame on someone else."

"Not sure I'd say always, Kalli, but let's call a truce for this morning." Taking her plate and silverware in hand, Nelli rose from the table. "We need to leave for church in forty-five minutes. We don't want to be late."

"Mama, are you serious about all of us going?" Nicola asked.

Nelli rinsed off her plate and put it in the dishwasher. "I'm not going to force anyone to go, but I'd be a happy mama if I had all my girls sitting with me."

Kalli got up from the table and smoothed out her dress. "As you can see, I'm ready."

Jilli drank the last of her coffee and carried the cup to the sink. "I'll be ready in plenty of time, Mama." She kissed Nelli on the cheek before heading up the back stairway.

Nelli turned to Nicola.

Nicola rolled her eyes. "Okay, I'll go. I was going to help you clean up, but if I don't start now, I'll never be ready on time."

"Go on," Kalli said grinning at her sister. "As usual, I've got this."

Nicola wrinkled her nose. "To save some time, I'm just going to ignore your childish comment."

Forty minutes later, everyone was ready and in Nelli's car heading to Ida's First United Methodist Church— the church all four had grown up in. Along with Nelli, Jilli and her family still attended. It was another gorgeous, sunny Georgia spring day. It only took them ten minutes to get to the church and settled in their pew. Nelli couldn't remember when she'd felt more blessed than on this day with her three daughters sitting beside her as they worshiped together.

Nelli was most excited for her daughters to hear the new minister who had only been with them since last June. They'd gone through several years of less-than-adequate preachers who had led to poor attendance and financial difficulties. Luckily, Reverend James Thompson and his wife and their two young children were appointed to serve this church. In only a few months under Reverend Thompson's leadership, church attendance had almost doubled and giving was on the increase.

What Nelli liked most about Reverend Thompson was his sermons. It was as if he knew exactly what words she needed to hear. His sermon today did not disappoint. The topic of his sermon was acceptance, and the Bible verse he based it on was one of Nelli's favorites, Proverbs 3:5-6.

Reverend Thompson recited the verse. "'Trust in the Lord with all your heart. Never rely on your own understanding. Remember the Lord in everything you do, and He will show you the right way.'"

Once again, Nelli felt as if he'd read her mind. She realized ever since she'd gotten the phone call from Jake Albright, she'd been leaning on her understanding, not the Lord's. She'd been praying about it, but she hadn't been trusting in the Lord to show her the right way. After listening to Reverend Thompson's sermon, she determined to change that.

It took Nelli and her daughters close to thirty minutes to get out of the church. It seemed everyone wanted to speak to Kalli and Nicola because it'd been so long since they had been there. When they finally made their way out the door, there were a few who lingered outside to catch the girls before they left.

"Whew!" Kalli said as she got in the front passenger seat. "That was exhausting. My shoulders hurt from hugging everyone. They wanted to let me know how sorry they were about Marshall dying so young."

Sitting in the back seat, Nicola massaged her face with both hands. "My face hurts from smiling so much. I think everyone wanted to tell me how they loved the pastries from Sweet Hart Bakery you brought to Bible Study, and how they think I should bring my bakery to Ida."

"You both have to admit it was flattering so many wanted to see and to talk to you," Nelli said as she started the car and drove out of the parking lot.

"Oh, I am!" Nicola agreed. "I love hearing someone tell me how much they like my product. That's what makes my business grow."

Kalli nodded. "Oh, I agree. So many said such sweet, nice things about Marshall, and many had only met him a few times."

Nelli looked right and left before turning onto Broad Street. "That's because they love you and hate such a terrible thing happened to you."

Kalli turned to her. "Mama, where are we going? Your house is in the other direction."

Nicola chuckled. "And you forgot Jilli!"

Nelli smiled. "We're going to The Steak House. Jilli is riding there with Ian and Drew."

Nicola leaned forward. "The Steak House! Do they still have their country buffet on Sundays?"

Nelli nodded. "They still do, with the best fried chicken in the South!"

Nicola sat back against her seat. "Yum! You're making my mouth water."

Jilli, Ian, and Drew were standing out front when Nelli pulled into a parking place. She hurried out of the car to join them.

"Where have y'all been?" Jilli asked. "I was beginning to get worried."

"I thought we'd never get away!" Nelli said. "It seems everyone wanted to talk to your sisters."

Kalli pulled Drew into a hug. "Good grief! I can't believe how tall you are! What's your Mama feeding you? Miracle Grow?"

Drew hugged his aunt back. "Aw, Aunt Kalli, it's been almost six months since you've seen me."

"Well, you're a good two inches taller than the last time I saw you, and that was only three months ago. Come here and give your Aunt Nicola a hug." Nicola embraced her nephew.

"Enough with the hugging," Ian said. "Eat now. Hug later. I'm starving. Let's get in line before they let the Baptists out of church."

The next hour was filled with good food and pleasant conversation. Nelli felt sorry for Drew, whose activities and ambitions were the focus of a great deal of questioning from his two aunts. She was proud of him when he answered most of their questions, even when she could tell he found some of their more personal questions embarrassing. As she looked around the table at her family laughing and talking, she was overwhelmed by the blessings God had showered on her. It was one of those times she wished could go on forever. Ian's chair scraping across the floor as he stood interrupted her thoughts.

"I'm sorry to leave the company of such beautiful ladies, but if Drew and I don't leave right now, he'll be late for baseball practice." Ian signaled for Drew to join him as he leaned over to kiss Jilli.

Nelli glanced over at the clock on the wall. "So sorry, Ian. I had no idea what time it is. Of course, we don't want the star pitcher to be late for practice."

"Oh, Grandma, I'm not the star pitcher," Drew said as he got up to give her a hug.

"You are to me," Nelli said as she welcomed her grandson into her arms.

After hugging Nelli, Drew went around the table and hugged his mother and each aunt.

Putting his hand on Drew's shoulder, Ian said, "Let's go, son," Turning to the others he added, "Please know I'm praying for y'all. Hopefully, by Tuesday night it will all be cleared up, and this whole thing can be put to rest."

Nelli smiled. "Thank you, Ian, for your prayers."

"See y'all later," Ian called as he headed out of the restaurant.

Kalli smiled at Jilli. "I hope you know how good you have it with Ian."

Jilli beamed. "I do. Believe me, I do."

CHAPTER TWENTY-TWO

It was all Kalli could do to not show her impatience as her mother drove them back to the house. She wasn't used to long, leisurely meals when she had work to do.

As soon as they walked in the house, her mother headed for the back stairs. "I'm beat. Y'all do what you want this afternoon, but I'm going to take a much-needed afternoon nap."

"That's a good idea, Mama. I think after I change, I'll grab my book I've been wanting to finish and head out to the porch to read." Jilli followed their mother up the stairs.

Nicola turned to Kalli. "After I change my clothes, I think I'll go for another walk. Do you want to join me?"

"I'd love to, but I have a bunch of reading and paperwork waiting on me," Kalli said. "I'll take you up on your invitation another time."

Kalli went up to her bedroom hoping to catch up on her reading and prepare for the introductory writing course she'd been asked to teach summer session. As soon as she got to her room, she kicked off her high heels and stripped out of her dress. She sat down on the chair opposite her bed to pull off her pantyhose. As she felt the relief of being rid of the constraints of her clothing, she thought back to Marshall's funeral when she'd last worn this dress. When she came home that day after his funeral, she considered tossing the dress in with Marshall's clothes she was donating to the local shelter. But it was a new dress, and her practical mind had insisted she keep it. Seeing the dress now, crumpled up on the bed where she'd tossed it, she didn't like the memories it brought back to her mind. She decided it would not be returning to her closet, but would become a donation.

Kalli went to the dresser where she'd unpacked her comfy jogging pants and two-sizes-too-large shirt and put them on. She took her laptop out of her leather messenger bag along with the course materials. She'd been assigned this introductory course to teach by the job-stealing department head, Kip Kidman. He knew full well she'd always taught the advance courses in journalism, never a beginning course. It seemed to her to be his way of making sure she understood the power he had over her career.

She spread everything out on the small corner desk and began looking through the materials. She tried to concentrate on what was in front of her, but found her mind kept wandering back to the chaos Jake Albright's unbelievable story of her father being a POW had brought to her family.

After thirty minutes, Kalli gave up on planning for the summer session and curled up on her bed. As she lay there, disturbing images of her injured father being taken prisoner and put through relentless torture filled her mind. Tears rolled down her cheek and onto her pillow. She hated how this man had put such ideas into her head. She closed her eyes praying sleep would come to take away her troubling thoughts.

Kalli could hear a tune she recognized seeming to come to her from far off in the distance. She tried to recall where she'd heard it before. She sat straight up in her bed as her ringtone pulled her from the darkness of a deep sleep. Her eyes darted around the room as she tried to remember where she was. Through the dimness of the room, she recognized the light from her ringing cell phone coming from the bedside table.

Kalli picked up her phone and pressed the screen to accept the call. "Hello?"

"Dr. Abbott, I hope I'm not disturbing you on this Sunday evening, but I thought it was important I call you. This is Whit."

Kalli came fully awake. She swung her legs over the side of the bed. "You're not disturbing me at all, Whit. I'm just surprised to hear from you on a Sunday. Don't you even get Sundays off?"

He chuckled. "I do, but I assumed from our conversation the other day you wanted what I could find ASAP. I was able to retrieve this information on my home computer through an online portal."

"Are you telling me you've found something important?"

Taking a less formal tone, Whit answered, "Yes, Kalli, as a matter of fact I have. However, I'm afraid it might not be what you were hoping I'd find."

Kalli sighed. "Truthfully, Whit, I'm not sure what I was hoping you'd find. So, I'm ready for whatever you have to tell me."

"First of all, I've checked into Steven Albright's service record."

Kalli got up from the bed and took a seat at the desk. She found her pen on top of her notebook where she'd left it. She pushed everything else to the side and put her cell phone on speaker as she waited for Whit to continue.

"In June of 1968 Steven John Albright joined the United States Air Force as a lieutenant after graduating with honors from the Citadel. He attended flight school where he was trained to fly the Cessna A-37 Dragonfly, better known as the Super Tweet. Upon graduation from flight school he received the commission of captain. In 1968 he was sent to Vietnam where he flew ten successful missions before being shot down over North Vietnam in January of 1969."

Kalli was writing down everything Whit was telling her. She knew in her heart his next words were going to tell her what she now realized she'd hoped would not be true. She held her breath as she waited for him to finish.

"After being shot down, he was captured by the Vietcong and listed as a prisoner of war."

Kalli let out her breath. "I was afraid you were going to say that."

"I hate to tell you that. I could tell from our conversation the other day you were hoping the story his son told of his father being a POW would turn out to be false."

Setting down her pen, Kalli put her head in her hands. "That only makes one part of his story true. That doesn't mean that Dad was also a POW. Right?"

"Well, maybe."

Kalli could hear the hesitancy in his voice. "Maybe? What does that mean?"

"It seems it's not as clear-cut as I'd hoped it would be." Whit cleared his throat. "I also looked through your father's military records. Actually, I had one of my aides do a thorough investigation. He came to me twice with concerns. At first, he had a problem locating them. They were not filed as they should have been—it's not unusual to run across filing errors of military records. But then he came to me a second time saying his request for access had been denied."

"Denied? That doesn't make sense."

"It didn't to me either. That's when I took over. Kalli, do you know what information your mother was given when they informed her of your father's death?"

"I can tell you I know more today than I did three days ago. I was only eight when Dad was killed. Mama never really talked about it. I never wanted to ask, for fear of upsetting her. But after the infamous phone call, I've learned a great deal more."

"Can you tell me more?"

"The Army first contacted Mama that Dad was MIA. Then about a month later, officials came to our house to inform her he'd been killed in action. She was told he'd been on a rescue mission to transport wounded soldiers after they'd been ambushed. They said his helicopter crashed and burned over a dense part of the jungle, which was the reason it'd taken so long to locate the crash and his body. Dad's flag-draped remains were then sent home. At Mama's request, his casket was never opened. She didn't want to see the injuries he must have sustained. She had his body cremated, and we spread the ashes at the farm."

"Do you know if your mother ever received any of his personal effects, such as his military ID tags, sometimes referred to as dog tags?"

"No, she said she'd assumed they'd been lost in the crash or maybe even stolen."

"Hmm."

A dread came over Kalli. "Whit? What's going on?"

"I can't tell you everything, because some of it is classified." Whit blew out a breath. "I'll tell you what I can, Kalli."

"Please, Whit, tell me everything you can. I wouldn't want you to get in trouble, but I do have the right to know what happened to my father." As Kalli picked up her pen, her hands were shaking.

"According to eyewitness reports, your father's helicopter made another stop that day against the orders he'd been given. The official report says he received a distress call, but when he requested permission to give aide he was told to proceed to the point, which meant he was not to heed the call. However, eyewitness reports claim his helicopter flew to the distress call coordinates, landed, and someone got off with medical supplies to help the injured. Another soldier from the field got on the helicopter, and it took off. The soldiers on the ground were told the helicopter would return for them, but they never saw it again."

Kalli put her shaking hand to her mouth. Her voice was almost a whisper when she asked the question she wasn't sure she was ready to hear the answer to. "Are you saying the crew member who got off the helicopter and stayed behind was my father?"

Once again, Whit hesitated before answering. "I'm not saying that it was, but I'm not saying it wasn't either. I can tell you that five of the soldiers who were left behind that day were Vietcong trying to get back to their unit when they were captured by the Vietcong."

Kalli's eyes filled with tears as it became clear to her there was a real probability the body the Army sent home to her family may not have been her father's. Her father might have died the way Jake Albright claimed he had.

"Kalli? Are you still there?" Whit's voice cut through her thoughts.

"Yes, I'm still here. It's just that. . ." Kalli's voice trailed off as she tried to control her emotions.

"I know it's not what you were expecting."

Hearing the concern in Whit's voice, Kalli could no longer hold her feelings in check as sobs began to wrack her body.

"I'm sorry I wasn't able to give you peace about what happened to your father. I can assure you and your family I'm not through looking into what happened to Chief Hart. I will get to the bottom of how a grievous mistake of this magnitude might have been made."

Through hitching breaths, Kalli managed to say, "Thank you, Whit, for letting me know what you did find out."

"You're more than welcome. I promise I'll keep you and your family up to date on what's happening with my investigation."

"I appreciate that and all you've done to help, Whit."

After Kalli ended the call, she put her head down on her arms and cried until she heard her mother's voice coming from the bottom of the stairs calling her name. "Yes, Mama?"

"Are you all right? You've been up there a long time. Come on downstairs and join us out on the porch."

With the heels of her hands, Kalli wiped the tears from her face and took a deep breath. "I'm fine, Mama. I'll be down in a minute."

Kalli made her way to the bathroom where she splashed cold water on her face. She grabbed a towel and studied her reflection in the mirror. *How am I going to tell Mama and Nicola and Jilli that Jake Albright's story just might be true?*

Kalli took out her contacts and put on her glasses hoping they would help to conceal her red eyes before going downstairs to join Mama and her sisters. Just before going out the front door, with her hand on the doorknob, she stopped to take in a deep breath and put a smile on her face. She opened the door to find Nicola and Jilli leisurely sitting in the swing. Mama was sitting in a white wicker chair that had been pulled over from the other side of the porch.

Facing the front door, Mama was the first to see Kalli. Greeting her with a smile, she said, "There you are. We were beginning to think you were taking a . . ." Rising from her chair, she hurried to Kalli. "Kalli, what is it? What's happened?"

Nicola and Jilli turned around to see what had alarmed their mother. Kalli knew it was obvious that she'd been crying. Without hesitation, they rose to gather around her.

Nicola put her arm around Kalli's shoulder. "Is Gabe alright?"

Overwhelmed by her mother's and sisters' concerns, Kalli could only stare at them as silent tears began to stream down her face. She had hoped she'd have more time to ease into a conversation where she could tell them in a gentle way what she'd just learned from Whit's phone call. Instead, she'd made it worse by not being able to control her emotions.

Taking her by the arm, Mama led Kalli to the chair she'd just vacated. "Come, sit down here and tell us what's happened to upset you."

Jilli rushed to pull another wicker chair next to Kalli's for Mama. She then joined Nicola on the swing. Mama sat down and took Kalli's hand in hers. "It's okay, Kalli. You can tell us."

Kalli looked up to meet her mother's dark brown, waiting eyes. "This isn't how I wanted to tell you."

Mama patted her hand. "Whatever you need to tell us, it's going to be okay."

Wiping her tears away with her free hand, Kalli looked from Mama to Jilli, and then from Jilli to Nicola. She sighed, and began her story. "I was upstairs in my room working on preparing for my next class when I got a call from Colonel Badger."

Kalli noticed all of them tense at the mention of Colonel Badger. For the next ten minutes— without any interruptions— Kalli reported to her mother and sisters the information Whit had given her about Captain Steven Albright and his speculation about their father. When she finished, she leaned back in her chair. She could see by the tears running down their faces that her news had upset her mother and sisters just as much as it had her. They sat in silence for several minutes.

Nicola was the first to break the silence. "So, if Jake Albright hadn't contacted Mama, the truth of what happened to Daddy would never have come to light?"

Kalli nodded in agreement. "That's right. There would have been no reason for Colonel Badger to look into the whole affair."

Jilli stood up and began to pace back and forth across the porch. "I wish he'd never called and just left us alone."

Mama slapped both hands down on the arms of her chair. "Don't you dare say that!"

The anger in Mama's voice shocked Kalli, and she looked at her, frowning.

"We need to know the truth of what happened to your father. We need to know what he did for his fellow soldiers. We need to know what he suffered. It's the only way we can truly honor his memory. I thank God for Jake Albright and his phone call."

Kalli leaned over to put her arms around her mother's shaking body. "You're right Mama. We do need to know the truth."

With arms crossed Jilli stared down at the floor. In a soft voice, she said, "I'm sorry, Mama. It's just that I don't know if I'm strong enough to know the truth."

Nicola reached up and smiled as she took Jilli's hand in hers. "Of course, you're strong enough. You're the daughter of Chief Nicholas Hart, the strongest of the strong."

CHAPTER TWENTY-THREE

The four of them spent their evening talking and speculating as to how the letter Jake Albright was bringing to them could put all their theories to rest. After supper, feeling exhausted from the day's revelations, they turned in early. Jilli wanted nothing more than to curl up in bed and let sleep carry her away from her thoughts and the disturbing images swirling around in her head. As she was just beginning to drift off, she was brought back from the brink of sleep by Morgan's ringtone on her cell phone. For a brief moment, she considered letting it go to voice mail once again, but reconsidered and accepted the call.

"Hey, Morgan."

" I've finally got a live voice to talk to! It's about time! I was beginning to think I was never going to reach you."

"I'm sorry. It's just that life has gotten a bit crazy around here."

"So, I hear. I just talked to Daddy. He told me about the strange phone call Grandma got about your dad being a prisoner of war. That's just so hard to believe."

Jilli hesitated, remembering what Kalli had found out. "Maybe not as hard as you might think."

"You mean, it's true? Your dad was a POW?"

"It's a real possibility, but we don't know for sure yet. We'll know more after we meet with this guy on Tuesday."

Wanting to change the subject, Jilli asked, "What's going on with you, Morgan? What's so important you're calling this late on a Sunday night?"

"I'm sorry if I've called you too late."

Jilli cringed, hearing the hurt in her daughter's voice.

"I can call back tomorrow if this is an inconvenient time for you."

Jilli hadn't meant to come across as harsh and uncaring, but it was obvious that was how Morgan had perceived it.

She softened her tone. "I didn't mean to sound so callous, Morgan. It's just been a rough couple of days. Of course, I want to know what's going on in your life."

Morgan cleared her throat. "I'm sorry, Mama. I've been so excited to share some big news with you. I was beginning to think it would never happen."

"I'm the one who's sorry, Morgan. I should have returned your call. I'm listening now ready to hear your big news."

Morgan blurted out, "I've been accepted to the Medical College of Georgia for this coming fall semester. Mama, I'm going to be a doctor!"

Jilli was speechless. At one time Morgan had talked of going to medical school to be a doctor like her father, but she'd changed her mind. She'd said more than once she wasn't willing to spend the time and energy it would take. "Morgan, I don't know what to say. I had no idea you still wanted to be a doctor."

"I knew this would be a shock, Mama. I only told Dad because I had to ask him to write a letter of recommendation to the college. I swore him to secrecy. I didn't want anyone else to know for fear I wouldn't be accepted."

Jilli shook her head at the realization of how much Morgan was like Ian. Tears of joy stung her eyes. "Oh, Morgan, I'm so proud of you! You'll be a great doctor."

"I think so too, Mama! I think being a nurse first will help me relate to my patients and to the staff."

"I have no doubt. I'm genuinely happy for you, Morgan."

"I'm excited, but also incredibly nervous. When I told the hospital my plans, they said they hoped I'd come back here when I finished."

"That speaks well of you. I know you're a fine nurse, and I have no doubt you'll be an excellent doctor."

"Thanks, Mama. I know it's late. I'll let you go."

Jilli chuckled. "You know how much an old lady like me needs my beauty sleep. I love you, Morgan. Congratulations."

"Love you too, Mama. Sleep tight."

After ending the call, Jilli immediately called Ian, hoping he was still awake.

"I was wondering if you were going to remember to call me like you promised or forget as you usually do."

"Oh, Ian, I just hung up from talking to Morgan."

"So, she told you her news. I've had a hard time keeping it a secret, but I promised her I wouldn't tell anyone."

"I understand. She told me she'd asked you to write a letter of recommendation. It was so good to hear such excitement in her voice. She hasn't seemed to be this excited about anything in a long time."

"She'll be a fine doctor. Did she tell you what area of medicine she wants to pursue?"

"Oh, my goodness! I didn't even think to ask. Do you know?"

"Pediatrics. You know what that could mean?"

From the excitement in his voice, Jilli knew exactly what it could mean. "That she'll come back to be in practice with you, right?"

Ian laughed. "You know me too well. You know it'd be my dream come true."

"I know it would, Ian. I'd love it if Morgan came back to Ida to practice medicine and raise her family. That is if she ever has time to have a family. But I think we might be getting ahead of ourselves."

"You're right. Guess I need to slow down a bit."

"We've had a lot happen in our family over the past few days. I think I need some time to adjust to all of it. I haven't even told you what Kalli found out today, but if you don't mind, I'll tell you all about it tomorrow. I just can't talk about it anymore tonight."

"Tomorrow will be fine, Jillian. You get some rest. You're going to need it to get through the next few days with your Mama and sisters."

"I hope you know how much I love you and thank God every day for bringing you to my life."

"Same here. Sleep tight, my love."

Jilli ended the call, set her cell phone back on the table beside the bed, and took very little time falling asleep.

Almost as soon as the door to her bedroom closed behind her, Nicola was undressed and in the shower. She stood with the hot, steaming water flowing over her body for a long time, praying the stress and uncertainty of this day would be washed away. From the time she'd first learned of Jake Albright's phone call, she'd sensed there was truth to his story. But until Kalli told them what Colonel Badger had discovered, she hadn't realized just how much that truth could hurt her mother.

When the water began to cool, Nicola stepped out of the shower and dried off with one of the HSI— Hart & Soul Inn— embroidered towels. Breathing in the scent from the freshly laundered towel brought back memories of days gone by when her job— along with her sisters— had been to prepare the rooms for the guests. At the time, she'd believed it to be such a burdensome chore. But now, as she looked back on those days, she smiled. The memories of how much the three of them had laughed and shared with one another as they worked to set up each room just like their mother had taught them were precious to her. It made her sad to think her own children might have been closer to one another if she'd had them work together to complete household chores.

Nicola was standing at the bathroom sink brushing her teeth with only the towel wrapped around her body when she thought she heard a tapping sound. When she opened the bathroom door to listen more closely, she was met by silence. As soon as she went back to the sink to finish brushing her teeth, the tapping resumed. Fear gripped her as it occurred to her a mouse may have gotten into her room. She hated mice, but knew they were a common problem in country homes. With her toothbrush in hand and her heart pounding, she stepped out into the bedroom. Body and mind alert, she scanned the room searching for the source of the sound.

She jumped at the sound of an insistent knock on her bedroom door followed by a heavily French-accented whisper. "Nicolette."

Nicola hurried to the door. "Alexandre!"

Alexandre stood at the open door, speechless. By the look on his face, she could see how he'd been silenced by the sight of his wife with toothbrush in one hand, her lips covered with toothpaste, and with only a towel covering her naked body. She reached out, pulled him into her room, and closed the door.

"What are you doing here?"

Alexandre gave her a sly smile. "Ooh la la!" He reached out to draw her into his embrace. "I think I have come to take you out of that towel!"

"Alexandre, stop!" Nicola put her hand on his chest and pushed him away. Mama and my sisters might hear you."

He pulled her closer to whisper in her ear. "I promise to be very quiet."

Nicola giggled. "At least let me rinse the toothpaste out of my mouth."

Alexandre opened his arms, releasing her. "As long as you hurry back to me."

Nicola returned to the bathroom. Ten minutes later she emerged dressed in her pajamas with her hair wrapped in the towel. She found Alexandre sitting in the blue wingback chair.

Smiling up at her, Alexandre put both his hands over his heart. "Why did you change? I like what you were wearing before."

When Nicola looked into her husband's exotic olive-green eyes and handsome tanned face, her breath caught in her throat. She leaned over and kissed him. "I'll just bet you do." She took her place on the window seat next to his chair. "How did you get in the house? How did you know which bedroom I was staying in? Why are you here?"

Alexandre held up his hands. "One question at a time. First, Mama let me in the house. I knocked on the door. Mama came. Mama let me in. Second, Mama told me in which room I would find you. And last." He got out of his chair and went on his knees in front of her. He held out his hands, reaching for hers. "I have come to apologize. I was not being fair to you."

Nicola stared at the palms of his open hands and crossed her arms. "It was more than you not being fair, Alexandre. You were mad at me. I've never known you to be so angry. It frightened me."

Alexandre bowed his head. "I know, mon amour. I was embarrassed to tell Maxwell we were not going to sell after I led him to believe we would. I am ashamed of my actions." He raised his head to look at her, his eyes glistening. "I was thinking all along we wanted the same thing, to sell. My Nicolette, I wasn't happy when you said it was not so."

Nicola uncrossed her arms and took his outstretched hands. "Alexandre, I thought you understood how much of my heart was in my bakeries. But after reflecting on what's happened over the past few days, I realize I wasn't honest with you. I let you set up that meeting, knowing I didn't want to sell our bakeries. I should have stopped you. I should have made my intentions clear to you. I'm the one who should be apologizing for not sharing my thoughts and feelings with you."

In one swift move, Alexandre pulled her into his arms.

Nicola held tightly to him as she began to cry with relief. "I thought you were trying to find a way to leave me."

Alexandre backed away and Nicola saw his distress. "*Tu es l'amour de ma vie.* You are the love of my life. I have no life without you."

"Oh, Alexandre, I love you." Nicola kissed her husband. It felt as if in that one kiss, their love was reborn.

After making love, they talked into the early hours of the morning. Nicola told him all that had taken place since she'd left home. He told her how he'd called Maxwell to tell him they would not be selling the Sweet Hart Bakery stores at this time, but to check back in ten years or so. Nicola giggled with relief when he said he could wait ten years before they sold the stores. Maybe, just maybe, in ten years she would be ready to sell. Who knew? If she'd learned anything in the past few days, it was how life could turn on a dime.

CHAPTER TWENTY-FOUR

Nelli awoke to a clap of thunder followed by a flash of lightning filling the entire room with light. Startled, she sat up and looked to her window. There was no light shining through, only darkness. She could hear the rain pounding against the side of the house. She squinted at the clock on her bedside table. It was five o'clock. She lay back down. Rolling over on her side, she curled up and pulled the covers up to her chin. Closing her eyes, she hoped for a few more hours of sleep.

After thirty minutes of restless tossing and turning, Nelli gave up. She shoved her feet into her slippers beside her bed and padded over to get her bathrobe from the chair in the corner. Opening her bedroom door as quietly as she could, she looked out into the hallway to see if the storm had brought anyone else out of their night's rest. Finding the hallway empty, she made her way to the back stairway thankful for baseboard motion sensitive lights illuminating her way. Once in the kitchen, she turned on the overhead light, made a pot of coffee, and popped one of Nicola's delicious leftover cinnamon swirl pancakes in the microwave to warm.

While she waited for the coffee carafe to fill, she wondered how Nicola had reacted to Alexandre showing up. She hoped his unannounced visit had been well received by Nicola. She was never quite sure how her middle daughter would react to the unexpected. Her mind traveled back to when she'd stood on a burning hot airport tarmac waiting for her red-headed, tennis star daughter she hadn't seen in over six weeks to emerge from the plane.

Nelli had been filled with confusion when Coach Cunningham stepped off the plane and the door had quickly closed behind him. She remembered the look on his face as he walked up to her to tell her that Nicola had made the decision, against his protests, to remain in France instead of returning with her team. He told her he'd encouraged Nicola to call home with her news and was sorry to find out she hadn't.

Nelli left for Paris the next day armed with the name of the hotel the team had been staying at and the name of the man Nicola had stayed for. After a day and a half of making phone calls and following leads, Nelli found her wayward daughter.

To say Nicola was less than thrilled by her mother's surprising visit would be an understatement. Nicola was furious. In no uncertain terms and in very disrespectful language, she made it clear she was not returning home, even after Nelli threatened to cut off her funding. Nelli left, and the two didn't speak to one another for almost three years.

The beep of the microwave announcing her pancake was heated brought Nelli out of her reverie. *Just in time*, Nelli thought. She could feel her blood pressure rising at the memory of that dark time of her life.

Nelli was finishing her breakfast when she heard footsteps on the back stairs. She looked up to see Jilli. She was dressed and ready for the day. Nelli smiled at her youngest daughter. "Good morning! I didn't expect to see you up and about this early."

Jilli walked straight to the coffeepot and helped herself to a cup. "This is exactly what I needed!" She kissed her mother's cheek before sitting down across from her. "Good morning, Mama. I couldn't sleep."

"Did the storm keep you up?"

"Not really. I got a call last night from Morgan. She's left me a couple of voice messages over the past few days, but I never had time, or maybe I just didn't take the time, to call her back. We finally got to talk last night."

"I hope nothing's wrong."

"No, in fact, everything seems to be going right for her." A smile lit up Jilli's face. "She's been accepted at the Medical College of Georgia in Augusta. Mama, Morgan's going to medical school to be a doctor."

Nelli's covered her mouth in surprise. "Oh, my goodness! That's what she's always wanted to be."

Jilli nodded her head. "I know, but I think she was too afraid to try right away. I think being a nurse has given her the confidence to go after her dream. She starts in the fall."

"Oh, Jilli, I am so happy for her." Nelli stood up, heading toward the phone on the kitchen wall. "I'm going to call her right now to congratulate her."

Jilli put her hand out. "Mama, it's only six in the morning. I think she'd appreciate it if you'd wait until later in the day to call her."

Chuckling, Nelli returned to her seat. "I think you're right. I'll wait."

Jilli took her cup to the sink. "Anyway, since I couldn't get back to sleep after Morgan called, I thought I might as well get up and get ready. I'm hoping to catch Ian and Drew before they leave the house."

"I think that's a great idea."

"Are you saying Jilli had a great idea?"

At the sound of Kalli's voice, Nelli turned to find her standing in the kitchen doorway.

"I do have one every now and then," Jilli said.

Kalli took a mug from the cabinet and filled it with coffee. "If you say so."

Jilli picked up her purse and briefcase she'd left next to the back door. "See y'all later."

Kalli watched Jilli walk out the door before joining Nelli at the table. "Where's she going in such a hurry?"

"Home."

Nelli told Kalli the news about Morgan.

"Good for Morgan. She's a smart one to go for her dream while she's still young."

"I agree. I'm going to call her later to congratulate her. Maybe we can all let her know how proud we are of her."

"Sounds good." Then Kalli frowned. "Mama, I thought I heard a man's voice late last night."

Nelli chuckled. "Oh, my, that's a whole other story!"

Jilli got to her house in time to see Ian and Drew off to work and school. Once they were on their way, she headed to her office. She was hoping to hear something from Aaron Bailer with information from his investigation of Steven and Jake Albright. After yesterday's revelations from Colonel Badger, she was anxious to see what Aaron might uncover about the pair. She couldn't imagine why Steven Albright hadn't told officials about her father being with him as a POW as soon as he'd been rescued. Why would he have kept it a secret for over fifty years? Had he made a deathbed confession to his son to clear his conscience of some wrongdoing? Those were the questions bouncing around in her head. She hoped Aaron might have some of the answers she craved.

Since it was an hour before Sade would be at work, Jilli found the front door to her office locked. Setting down her briefcase, she searched through her purse for her keys to the office door. She tried two keys before finding the right one to unlock the door. She couldn't remember the last time she'd opened the door for the day's business.

She walked through the door and stood staring through the dim light at the emptiness beyond. She found the stillness and the quiet of her empty waiting room comforting and peaceful. It was as if she were lost in time and space somewhere between the comforts of home and the demands of her job. She knew as soon as she flipped on the lights the peace of that moment would be gone. Closing her eyes, she asked God to bless her and all she held dear. Opening her eyes, she reached out her hand and flipped on the switch.

Jilli hurried through the waiting room to her office. She sat down behind her desk, opened her laptop, and signed in. She scrolled through her email searching for Aaron's name. Halfway down the screen, she found it. She smiled as she opened the email and read his message. It was brief and to the point. "Call me."

Glancing up at the clock on the wall, Jilli noted it was only a little past eight. Hesitating for only a minute, she picked up the office phone and placed her call. When there was no answer after five rings, she was about to hang up when she heard a familiar voice come through the headset.

"Aaron Bailer's Private Investigation Services. Aaron Bailer speaking."

"Aaron, this is Jilli, Jilli Hart. I'm calling about your email message."

"Thanks for calling. I've had some success in my investigation."

"Already? That's good to hear."

"If it's all right with you, I'd rather give you my report in person. Can we meet somewhere?"

Jilli was caught off guard by his request. She'd expected he'd send her a written report detailing what his investigation had uncovered about Steven and Jake Albright. "Sure, how about Rosie's Coffee Depot in fifteen minutes?"

"See you then."

After she hung up, Jilli's imagination took off. What information had his investigation uncovered that would require they meet in person? Glancing out the window, she decided she'd take a chance and walk the two blocks to Rosie's. If it started raining before she had to walk back, she could have Sade come pick her up.

Before leaving the office, she grabbed her umbrella just in case. In just a few minutes, she was sitting in a booth at the back of the coffee shop waiting for Aaron to arrive. She didn't have to wait long. When she saw him enter, she was transported back to her days when she'd believed him to be the best-looking boy at Ida County High School. It amazed her how little he'd changed since then. She smiled and waved him over to where she was sitting.

Aaron slid into the seat across from her. "Thanks for meeting me."

"I have to tell you, you asking me to meet in person has me more than a little curious as to what you've found out about this father and son duo."

Aaron placed his briefcase on the seat beside him. He took a file folder from the case and placed it in on the table. "I know how important this is to you, Jilli. I thought it best we meet so I can explain a few things rather than simply send you a report to read."

A waitress came to their table to take their order. Aaron ordered coffee. Having had two cups of coffee already, Jilli ordered hot chocolate.

"Before you begin, I need to tell you Kalli found out a couple of things about Steven Albright yesterday from her source at the Pentagon. It turns out he was a pilot and was shot down over North Vietnam in January of 1969. He was captured by the Vietcong and taken prisoner."

Aaron nodded his head. "That goes right along with what I have on Captain Steven Albright. Did Kalli's source also tell you that he escaped from the POW prison in May of 1969 and was rescued in the middle of July?"

"No." Jilli shook her head. "As far as I know, Kalli's source didn't mention that fact. We assumed he was rescued, but he didn't give those details."

"When he was rescued, he was alone. No one else was with him."

Jilli cocked her head to one side. "Okay, so he was alone. Why is that important?"

Aaron leaned in. "Because there were other prisoners, eyewitnesses, at that POW prison camp he escaped from. Several of the prisoners left behind swear there were six soldiers with Albright when he escaped. Jilli, seven people escaped, yet only one was rescued."

Biting her lip, Jilli asked, "What are you saying, Aaron?"

"I'm saying at the end of the Vietnam conflict, when those POW prisoners were released, they told the story of Captain Albright's escape, and they named the other soldiers who escaped with him."

"Are you telling me one of those other soldiers who escaped was my father?"

"Chief Hart was one of the names those released prisoners gave."

Jilli sat back against the seat, crossing her arms over her chest. "I find all of that hard to believe." She leaned in toward Aaron. "If all of what you're telling me is true, then why didn't the Army tell us? I don't see what they could gain by keeping it a secret."

"I don't have an answer for you, Jilli. I'm reporting what my investigation of Steven Albright turned up."

Jilli sat in silence, but her mind was churning with questions. "Did you find any record of Steven Albright giving an account of what happened to the six other soldiers?"

Aaron shook his head. "I didn't."

"Did any of those witnesses who saw my dad with Albright when they escaped have any idea what happened to him?"

Aaron put his hand over Jilli's. "I'm sorry, Jilli, but that's all I've turned up about Steven Albright's escape and rescue. I can keep looking for answers to your questions if you want me to continue my investigation."

Jilli looked away. She hadn't known what she wanted Aaron to find out, but this wasn't anything she'd expected. Now there were more questions and possibly more heartbreak for her whole family, but mostly for her mother. Tears began to sting her eyes as she thought of telling her mother what Aaron had discovered about Steven Albright.

"I can't answer those questions you asked, but I do have more information," Aaron said interrupting her thoughts.

Jilli turned back to him.

"Do you want to know the rest?"

Jilli slowly nodded. "Yes, I need to know all you've found out."

Aaron looked down at his notes. "It turns out Steven Albright didn't have such a great life after Vietnam. He worked for several airlines, but was fired from all of them. Each time he was cited for drinking on the job or reporting to work drunk. He did some odd jobs and even flew for a crop-dusting company, but he never stopped drinking. His wife left him, taking their only child, Jacob, age eleven, with her. It appears he was never involved after that in his son's life on any level. Steven Albright died four weeks ago at a veteran's hospital in Georgia of end-stage alcoholism."

Jilli sat silently for several minutes as she processed this. She cleared her throat. "What did you find out about his son?"

"In spite of his father, it looks like Jacob, or rather Jake, as he's called, has had a good life." Referring to his notes once again, Aaron continued. "Jake is fifty-nine years old. He's an aeronautical engineer for Boeing in Huntsville, Alabama. Graduated from the University of Florida. Owns his home, no mortgage. He's a member of the Huntsville First United Methodist Church. He's also a member of the Rotary Club of Greater Huntsville. He served as president for two terms. He was married for thirty years until his wife Valarie died of ovarian cancer three years ago. He has one daughter, Lisa, twenty-seven years old, who also lives in Huntsville. She's married with two children. She has a degree in elementary education and taught for a while just like her mother. She now stays home with her children. Her husband Arthur is the vice president of The First National Bank in Huntsville."

Jilli's eyes widened. "Well, that's not at all what I expected."

Aaron raised his eyebrows. "Really? What did you expect my investigation would find out about Jake Albright?"

Jilli shrugged. "I guess I thought you would find out my sister was right about him being a loser looking to hit up a military widow for some money by giving her some made-up story about her husband being a POW." She held her palms up. "Looks like Kalli was way off base."

"She sure was. By all accounts, Jake Albright is an upstanding, highly respected, all-around-good-guy."

Jilli tapped her fist against her lips. "That's good, and that's bad."

"How do you mean?"

"I mean it's good he's not coming to try to swindle Mama." Frowning, Jilli looked up into Aaron's eyes. "But it's bad in that he must honestly have some sort of proof Daddy was a POW and didn't die in that helicopter crash like we were told."

CHAPTER TWENTY-FIVE

Aaron left as soon as he finished giving Jilli his report. She remained, barely noticing that her hot chocolate had grown cold. She didn't know exactly how she felt about all she'd learned from Aaron's investigation. She no longer believed her father had been killed in a helicopter crash. She no longer questioned Jake Albright's claim her father had been a prisoner of war. However, what she did question was how her father had died. That question weighed heavily on her heart.

It wasn't until Jilli left the booth and was standing at the front door of the coffee shop that she noticed the rain had returned. It wasn't one of those soft, gentle spring rains, but a hard and fast downpour. There was no way she could walk back to her office through the deluge. She took out her cell phone to call Sade to come pick her up, but reconsidered. She didn't want to go back to her office. She wanted to be in the comfort of the home she'd grown up in. She wanted— needed— to be with her Mama and sisters at the Hart & Soul Inn.

Looking down at the phone in her hand, she selected the number from her contacts.

Kalli answered with a cheerful voice. "Hey, baby sister. You sure got up and going early this morning."

"Can you come get me?"

Kalli's voice dropped. "What's wrong, Jilli? Are you all right?"

"To tell you the truth, I'm not sure how I am. I just met with Aaron Bailer, you know, the private investigator I hired to look into Steven and Jake Albright's pasts."

"I take it he didn't find sweetness and butterflies."

"Not really."

"Tell me where you are."

"I'm at Rosie's Coffee Depot."

"I'll be there in ten."

"And Kalli, please don't say anything to Mama."

"Mum's the word."

After ending the call, Jilli sat down at the table closest to the door and ordered a cup of hot tea. As she waited for the waitress to bring her order, she couldn't stop thinking about what might have happened to her father after he escaped with Captain Albright. Had he been recaptured and tortured? Had he lost his way in the dense jungle? It broke her heart to imagine the atrocities her father may have suffered. She'd only taken a few sips of her tea before she noticed Kalli's car pull up to the curb in front of the restaurant. She left her cup and payment on the table and hurried out through the pouring rain to Kalli's car.

"Oh, Jilli, why didn't you think to bring an umbrella with . . ." Kalli must have seen the sorrow on Jilli's face. She leaned over and pulled Jilli into her arms. Jilli welcomed her embrace as she began to softly cry against her sister's shoulder. The two sisters held on to one another for several minutes.

It was Jilli who pulled away first. Sitting up, she wiped her tears away with the flat of her hand. "We better go before you get a ticket for parking illegally."

Dabbing at the tears in her own eyes, Kalli put her car in drive and pulled away from the curb. "If I do, you're going to pay for it."

"Oh, you think so, do you? It's your car. You can pay the ticket," Jilli teased.

Kalli began to giggle. It wasn't long before Jilli joined her. Their laughter cleared the tension from the car. When they'd both calmed down, Kalli asked, "Jilli, what in the world did Aaron discover that has you so upset?"

For the rest of their ride home, Jilli recounted all Aaron had told her. She finished just as Kalli pulled into the driveway of the Hart & Soul Inn. Kalli parked the car next to Alexandre's and turned off the engine. In the stillness of the car, Kalli turned to Jilli. "Well, at least we know Jake Albright isn't some kind of scallywag."

Eyes wide, Jilli stared at her sister. "Scallywag? Where did you get that word from? A Civil War dictionary?"

Kalli chuckled. "I don't know. It just came to me."

"Well, don't let it follow you in the house." Jilli opened her door and was about to exit the car when she remembered something. She sat back down and closed her door.

"What's wrong?" Kalli asked.

Jilli placed her hand on her chest. "I think I'm losing it."

"I'll be the judge of that."

"I just realized my car is still parked at my office."

"Do you want me to take you back to town to get it?"

Jilli thought for a moment. "No, I'll have Ian bring it to me."

Kalli opened her door and stepped out of her car. She looked back at Jilli. "By the way, I think forgetting your car is the first stage of losing it!" With that, she slammed her door shut.

Jilli followed Kalli into a kitchen buzzing with activity. Nicola was at the stove stirring a huge, bubbling pot while Alexandre stood at the counter slicing a long loaf of bread. Mama was setting the dining room table with napkins, spoons, and knives.

Closing her eyes, Kalli took in a deep breath. "Something smells wonderful."

Nicola turned to her sisters with a big grin on her face. "It's Topsy's vegetable soup."

Jilli went to the stove to check out the large pot Nicola was stirring. "Please tell me you're not making a joke. You know it's my favorite. I haven't had her soup in ages."

Nicola continued stirring. "Not kidding. I decided on this awful, dreary day that Topsy's soup was the perfect thing to brighten up everyone's outlook on life. After all, as Topsy used to say—"

Kalli and Jilli and Nicola said together, "It's the best bowl of soup in the South." All three laughed as they shared a favorite memory of their great-grandmother.

"I could sure use something to make my day better," Jilli said as she planted a kiss on Nicola's cheek. She made her way to where Alexandre was occupied with placing buttered bread slices on a foil-lined cookie sheet and held out her arms to him. "It's so good to see you, Alexandre. When did you get here?"

Alexandre took the towel from his shoulder and wiped his hands. He embraced Jilli as he planted a kiss on each cheek. "I snuck in last night. I'm happy to be here with you lovely ladies."

Jilli curtsied. "Thank you, Monsieur."

Alexandre bowed. "Merci."

"Okay, that's enough of that!" Nicola pointed at her husband with her spoon. "You need to finish with the bread." Turning to Jilli, she added, "And you can fill the glasses with ice."

Jilli saluted before going to the refrigerator as her sister asked.

Rubbing her hands together, Kalli asked, "Okay, what do you need me to do?"

"Why don't you get the soup bowls? As soon as Alexandre finishes heating the bread, we'll be ready."

Before long, everyone was seated at the dining room table with a steaming bowel of Topsy's vegetable soup in front of them.

Mama cleared her throat. "Looking down this table at my beautiful daughters and handsome son-in-law. my heart is filled with pure joy. I feel so fortunate to have y'all here together with me during this trying time. Let's thank God for our many blessings."

Jilli took Kalli's and Mama's hands in hers and bowed her head as Mama prayed, "Our Father in Heaven, we give thanks for the pleasure of gathering together here today. We give thanks for this food prepared by loving hands. We give thanks for life, the freedom to enjoy it all, and all the blessings you have showered upon us. As we partake of this food, we pray for health and strength to carry on and live as You would have us. This we pray in the name of your son, Jesus Christ. Amen."

Everyone at the table added, "Amen."

Kalli was the first to fill her bowl with soup. "I hope it's as good as it smells." After taking a bite, she announced, "Oh, my gosh! It's even better!"

Jilli chuckled and then began eating. For several minutes only the sound of spoons hitting the rims of bowls could be heard.

Jilli decided it was time to break the silence. "To what do we owe the honor of having you join us, Alexandre?" she asked as she reached for another piece of bread. "Is it that you just couldn't take another day away from your beautiful wife?"

"Yes, Jilli, you are so perceptive." Alexandre took Nicola's hand in his and kissed it. "I am not so very happy without my beautiful wife."

Jilli smiled. "I understand. I know Ian would also be glad to see you. I believe this is one of his early days if you want to stop by his office this afternoon around four."

Alexandre returned her smile. "Thank you, I will be glad to see Ian as well."

"So, why were you up and out so early this morning, Jilli? Having a secret rendezvous?" Nicola asked.

Jilli looked down at her bowl of soup. She was hoping she could put off telling Mama and Nicola what Aaron's investigation had turned up, but decided now was as good a time as any to tell them. "Something like that." Clearing her throat, she looked up. "I met with Aaron Bailer. He's the private investigator I hired to look into the background of Steve and Jake Albright."

"Aaron Bailer." Mama rubbed her chin. "There's something familiar about his name."

Jilli glanced over at her mother. "He was the captain of the debate team at Ida County High School."

"That's where I've heard it before. But I thought I heard he left town after high school."

"He did, but he's back and has opened his own business—Ida Investigation."

Nicola tapped her fingers on the table. "Get on with it, Jilli, I want to hear what he found out about the pair."

"It turns out Jake Albright—his full name is Jacob—grew up to be a fine, upstanding man, but without much help from his father. Jake is fifty-nine years old. He's an aeronautical engineer for Boeing in Huntsville, Alabama."

"Well, that's good news," Nicola said as she glanced at Kalli. "I knew I was right. See, he's a good person."

"Let Jilli finish." Kalli turned to Jilli. "Go ahead. Tell them the rest."

Mama put her hand to her chest. "Oh, dear, that doesn't sound good."

"It isn't." Jilli stared down at the table. "As you already know, Steve Albright was captured by the Vietcong after he ejected from his plane. What Colonel Badger didn't tell Kalli, or maybe doesn't even know, is that the men who were in the POW camp with Captain Albright claimed that when he escaped there were six other soldiers who escaped with him." Jilli paused as she looked around the table. "However, when he was rescued, he was alone."

All eyes were on Jilli, waiting for her to continue. Her eyes met her mother's. "Those POW witnesses reported that Chief Nicholas Hart was one of the soldiers who escaped with him."

Jilli watched as her mother's hand went to her mouth.

In a shaky voice barely above a whisper, her mother asked, "Did Mr. Bailer find out if Captain Albright said anything about what happened to your father?"

Jilli shook her head. "No, because Captain Albright claimed he'd escaped alone." She went on to tell her family everything she'd learned from Aaron's investigation of Steven Albright and his tragic civilian life. When she finished, she sat back against her chair, emotionally exhausted.

Nelli sat silently with her head bowed for several minutes. She stood and looked down the table at her daughters. When she spoke, it was with a clear, strong voice. "I believe tomorrow Jake Albright will bring us the truth about what happened to your father." She picked up her bowl and glass and left the dining room. A few minutes later, Jilli heard her mother's footsteps on the back stairway.

CHAPTER TWENTY-SIX

On unsteady legs, Nelli made her way up the back stairs. She stood in front of her bedroom door with her hand on the knob. She wasn't sure her bedroom was where she wanted to be. If this were a bright, sunny day, she would go to the plantation pond, but on this dreary, rainy day she didn't see that as an option. She withdrew her hand and proceeded to the room at the end of the hall. She opened the door and stepped into her office.

It was the second time in a week she'd entered this room after months of abandonment. As her eyes adjusted to the gray light, she could see it was as she'd left it only days before when she'd been searching for documents to prove Jake Albright wrong in his declaration of her husband's imprisonment in Vietnam. She sighed, recognizing how things could change in just a few days. There was a strong possibility that tomorrow she would be handed a letter proving that her husband— her Nicholas— had in fact been a prisoner of war.

Ignoring the open file cabinet drawers, Nelli walked to her desk and sat down. She could see it was covered with a thin layer of dust.

She brushed her hands across the top to remove as much of the dust as she could then wiped her hands on her pants. She opened the middle drawer and took out her favorite writing pen. It was one she'd gotten for Christmas from Jilli when she was only ten years old. Her youngest daughter told her she'd chosen it special for her because the top half of the pen was filled with sparkling "jewels." Nelli could see they were colored glass, but when Jilli said, "The sparkle reminds me of you, Mama," the pen became her favorite. She'd replaced the pen's cartridge so many times she'd lost count.

From the side drawer, she pulled out her neglected journal. For most of her life, she'd religiously written her thoughts down every single day. She could remember nights she'd written in her journal when she could barely hold up her head. She wasn't sure why, but over the past few months she'd stopped writing. Today, she had so many thoughts and emotions going through her mind. She knew the only way she could sort them all out was to put them down in writing.

Nelli turned to the first blank page and began to write. At first, she simply wrote about the events of the past few days, but soon, as it often had, her written words became a letter to her husband.

My Dearest Nicholas,

My heart is heavy as I write these words. For over fifty years I willingly and completely accepted as truth what I have now found to be a lie. When the Army informed me you'd been killed in a helicopter crash, I believed without questioning. I was comforted that death had come quickly and you had not suffered. Now, over the past few days, the veracity of the Army's claim has come into question. There are witnesses who tell a different version of the events leading to your death.

There are no words in the English language—or any language for that matter—strong enough to describe my pain and suffering when I was told you were gone from this world. The heartbreak I felt knowing I would never again hold you or be held by you or accept your tender kiss upon my lips or hear your deep laugh or see your sweet eyes smiling down on me in love is beyond description. At first my heart and mind fought against accepting your death. It was only with the help of God and the love of three little girls that acceptance finally came. With my acceptance came a sense of peace, and my life continued without you.

Now, the very peace I've held on to for years has been shattered as a stranger who believes I should know the truth has come forward with a different version of your death. I haven't heard his account of the events leading up to your death, but I have learned enough to question what I was told by the Army. In his story, you were a prisoner of war held in a Vietcong prison camp. I've heard and read personal accounts of those who were held as a prisoners of war in Vietnam. I am sickened realizing you must have suffered those same inhuman cruelties at the hands of your captors while I believed you were resting in the arms of sweet Jesus far beyond such horrors.

I don't know what I will learn tomorrow when I am given this altered account of events, but I do know it will shatter the peace I have had these past fifty years. I must believe I will find that peace once again. It may not come to me right away, but it will come, because God is still right here beside me. With His help and the love of those same three girls, I know peace will come to my heart once again.

Nicholas, I will forever and always love you. My heart will always ache for you and the life we could have had together. I am eternally grateful to you for blessing me with the best part of you, three wonderful, loving daughters.

Love always, Nelli

Nelli put down her pen and read through all she'd written. Satisfied, she closed her journal and placed it back in the side desk drawer. Resting her elbows on her desk, she rested her head in her hands and prayed out loud.

"Lord, I never imagined so much could change in so few days. It breaks my heart to think of Nicholas suffering as a POW, and I wasn't even aware of it. Questions keep running through my mind. If I'd known, was there a chance, even a slim one, I could have saved him? Did they hurt him? Was he frightened? Did he think I'd abandoned him?"

A sob broke loose from Nelli's chest and tears rolled down her cheeks and onto the desk. "My heart aches, and I'm so very tired. I need Your help, Lord. I pray for strength in my weakness. I pray for faith in my fear. I pray for courage to face the truth of what happened to my beloved Nicholas. I pray for my questions to be answered."

She paused, taking a shuddering breath. "I find comfort in knowing deep in my heart Nicholas was never alone, because You were always there with him. I pray I can find a blessing in learning the truth about his death. I thank You for Your unwavering love for Nicholas, for me, and for my family. In Jesus' name, Amen."

When Nelli finally emerged from her office, she headed straight to her room to freshen up. She didn't want her daughters to know she'd been upset and crying. For all their lives, her daughters had looked to her to know how to react to bad or good news. It was important she show them her strength now, not her weakness, as they all dealt with this life-altering event.

Nelli went into her bathroom, where she washed her face, took down her hair, brushed through it, and in two swift motions pinned it neatly on top of her head. When she was satisfied with the way she looked, she went to her closet. She'd never been a shopper, especially not a clothes shopper. She thought shopping was the most boring activity anyone could participate in. If she had anything new and stylish in her closet, it would be something her daughters had purchased for her. Since they were teenagers, they'd tried in vain to make their mother dress in the style of the day. Nelli always thanked them for their offerings, and then put them in the back of her closet, usually without removing any tags. She decided today she'd pull something out of the back. It would make her daughters happy to see her dressed in something more stylish than her usual jeans and T-shirt topped with a flannel shirt that had most likely been her brother's.

Nelli put on her black pants with the elastic waist. She then chose a light blue blouse and even found the colorful scarf Kalli had given her last Christmas to tie around her neck. She was trying to decide if she should tuck her shirt in or leave it out— she had no clue which was in style these days— when there was a knock at her bedroom door.

Nelli turned toward the door. "Come on in. You can help me with—" She stopped midsentence when she took in the look on Kalli's face.

Kalli rushed into her mother's arms as she began to cry. "Oh, Mama, it's just all too much."

Nelli wrapped her arms around her daughter and patted her back. "I know it is, but it's all going to be okay."

Kalli took a step back. "How can you know, Mama? The Army gave us false information, lies, when they may very well have known the truth about Daddy all along. Why would they do that to us?"

Nelli tenderly placed her hands on each side of Kalli's face so she could look into her eyes. "I wish I knew the answer, my dear, but I don't. What I do know, or rather what I do believe, is God must have a reason for Jake Albright coming into our lives now to bring us the truth of what happened to your father after all these years. We need to trust in God's timing."

Kalli wiped at her tears with her shirt sleeve. "Oh, Mama, I feel like such a fool. I was so sure Jake Albright was a loser who was feeding you this made-up story so he could get something from you. I said such terrible things about him. Now, Jilli finds out he's a good guy who's had a difficult life."

Nelli chuckled. "Oh, Kalli, you're always so hard on yourself. You didn't do anything bad. The reporter in you was simply looking for facts, and the only facts we had turned out to be partial facts. That's not your fault. We all believed what the Army told us. Why wouldn't we? We had no reason to doubt their information. But because of your digging, we've learned so much about what happened in Vietnam to your father. And tomorrow, when Jake comes, we'll know even more. Now, help me decide which way I should wear this blouse."

Kalli kissed her mother's cheek. "Thanks, Mama." She stood back to study her mother's outfit. "Definitely out."

Nelli smiled at her daughter. "That's what I thought."

"By the way, I love the scarf."

"Thanks. My stylish daughter gave it to me."

They both laughed as they walked out of Nelli's bedroom arm in arm.

CHAPTER TWENTY-SEVEN

Kalli lay awake in her bed watching through her bedroom window as the long, dark night faded into a brilliant, fresh day. She wasn't sure she'd slept at all. She'd spent a restless night filled with a nervous apprehension as she anticipated what information the letter Jake Albright had in his possession might contain about his father.

When she and her mother had come downstairs yesterday afternoon, Jilli and Nicola were in the middle of making plans for a night out with their husbands. Of course, they'd invited her and Mama to come with them, but they'd declined, wanting to spend a quiet evening together. Neither wanted to spoil a fun couples' night out.
After fixing a comforting supper of chicken noodle soup and pimento cheese on crackers, Kalli and her mother spent the rest of the evening on the front porch swing reminiscing. She was surprised at how much of her childhood she could recall. As she recounted stories from her growing-up years, she realized just how much time she'd spent with her great-grandmother Topsy. She was transported back through her

memories to the hours she'd spent at Topsy's little house listening to her stories and learning about her family's history. Despite everything she and her sisters had suffered at such a young age, she believed her childhood to have been a happy one.

After telling a story she remembered from her time with Topsy, Kalli noticed how quiet her mother had become. She put a comforting hand on her mother's knee. "Mama, are you alright?"

Nelli reached up to put her hand over Kalli's. "Oh, Kalli, for so many years, I've worried you and your sisters wouldn't have fond memories of your time growing up here with the tragedy of your father's death and me always busy with running Hart & Soul." A tear slid down Mama's cheek. "But after listening to you tell your stories and seeing the excitement and wonder on your face, I think all my worrying was senseless." She sighed. "I can't tell you what it means to have that worry taken away."

Kalli wiped the tear from her mother's cheek with her thumb. "Oh, Mama, we all loved growing up here. Sure, there were some tough times, but we always knew we were loved, and that's what really mattered to us."

After such a satisfying, relaxing evening, Kalli was sure she'd fall fast asleep as soon as her head hit the pillow. But to her dismay, that didn't happen. Instead, she lay in her warm, comfortable bed, wide-eyed, with her busy brain full of random thoughts. She was awake when Jilli, Nicola, and Alexandre got home a little after midnight. She considered opening her door to ask how their time together had been, but changed her mind. If she did that, her sisters would think she'd been waiting up for them. They might worry she was feeling left out, which she wasn't at all. Then she'd have to contend with them fussing over her.

Kalli watched her bedside clock throughout the night as the hours slowly ticked by. When the first rays of the morning sun filtered in through her window, she almost jumped out of bed. Once showered, she took extra time with her makeup and hair, wanting to look her best. Years ago when she'd been a busy young mother with a career, husband, and child demanding her attention, she'd cut her crowning glory of long, thick brown hair into a short, blunt bob which required very little time to style. She'd continued with the style, afraid to make any changes. Now she wondered if she should let it grow out again.

Looking though the clothes she'd packed, she decided on her cornflower blue tunic, hoping its fullness would camouflage her expanding waist, and her stonewashed jeans. She wore her gold locket with matching earrings Marshall had given her for her birthday only a few days before he'd been killed. She put on her most comfortable navy flats. She smiled at her reflection in the mirror on the back of the door, satisfied with the way she looked. She headed down the back stairs to start her day.

Kalli was about to start making breakfast for everyone, but she could almost hear the morning calling her outside. Since no one else seemed to be awake, she decided to answer the call. She took one of her mother's flannel shirts from the hook next to the back door. Her rather new navy flats wouldn't do with the ground most likely muddy from yesterday's showers. She hurriedly stepped out of her shoes into her mother's too-small rubber boots and out the back door. Her breath caught in her throat when she looked to the east at the glorious golden Georgia sunrise. Her eyes filled with wonder at the awe-inspiring sight. It was almost as if God was sending her a personal message, telling her today was going to be a good day.

Kalli raised her hands in praise. "Thank you, God, for this day!"

As she watched the sun rise above the horizon, Kalli knew where she needed to be to start this day—Mama's bench. She turned away from the sunrise and headed to where the edge of the woods met up with the plantation pond. It was as if her father were calling her there. With a sense of urgency, she walked as fast as she could manage in her mother's boots until she was standing beside the bench. She ran her hand along the bench's arm, marveling at how well it had endured through well over fifty years of hot Georgia summers and cold, rainy winters. She wondered if her father ever imagined it would still be here after so many years.

Feeling the chill of the morning air, Kalli turned up the collar on her mother's shirt and sat down. Taking in the view, she marveled at the wonders of nature surrounding her. She could see the water from yesterday's rain dripping from the leaves of the trees. The morning sun glistened on the drops, making them look like precious diamonds as they fell to the ground. Soft, new green shoots of grass were springing up around the edge of the pond. She closed her eyes, concentrating on the early morning sounds as the waking birds sang their special songs and a gentle breeze rustled the leaves on the trees. It was at times like this, sitting in the beauty and tranquility of the country, that Kalli wondered why she lived anywhere else but here.

With her eyes still closed, Kalli began to imagine what her life would be like if the two men most important in her life were sitting on this bench on this very day right beside her. She'd have her father on her left and her husband Marshall on her right. She placed her left hand and right hand on each side of her and tried to conjure their images in her mind. Her father would be eighty-seven years old now. His once bright red hair would most likely be gray. He'd always worn his hair in a short, sharp military cut, and she was sure he'd have kept it in that same style. He'd still have those beautiful, sensitive, azure-blue eyes that sparkled when he smiled and literally danced when he laughed. His hands would be scarred and rough from years of hard work, but still gentle and loving. She could almost feel the weight of his hand on hers.

On her right would be her Marshall with his light brown unruly hair. She smiled remembering how it always seemed to need a trim. His face might have a few more lines in it from worrying about the state of the world, but his brown eyes would have the same tenderness shining with love for her and their son. She remembered the calluses on his hands from his woodworking projects and how she used to trace with her finger the veins that roped through the top of his hands. With her whole being she wished for those hands of his to be holding hers.

With her eyes still closed, Kalli clasped her hands. She silently prayed for God to bless her with the strength and wisdom of her father and her husband as she listened to what Jake Albright had to tell her family. She prayed for an accepting and forgiving heart. She thanked God for the love her father and husband had given her and for the beauty and wonder of this day.

Kalli opened her eyes, breathed in the fresh clean air, got up, and walked back to her mother's house ready for the day ahead and all it would bring.

Breakfast that morning was cereal and toast. Nelli was joined at the table by her two younger daughters and their husbands. All were still in their pajamas and teasingly fought over first dibs to the coffee. They were discussing the evening before when Kalli came through the back door.

"Is that my shirt?" Nelli asked as she stared at her daughter. "And my boots? Aren't they a little small?"

Kalli stepped out of her boots and stood on one leg as she rubbed her toes. "Yes, ma'am. Much too small."

"Where have you been?" Jilli asked before she took a bite of her toast.

"Nowhere, really, just walking around." Kalli slipped on her shoes and then hung Nelli's shirt back on the hook.

"Well, you look nice for a walkaround," Alexandre observed with a smile.

Kalli returned his smile as she poured herself a cup of coffee. "Merci."

"So, Mama, what time are you expecting this Jake guy?" Nicola asked.

Nelli put down her coffee cup. "He didn't say exactly what time he planned to be here. I'm hoping it'll be sometime around noon. I'm not sure I have the energy or patience to wait all day."

Kalli shook her head. "Me either. I want to get it over with. I barely slept a wink last night just thinking about all of this."

"Me either," Jilli agreed. "I must have looked at the clock next to my bed fifty times."

Nicola put her hand over Alexandre's as she smiled up at him with a knowing smile. "We slept like babies. Didn't we?"

Alexandre bent down to kiss her hand. "Oui, mon amour."

Jilli wrinkled her nose. "Oh, please, y'all are going to make us all sick."

Nelli looked at Nicola and Alexandre. "I, for one, think it's sweet."

Kalli rolled her eyes. "Well, I, for one, am ready to get on with our lives. It's like since that phone call we've all been living in limbo, and I'm tired of it."

"I second that," Jilli chimed in.

Their conversation was interrupted by the ringing of the kitchen telephone. Nelli got up from the table to answer. "Hello."

"Hello, Mrs. Hart, this is Jake Albright. We talked the other day."

Nelli turned to look at her daughters. "Yes, Mr. Albright, I remember. I've been expecting your call."

"Yes, ma'am. I'm wondering when would be a good time for me to meet with you."

Nelli put her hand over the receiver and whispered, "He wants to know what time to meet today. What should I tell him?"

Jilli and Nicola shrugged and looked to Kalli.

Kalli whispered back, "Tell him we'd like to meet at one o'clock."

Nelli cleared her throat as she removed her hand from the receiver. "Would one o'clock this afternoon be convenient for you, Mr. Albright?"

Jake answered without hesitation. "One o'clock would be fine with me."

"Mr. Albright, I think you should know that my three daughters will also be here for our meeting."

"That's fine. In fact, I'm glad you have them with you. I'll see you at one."

"Do you need directions to my house?" Nelli asked.

"No, ma'am. I have your address. I'll put it in my GPS."

"Then we'll be expecting you. Drive carefully, Mr. Albright. Goodbye."

"Goodbye."

Nelli hung up the phone and looked to her daughters. "Well, it looks like we'll be having company today."

Jilli stood up and put a comforting arm around Nelli's shoulder. "Are you okay, Mama?"

Nelli patted her daughter's arm. "I'm fine. I'm so glad y'all are here with me. I don't believe I could get through this without my three precious daughters by my side."

Nicola got up from the table and hurried to Nelli's side. "We wouldn't want to be anywhere else, Mama." She leaned over to kiss Nelli's cheek. "I'm glad we're here too."

Kalli stood. With cup in hand, she walked to the coffeepot. "Well, I'm glad he agreed to meet at one. I was worried we'd have to wait all day long to hear what he has to say. Then we can put this behind us."

Nicola's eyes narrowed as she turned toward her sister. She spoke through gritted teeth. "Kalli, I can't believe you just said that. This meeting isn't going to make anything go away. In fact, it's only beginning. The beginning of learning to live with a new truth of what Daddy went through in Vietnam."

Kalli put up her hands. "Okay! Okay! I'm sorry! I didn't mean it like that. I meant we could be done with wondering what really happened."

"Let's not do this now, girls." Nelli broke through the tension between the two sisters. "Today we need to be united and strong. That's what your father would want from his daughters. And, truthfully, it's what I need."

Nelli held out her arms to her daughters. Without hesitation, Kalli and Nicola rushed into them.

CHAPTER TWENTY-EIGHT

As soon as breakfast was put away and the kitchen set back in order, Mama, Jilli, and Nicola headed upstairs to get ready for the day. During breakfast Alexandre had received a frantic call about one of the ovens at their Madison Sweet Hart Bakery. His plan had been to stay to support Nicola, but after receiving the call, he'd left as soon as he'd showered and dressed.

With everyone upstairs, Kalli found herself sitting alone in the kitchen. She went to the kitchen drawer next to the telephone where her mother kept pens and paper to take down phone messages. She took out a notepad and pen and returned to the table to write down questions to ask Jake Albright. In her journalism classes, she'd always stressed to her students the importance of being prepared. By nine thirty, she had just finished writing her last question when she heard her mother along with her sisters coming back down the stairs.

Kalli looked up from the kitchen table as they entered the room. Nicola was looking fashionable in her slim white ankle pants and emerald-green button-down shirt which set off her fiery red hair cascading over her shoulders. Her mother, once again looking unusually stylish, was dressed in the same light blue shirt, scarf, and black pants she'd worn the night before. Unsurprisingly, her youngest sister was looking gorgeous. She was dressed all in black, highlighting her shoulder-length straight blond hair that provided the perfect frame for the exquisite diamond pendent she wore around her neck.

Kalli smiled at her mother and sisters. "Well, if nothing else, we're a good-looking group of women."

"I agree with that," Nicola said. "Now, are we just going to sit around here waiting, or are we going to share our beauty with the outside world?"

Jilli spread her arms out. "I say we go out into the world." She put her arms down. "What do you say, Mama? It's really up to you."

Nelli's mouth slowly turned up into a sly grin. "I say let's share our good looks with the world."

They all laughed.

"Where should we go?" Nicola asked.

Jilli glanced at the kitchen clock. "What about going over to Kerry? It's only about ten minutes away. We'll have plenty of time to look around the downtown shops. We can eat an early lunch at the Rustic Bistro. No doubt we'll be back in time for our meeting."

Kalli looked at her mother. "You want to do that, Mama?"

Nelli nodded. "Sounds good to me."

Because Jilli was the one most familiar with the area, it was decided she'd drive. Even though Kalli and Nicola had grown up in Ida, it had been years since they'd been to Kerry. The four took their places in Jilli's car with her Mama sitting in the passenger's seat and Kalli and Nicola in the back seat. They spent the morning looking through Kerry's antique and specialty shops. Kalli couldn't believe how much the town had changed since she'd driven the streets as a teenager. A little after eleven the four were seated at a table at the Rustic Bistro, enjoying their meal.

Kalli sat back in her chair. "Whew! I don't know about any of you, but my feet are tired. I'm not used to walking on hard concrete sidewalks. I should have worn my tennis shoes."

Nicola laughed. "Well, at least you didn't wear your high heels."

"True."

"So, girls, what do you think of the new Kerry?" Jilli asked.

"I like it." Speaking in a low voice, Nicola leaned in. "In fact, I'm thinking they just might need a Sweet Hart Bakery in their little town." A teasing smile crossed her face. "We've even batted around the idea of putting a Sweet Hart Bakery in Ida now that the Coffee Cup has closed down."

"I really like that idea," Jilli said excitedly. She put a hand over her mouth. "Sorry, I didn't mean to shout. But that would mean you'd be coming down here more often."

"I'd like that," Nelli said, smiling at Nicola.

Nicola returned her smile. "I'd like that too, Mama."

Kalli crossed her arms over her chest. "You know, I'm not sure how much longer I'll be teaching. Maybe I should come down this way to retire. After all, there's nothing up there to hold me."

Jilli put her hand on her chest. "Oh, be still my heart!" She laughed. "Mama, how would you like it if all of your daughters came back this way to stay? Could you handle that?"

Nelli put her finger on her chin as she squinted her eyes in thought. "Hmm, I'm not sure. It might take me a while to get used to the idea."

"Well, if you aren't sure, Mama, I can find somewhere else to retire to," Kalli teased.

"I'm kidding!" Nelli reached out to grab her wrist. "I'd love it! It'd be my best dream come true."

Kalli patted her mother's hand. "We'll just have to see what works out, but it's something I'm truly considering."

Jilli clapped her hands together. "How exciting! Now, how about we top off our morning with a slice of the Bistro's famous three-layer German chocolate cake and a cup of coffee?"

When the living room clock struck one, Nelli, Kalli, Nicola, and Jilli were gathered on the front porch awaiting the arrival of Jake Albright. Their trip to Kerry had been the perfect distraction, but now Kalli was focused on the changes the next few hours would bring to their lives. Since no one seemed to be in the mood for idle chatter, the only sounds were the birds in the trees calling to one another and the creak of the swing as it moved back and forth.

Kalli stood when she heard a car turning off the highway onto their drive. She watched as a silver car slowly traveled down the long, tree-lined driveway. It came to a stop at the wide sidewalk at the front of the house. She held her breath as a tall, slender, gray-haired man with a neatly trimmed gray beard and mustache climbed out of the car. He was dressed in a navy-blue sports coat with a white button-down shirt over blue jeans. His white teeth stood out against his tanned face. She turned back to her mother, who waved her forward. She made her way down the front steps and out to meet this man whose unexpected phone call only a few days before had torn apart her world. Mr. Jake Albright.

Holding out her hand to him, Kalli smiled. "Mr. Albright, I'm Kalliope Hart Abbott, Nicholas Hart's oldest daughter." She had no idea why she'd used her full name or felt the need to mention she was the oldest except for the fact she was unnerved by the unexpected attractiveness of the man standing before her. He was nothing like the small, hump-backed, pinched-face man she'd imagined ever since she'd first heard his name. When he removed his aviator sunglasses, revealing the most vivid deep-sea-blue eyes Kalli had ever seen up close and smiled down at her, her breath caught in her throat.

Jake took Kalli's outstretched hand in his. "It's a pleasure to meet you, Kalliope Hart Abbott. I'm Jacob Steven Albright, but you can call me Jake."

Kalli gave a nervous laugh. "Nice to meet you, Jake. You can call me Kalli." Her face reddened as she realized how close her laugh had been to a flirting, girlish giggle. Embarrassed, she released his hand.

She looked back and saw Nicola and Jilli hurrying her way. Stepping around Kalli, Nicola introduced herself. "Jake, I'm Nicola, and this is Jilli. Won't you please join us on the porch?"

Jake followed the sisters up the front steps and onto the porch to where Nelli was waiting for them. He took Nelli's hand in his. "Mrs. Hart, I'm sure my phone call has brought up some hard memories and disturbing questions. I hope my visit today will help answer your questions and bring you peace."

"Thank you, Mr. Albright. I hope so too." Nelli gestured to the chair next to her. "Please have a seat."

"Thank you, ma'am." Jake sat down in the white wicker rocker.

Nelli smiled at him. "I'm sure you're parched after your trip. May we get you something to drink?"

"How nice, thank you."

Nelli turned in her seat to look at her daughters who were still standing. "Would one of you please get Mr. Albright some iced tea?"

Kalli quickly volunteered. "I'll get it."

Without missing a beat, Nicola added, "I'll help her."

"Can you believe that's Jake Albright?" Kalli asked Nicola as soon as she was sure she couldn't be overheard by their guest sitting on the porch,

Nicola put her hand to her mouth. "I never imagined he'd look anything like that!"

"I know! I almost fell over when I saw him get out of his car."

"You mean, you almost fell into his arms!"

Kalli playfully hit her sister's arm. "I did not!" Then in a more serious tone asked, "Did I?"

Nicola rubbed her arm. "Oh, Kalli, I hate to tell you this, but it was so obvious you were attracted to him."

Kalli covered her face with her hands. "Oh, I was, wasn't I? But did you see those Paul Newman eyes of his? Oh, Nicola!"

"And you were the one who's been saying such ugly things about him all week."

"Well, he may be a handsome guy, but I'm not taking anything back I've said about him until I find out what he has to tell us."

Kalli took down five glasses from the cabinet and filled them with ice. She went to the refrigerator to get the tea while Nicola put the lemon cookies they'd bought at the Rustic Bistro on a plate. Once Kalli had poured the tea, she put the glasses on a tray. "Are you ready?"

Nicola nodded. "As ready as I'll ever be."

Kalli carefully picked up the tray and smiled at her sister. "Here we go."

Before Kalli walked out onto the front porch, she could hear her mother's voice. She sighed. "Good grief, Nicola! I think Mama's giving him the complete history of the Tucker Plantation!"

"He must have made a comment about the house which set her off into giving him the whole spiel." Nicola rolled her eyes. "Just like old times when we had guests staying here."

Kalli placed a smile on her lips as she stepped out onto the porch. Once everyone had been served, she took a seat on the swing next to Nicola, sipped her iced tea, and tried to patiently listen to her mother tell about her family even though she was more anxious to hear what Jake had to tell about his family.

Nelli finally concluded her recital with a sweep of her hand. "Now, this once grand plantation house is simply my home."

Kalli watched as Jake glanced around taking in the porch and the magnificent tree-lined driveway. She thought she could hear a touch of awe in his voice when he spoke,

"Well, Mrs. Hart, I must say this place is anything but simple."

"Thank you, Mr. Albright." Nelli sat back in her chair as she sipped her iced tea.

Jilli, who had been silent as her mother told her story, leaned forward in her seat to look at Jake. "Now that you've learned more about our family, what are you here to tell us today?"

Just like a lawyer, getting to the point, Kalli thought.

Jake set his iced tea down on the table next to his rocker, opened his jacket, and pulled an envelope from the inside pocket. He turned in his seat toward Nelli. "Mrs. Hart, I know I'm a total stranger who called you out of the blue with disturbing news about your husband. Believe me when I tell you I never wanted to upset you or your daughters."

He held the envelope in his hands as he spoke. "You see, my father was an alcoholic, a drunk, who was never a real father to me. My mother divorced him when I was young. I didn't see him for well over thirty years. I was sure he was an uncaring, selfish man who never wanted to be my dad."

He stared down at the floor and began stroking his beard with his free hand. After a minute he looked up and continued, "Then one day I got a voice mail from a nurse at the Carl Vinson VA Medical Center in Dublin, Georgia, telling me my father was dying and was asking for me. He was really nothing to me. I didn't want to see him, so I deleted it. When she called two more times stressing the urgency of my visit if I wanted to see him before he passed, something deep down inside of me told me I needed to see him. So, I went. By the time I got there, he was in bad shape. Years of abuse to his body had caught up with him. He was weak and could barely speak above a whisper."

Jake took in a deep breath. "Looking at him in that bed and seeing him as a dying, shriveled up old man, I couldn't hate him anymore. I just felt sorry for him. He'd let alcohol take his life and his only son away from him."

Jake held up the envelope. "With his dying breath, he asked me to find you to give you this letter. I have to tell you; my first inclination was to burn it. I couldn't imagine he had anything worthwhile to say or that anyone would be interested in what he'd written."

Jake lowered his head. After what seemed like a full minute, he looked up to meet Nelli's eyes. "But after I read it, I knew this was something you needed to know about your husband. I knew, just like my father finally knew, it's time for the truth to be told about Chief Nicholas Hart. I'm just so sorry he didn't tell it sooner."

Kalli could see tears glistening in Jake's eyes as he handed the envelope over to her mother. She looked on as her mother accepted it with shaking hands.

"I'm sorry too, Jake. I don't know what's in this letter your father has written, but I intend to read it very carefully."

Looking to her daughters, she added, "By myself."

She slowly stood. "Now, if y'all will excuse me."

Kalli had assumed the four of them would read the letter together. She frowned as she watched her mother get up from her chair, walk down the front porch steps, and disappear around the corner of the house.

CHAPTER TWENTY-NINE

When Nelli first stepped off the porch, away from Jake and her daughters, she wasn't sure where she was going. She only knew she had to read the words Steven Albright had written on his deathbed without her daughters watching her reaction. Before she was aware of where she was going, she was halfway there—the spot where she felt closest to Nicholas. Their bench.

As soon as Nelli reached her special spot, she slid onto the bench and placed the envelope on her lap. As she walked to this spot she'd resisted the urge to rip the letter from its envelope and read it. But now, looking down at the envelope containing the letter Steven Albright had written telling her how her husband had died, she wasn't sure she was strong enough for the truth.

Her heart was beating so hard it felt as if it might pound out of her chest. What was it about this letter that frightened her? She placed her hands over the envelope and took two deep, calming breaths. She bowed her head, closed her eyes, and prayed.

Dear Father in heaven, I'm not sure why I'm afraid to learn the truth of what happened to my beloved Nicholas. I guess a part of me found some peace in believing the Army's story of how his life ended in an instant, without suffering, when his helicopter crashed. Now, here is this letter which will most likely tell a vastly different story. One where he was tortured, and his life ended in violence at the hands of the enemy. Lord, I'm not sure I'm strong enough to handle this. I'm calling on You to please give me the strength and courage to open this letter and accept the truth of how Nicholas died. I ask this in Jesus' blessed name, Amen.

Opening her eyes, Nelli looked up at the surrounding trees with their branches swaying in the afternoon breeze. One of the Bible verses Topsy often recited to her as a child when she'd been frightened came to mind. *"For I hold you by your right hand— I, the Lord your God. And I say to you, 'Don't be afraid. I am here to help you.'"*

There was not a doubt in Nelli's mind that recalling this Bible verse was God's answer to her prayer. Imagining Jesus' steady, comforting hand holding hers, she picked up the letter and took it from its envelope.

This letter is intended for Chief Nicholas Hart's widow and his family. I swear everything I've written in this letter is God's honest truth of what happened to Chief Nicholas Hart.

I guess you could call this letter my deathbed confession, since I'm sure I will be dead by the time you read this. I don't want to go to my grave without telling you the truth about what happened to your husband in Vietnam. When I was rescued, I believed I could live with the half-truths and lies I gave to those who rescued me. Much too late, I learned how hiding the truth can ruin a person's life. So many times over the years I've wanted to shout out the truth, but shame and fear held my tongue. I tried to find peace and comfort in each drink I took, but I only found torment and grief at the bottom of every bottle. What I did in Vietnam to your husband has cost me my family, my livelihood, and, ultimately, my life.

I don't know what the Army has told you about Chief Hart's death, but I know whatever they told you wasn't how he died. I know this for certain because they don't know the truth. I am the only person in this world who knows how Chief Hart met his end, because I am the person who allowed his life to be ended. I never intended for things to turn out as they did, but I now understand how my intentions matter little when it comes to the death of a man who believed I was his friend.

I know it may be hard for you to believe after you've read this letter, but I considered Chief Nicholas Hart—Nick as I called him— my friend, my good friend. As POWs, we went through a hell beyond anything you can imagine. There are no words to describe it. I was captured after my plane went down a few days after Nick and five guys from his crew were caught by the North Vietnamese. I have no doubt I would have died those first weeks when we were being dragged from one hell-hole jungle prison camp to another if it weren't for Nick. He helped me when I was sure I couldn't take another step.

There were times when I didn't want to wake up in the morning. I figured the war would last another five years or so, and I'd probably die anyway. So, what difference would it make if I died right then? I was sure I'd never see my wife and son again. It was Nick who gave me comfort and courage by quoting scripture. A verse he said to me and those around us over and over until we all knew it by heart was from Deuteronomy chapter 31 verse 6:

"Be strong and take heart, and have no fear of them: for it is the Lord

your God who is going with you; he will not take away his help from you."

Nelli's breath caught in her throat. With her heart racing, she reread the Bible verse written by a man she now knew without a doubt had been with Nicholas as a prisoner of war. The letter fell as her hands flew to her mouth. There was no way Steven Albright could have known this was the verse she and Nicholas often quoted to give one another hope and strength. He couldn't have known how this verse contained the two words she and Nicholas had ended every letter they'd ever written to one another while he was in Vietnam—*Take Heart*. Taking a calming breath, she picked up the letter and continued to read.

I can't tell you how many times I repeated that verse. Every night I listened to Nick's prayers not only for himself and for his family, but for all of us. There were times I thought I felt Jesus was right there with us. That's how good Nick's prayers were.

There were seven of us kept together in a cage on stilts about three feet off the ground. The stilts were surrounded by ten-inch logs. Right away, Nick started talking about how we could escape. He made a calendar and scratched off each day. We decided our best chance of escape would be when the rains came in May, around the middle of the month. Nick never doubted we'd escape. His talking about it night after night gave us hope and kept us alive.

In March we started hiding rice in bamboo containers stashed above our heads. Now and then we picked up empty ammunition clips that the guards had discarded and hid them as best we could. During times when the guards were busy or distracted, we rubbed bamboo together to make a small fire, heated the clips until they were soft, then pounded them with rocks into little knives.

The rains did come in May, just like we hoped. It rained like the devil all day and night, which caused the food we'd stored up begin to mold. The rains also caused the guards' tempers to flare more than ever, which brought on more torture. We knew we had to make our escape soon before they decided the easiest thing for them to do was to kill us all.

About five o'clock each afternoon the guards would walk to the kitchen, pick up their food in turtle shells, then walk back to their hut. Our plan was to cut a hole in the floor. Then we could wiggle through the hole and drop to the ground 3 feet below. We could then dislodge one of the stacked 10-inch logs that surrounded the stilts and sneak across the open space to the guards' hut. If we could grab weapons, we could capture the guards when they returned from the kitchen.

God sent us two blessings the night of our escape: the deafening sound of the pounding rain and fewer guards. That morning, we couldn't believe it when we saw eight guards leave the camp. We guessed they'd been sent from camp to pick up supplies, but we never knew for sure. We just knew we had fewer guards watching us. Turning what was left of our shirts into rucksacks, we filled them with the rice we'd been saving and our pitiful handmade weapons.

We didn't have much time. Nick dropped to the ground through a hole it had taken us days to carve out, and dislodged one of the 10-inch logs with a rock and a bamboo stick. Another guy cut a tiny hole in the wall so he could watch the kitchen.

As soon as Nick reached the porch, the rest of us started coming through the hole. Nick grabbed two M-1s, a carbine, ammunition, and a couple of machetes. He passed them out to the rest of us, and we turned to face the kitchen.

All of a sudden, the guards were running out of the kitchen and shooting at us. I felt the bullets fly by my head. We yelled, "Ute, ute" for them to stop, then returned their fire. Five guards fell dead in their tracks. Three of them fled into the bush.

None of us had been hurt in the exchange of fire. Still, we were in trouble. We knew there was a village only a mile or so from the camp. If those three guards had gone to get help, search parties would be after us in half an hour.

Five minutes later we were moving out on the trail. We ran and ran until we were deep in the jungle. We stopped and knelt down to pray. Then two of the guys headed east. We gave them an M-1 and some ammunition. We never saw them again. The remaining five of us walked south to the closest ridge. By this time, our feet were swollen and bleeding.

We spent the night near a creek. It rained, and leeches swarmed all over our bodies but we were too exhausted to care. We got up again at dawn and decided to split into two groups. Nick and I would stay together. We gave the other guys the other M-1 and twenty-four rounds of ammunition in return for one of their machetes. Then we shook hands and wished them luck.

Nick and I had no idea at all of our position, so we decided to follow the creek. It was rising now because of the rain. In some places it was only five feet wide, in others, more than 100 feet and very deep.

On the third or fourth day we built a raft of banana trees. It took us eight hours. We floated along for several hundred yards. Then we heard a waterfall. We jumped and swam as fast as we could to the shore. The raft swept over the falls and splintered.

Our carbine along with the ammunition was gone with the raft, but we still had our machete although we didn't dare cut a trail. If we couldn't go straight through a section of bush, we'd go around it or try to bend it or crawl under it on our stomachs. Our arms were numb. The skin had been ripped from our feet and legs, and we could see bone.

After about fourteen days of walking, we stumbled upon a village. We hid out in the jungle and watched the village all day. Our plan was to sneak in that night and take any food and water we could find. From what we could see, it looked like there were only women and children along with a few old men in the village. I was so hungry. I wanted to go in right then and there and take whatever they had, but Nick convinced me that would never work. So, we did what he thought was best and waited until nightfall when everyone was asleep.

That night we crept into the village. All day long, I'd had my eye on the three dogs I'd seen walking around. Even though they were skinny, I was sure the meat from just one of those dogs could give us the strength we needed to make it out. I had my homemade knife out ready to slit the first dog's throat. Just as I was about to grab the dog, Nick stopped me. He pointed to a small girl about four or five years old standing near one of the huts only a few feet away. She was looking directly at us.

*Smiling at her, Nick crouched down. He greeted her in a soft, cooing voice. "*Chao chau', cô bé.*" Which in Vietnamese means "Hello, little girl."*

The girl came closer and crouched down across from him, but she didn't say anything. I will always remember her big brown eyes staring up at Nick in wonder. For all I know it could have been the first time she'd ever seen an American.

Nick patted his chest and whispered, "Nick."

She smiled and pointed to him and said, "Nick."

I was standing behind him and I was feeling more than a little antsy about him taking the time to have a conversation with that kid. Hunger and fear had taken over my mind. I know that sounds like a terrible excuse, but it's the truth. I knew we needed to kill that kid before she got us killed. I tapped Nick on the shoulder and told him how crazy this was and that he needed to get rid of the kid. We needed to grab the food and get out of there before someone came looking for us.

Then we heard a woman say, "Qui? Bạn ở đâu?"

Before Nick could stop her, the kid stood and turned away. I reached out with my machete ready to silence her forever. I couldn't believe it when Nick knocked it away.

The little girl began screaming. Suddenly, a black-haired man in a loincloth started running toward us. He carried a long machete — curved at the end. "Amerikali, Amerikali," he yelled. We nodded our heads, smiling, and said, "Sentai, Sentai" ("hello, hello"). But the man kept running towards us. I jerked back to pick up my machete.

The man's knife was already moving through the air. The first blow hit Nick on the leg. The second cut into his shoulder just below the neck. Nick turned and reached out to me as he fell to the ground. I know he wanted me to use my machete to stop the man, but I just stood there with my mouth wide open watching as the man's machete come down on Nick blow after blow until his life was ended.

Then the man turned to me as if he'd noticed me for the first time and began to swing his machete at me. The tip of his knife missed my throat by half an inch. I turned and took off running. I ran until I couldn't run any more.

When I was far into the jungle, I dropped down on the ground. My heart was beating so hard, I was sure it would pound right out of my chest. I sat there all night with my whole body shaking. Hunger and fear played games with my mind that night. I kept expecting Nick to break through the dense jungle and plop down beside me at any minute. It wasn't until I saw the first rays of the sun break through the jungle canopy that reality hit me. I had watched my best friend die and hadn't done anything to stop it from happening.

I thought about burning that village to the ground or sneaking back there in the night and killing the dark-haired man with the machete. I wish I could tell you I went back to the village to avenge Nick's death, but I am not a brave man. It was that day I learned the truth about myself. I'm a coward. I ran away from that village and the truth about what happened to Nick.

I know now the decision I made that day set in motion the path for the worthless life I've lived. I've wished a thousand times over I could go back to that moment when the man came charging at Nick. I wish I had stepped out in front of Nick and used my machete to defend him and take the life of that cruel man. Instead, I allowed my fear to stop me from taking action as I watched my friend die. He was my friend, and I let him down in the worst way possible.

I'm not sure what happened to me after that. My shame has blocked it from my memory. I've been told that weeks later a plane spotted me and a helicopter came for me, but I don't remember those events. What I will always remember is the smile on Nick's face as he spoke to the little girl and her big brown eyes looking up at him in wonder. It has haunted my dreams every night since.

I should have told this story as soon as I came back, but, as I said before, I'm a coward. I guess the truth is, I was too much of a coward to even face myself with the truth. I tried to numb my brain and drown the truth any way I could. I wish with all my heart and soul I could tell Nick how sorry I am for what I did. Since I can't ask him for his forgiveness, even though I have no right to, I ask for your forgiveness. Please forgive me for what I allowed to happen to your husband.

With my sincere apology,
Steven Albright

Tears were streaming down Nelli's face as she read the letter through two more times trying to make sense of Steven Albright's actions. Now she had a vivid picture of what Nicholas must have suffered not only as a POW, but in the village where the man he believed to be his friend watched as he was mutilated, without lifting his own machete to stop it from happening. She reread the last paragraph of Steven's letter. His asking for her forgiveness was an unbelievably bold request. He was asking a great deal of her. At this moment, she wasn't sure she had it in her to forgive him for what he'd failed to do for her husband. How could she forgive someone Nicholas believed to be his friend and trusted would do the right thing by him?

Nelli folded the letter and put it back in its envelope. She set it down on the bench beside her. Feeling a chill in the afternoon breeze, a shiver ran through her body. She picked up the envelope and held it close to her heart. Looking up to the sky, she stood and cried out, "Oh, Nicholas, my love, I'm so sorry. What courage it must have taken to escape and live each day with the fear of being captured and taken as a POW again or killed for your efforts. I know you were trying to get back to me because you didn't want to break your promise of returning to me. My heart breaks knowing a man you trusted and believed to be your friend could do such a thing to you. It's not fair he was the one to survive instead of you. He should have been the one who died, not you. The life he chose for himself was a wasted, worthless one. If you had been the one to live, your life would have been a worthwhile life as well as a blessing to all of us."

Sobbing, Nelli held the letter away from her. She crushed it and held it up to the sky in her fist and screamed out, "It's not fair. Why, God, would you allow this to happen to Nicholas? Steven Albright should have been the one to die!"

Nelli threw the letter as far away from her as she could. Wailing from the pain and grief of her broken heart, she collapsed onto the bench. After what seemed like hours of crying, she had no more tears left to shed. Wiping her face with the hem of her blouse, she sat up. It was hard to believe how much time and how much life had passed since she and Nicholas sat together on this bench. Now, as she sat alone on their bench, a heart verse came to her. *"Love bears all things, believes all things, hopes all things, endures all things."*

The facts were the same as they had always been: She had loved Nicholas, and he had loved her. Even though her courageous, strong, determined Nicholas hadn't been able to keep his promise of returning to her, she now knew he'd done all that was humanly possible to get home to her. She got up and picked up the letter she'd thrown, thankful it hadn't gone into the pond. Sitting back down on the bench, she placed the letter on her lap and began smoothing out the wrinkles.

Nelli now knew without a doubt that through some divine miracle it had been her Nicholas who'd sent Jake Albright to her with his father's letter. He'd wanted her to know the truth as to why he hadn't been able to keep his promise to return home to her, and now she did. She also knew one day she might be able to do what Steven Albright had asked of her, to forgive him for what he'd done—or rather not done—to save her husband's life. But not today. Today, she needed to share this letter with her daughters. She imagined they were anxiously awaiting her return. They needed to know the hero their father had been. They needed to know the truth as to why they'd grown up without him in their lives.

Nelli rose from the bench, took a final look up at the swaying trees, and breathed in the fresh, crisp air. This would be a day she would remember for the rest of her life. The day she learned the cold, hard truth about her husband, her hero.

CHAPTER THIRTY

Jilli watched in disbelief as her mother disappeared around the corner of the house after Jake placed the envelope in her hand. She turned to Nicola, who was sitting closest to her. "Where do you think Mama is going? I thought we'd all huddle up and read the letter together!"

Nicola shrugged. "Don't ask me. I thought the same thing."

Jilli put her hand to her chest. "I have to admit, I'm shocked and a little hurt Mama left with it."

Kalli stood up from the swing, walked to the side of the porch, and leaned out over the railing trying to catch a glimpse of where their mother was headed. "Well, it's obvious Mama wants to be alone when she reads it." She turned back to her sisters. "I'll give you two guesses as to where she's headed and the first one doesn't count."

Jilli and Nicola looked at one another and answered in unison, "The bench."

Kalli nodded her head. "No doubt."

"The bench?" Jake asked sounding confused.

Taking her seat on the swing once again, Kalli explained, "It's a bench my father built for her out of one of the cypress trees from the plantation when she was pregnant with me. He set it at the edge of woods and the plantation pond. He put it there for a place for her to rest when they walked out there together. As far as I know, it's stayed in the exact same spot for well over fifty years."

Nicola picked up the explanation. "Mama has always gone there when she gets upset or wants to think or just to be alone."

Jilli added, "It's her favorite spot in this whole wide world."

Kalli and Nicola nodded in agreement.

Jake sat back in his chair. "Wow! That's special. Your mother must have loved your father deeply."

Kalli looked off down the driveway. "Not loved, but loves." She turned to look at Jake. "Our Mama has never stopped loving Daddy. He may be gone from this world physically, but he's never been gone from her heart."

Jake's shoulders dropped with a sigh. "That's just something I can't relate to. I don't know if my mother and father ever really loved one another. I do know they didn't like each other."

Jilli glanced over at Jake. "I'm sorry to hear that. That must have been tough."

Resting his elbows on his knees, Jake hunched forward. "I don't think you can even imagine what growing up with two people who hate one another is like. When Dad first got back from Vietnam, things were good, or at least they weren't bad. But when he started to drink and lose job after job, things went from bad to worse until one day Mom met me at the door with our bags packed when I got home from elementary school. We walked out and never went back. Dad didn't even try to stop us. He just closed the door as we walked away."

Jilli bit her lip. "That's so sad."

Jake shrugged. "Well, it is, and it isn't. My Mom was a good, strong woman who raised me to be a good, strong man. It's true, my father never wanted to be a part of my life, but that was his choice, not mine." Jake smiled. "His excellent example of how to be a terrible husband and father showed me how all I needed to do to be a good husband and father was the opposite of him. So, it turned out for the best for me."

Kalli laughed. "I never thought about how a bad example could be used that way."

"Like I said, Dad was never really a part of my life. That's why I was so surprised when the nurse from the VA called and told me my father wanted to see me. That was totally out of character for him. But after I read his letter, I understood why he'd written it and why he'd lived the life he had after coming back from Vietnam."

"Which brings us back to the letter and why you're here today." Jilli folded her hands together. "Jake, what does your father say in that letter? What secret does he reveal about what happened to our father?"

Jake slowly shook his head. "I'm afraid I can't tell you that. The letter was written to your mother. It's up to her to tell you what it says. I'm not going to."

Jilli rushed to her feet so fast the swing flew back and hit the house. "You've read it!" She felt the heat in her face as she confronted Jake. "If it was meant for our Mama, what gave you the right to read it?"

Jake stood up. Clearly irritated, he snapped back, "Because I needed to know what turned my father into an angry, bitter, worthless human being."

Turning his back on them, Jake hurried from the porch. Jilli watched as he walked away from the house and down the driveway. Wrapping her arms around her shaking body, she turned back to her sisters. "Well, I guess I asked the wrong question."

Nicola stood and put an arm around her. "You hit a nerve, that's for sure."

Jilli looked out at Jake as he retreated down the drive. "Maybe I shouldn't have said anything about his reading the letter. But it just flew all over me how he knows what's in it and we don't. I hope I didn't make him mad enough to get in his car and leave. I imagine after Mama reads the letter; she'll want to talk to him."

Kalli ran her hands through her hair. "Not knowing what's in that letter is driving me crazy. I still can't believe Mama left us behind to read it on her own."

Jilli patted Kalli on the back. "We all want to know what's in the letter, Kalli, but it's Mama's prerogative to do whatever she wants to do with it."

"She's right, Kalli," Nicola agreed. "This should be about Mama, not us."

Kalli stood and stepped away from her sisters. "Really? You really think this only involves Mama? We all had to grow up without a father because of whatever that letter says. We have as much right to read that letter as Mama does." Pointing at the figure retreating down the driveway she added, "And a heck of lot more than he does!" She turned on her heel and stormed through the front door, slamming it behind her.

Speechless, Jilli stared at her sister's back as she disappeared into the house.

It'd taken Nelli a little over five minutes to make her way back to the house. She slowly walked up the back steps. She'd just put her hand out to pull the back door open when Kalli came rushing out, knocking her off balance. Kalli grabbed hold of Nelli's flailing arms, stopping her from falling backwards down the steps.

"Mama! Are you all right?"

Nelli's heart was pounding. "Oh, my! I would have surely broken my neck if you hadn't grabbed me."

Still holding onto Nelli, Kalli eased her down the steps and helped her sit on the bottom step. "Oh, Mama, I'm so sorry! I didn't see you."

Using the envelope she still held in her hand to fan herself, Nelli looked up at Kalli. "I know you didn't. It seems to me you were in a mighty big hurry to get out of the house."

Kalli sat down next to her. "I was. And it's all that Jake Albright's fault."

Nelli cocked her head to the side. "How so?"

Kalli blew out a forceful breath. "He just makes me so mad."

"What did he do this time?"

"Oh, it's all because of that letter he brought with him."

Nelli looked down at the envelope she held in her hand and slowly shook her head. "I'm thankful he brought this letter to us, Kalli."

Kalli silently waited for her mother to continue.

"Steven Albright may have been a coward most of his life, but at the end, he found the courage he needed to finally give us the story he should have told over fifty years ago." She looked up into Kalli's angry eyes. "Jake's father did a brave thing by writing this letter to us. He could have died without letting us know the truth about your father."

With trembling hands, Nelli placed the envelope in Kalli's hand. "It's a hard letter to read, Kalli, but it's a story you need to know."

Putting a hand on Kalli's shoulder, Nelli stood, walked up the steps, and into the house, leaving her oldest daughter alone.

CHAPTER THIRTY-ONE

Nelli's hands were still trembling as she closed the back door. She knew she'd done the right thing by leaving Kalli alone to read the letter. She'd need time to adjust to the shocking story of all her father had suffered. Folding her hands together to stop them from shaking, she stepped into the kitchen. Turning to look out the kitchen window, she noticed the sun was setting. Sighing, she wondered how she could have been unaware of the daylight slipping away.

Turning on the light, she glanced up at the kitchen clock. She drew in a sharp breath. She'd been gone for over an hour. A dreadful thought came to her. *Has Jake left?* She hadn't asked him to wait for her. He might not have realized how much she would need to talk to him about his father after reading the letter.

Nelli walked through the kitchen, through the dining room, into the living room, down the hall, and out the front door to where she hoped she'd find Jake where she'd left him. She looked to the chair where he'd been sitting, but it was empty, and her heart sank. Holding her hand to her chest she asked Nicola and Jilli, "Where's Jake? Please, don't tell me he's gone?"

Nicola and Jilli stood up and came to stand beside her.

"Mama, are you okay?" Nicola asked.

"Come, sit down," Jilli said as she helped Nelli to the white wicker rocker. She knelt down in front of Nelli and took her hands in hers. "Mama, Jake hasn't left. He's still here."

"Where is he?"

Nicola put her hand on Nelli's shoulder and gave it a comforting squeeze. "He's just taking a little walk, Mama. I'll go get him for you." She hurried down the front steps and out onto the tree-lined driveway where she could see Jake leaning against one of the trees.

Jilli squeezed Nelli's hands. "What did the letter say, Mama?"

This was the question Nelli expected her lawyer daughter would ask, but it was not a question she had any intention of answering. She believed each of the girls should read the letter and decide for themselves what it said. Hoping she could use the coolness of the evening as a distraction, Nelli shivered. "I'm a little chilly, Jilli. Would you be a sweetheart and get a sweater from my bedroom?"

Jilli sat back on her heels and wrapped her arms around herself. "It has cooled down, hasn't it?"

Nelli nodded in agreement.

Jilli stood up. "Sure. I'll be right back."

Nelli called after her daughter as she left the porch on her way upstairs. "I'd like the navy one. It should be on the back of my chair in the corner."

Nelli remained seated in the wicker rocker watching Nicola and Jake make their way to the front porch. Her opinion of Jake had changed since reading the letter his dying father had written. From the first time she'd spoken to him until he'd handed her the fateful letter, she'd thought of him as somewhat of a troublemaker. After all, he'd challenged what she'd long ago accepted as the truth how Nicholas had passed from this world. She'd grown comfortable and felt at peace with that truth. From the very start, she hadn't wanted to believe any of what he'd claimed to be true.

Now, after reading the letter, Nelli saw Jake for the brave man he was. After the way his father had treated him his whole life, he owed his father nothing. He had every right to ignore his father's request to come see him. He had no obligation to get the letter to her. If he hadn't been a courageous, honorable man, she'd never have learned the truth of what happened to her husband in Vietnam. She appreciated Jake's strength and the courage it took for him to bring a letter proving his father's character was less than honorable to her family.

As soon as Jake stepped onto the front porch, Nelli stood up from her chair and held out her right hand. "Jake Albright, I want to thank you for bringing your father's letter to me. I know it couldn't have been an easy thing to do."

Jake took Nelli's outstretched hand in his. "No, ma'am, it wasn't easy, but I knew it was the right thing to do."

Nelli smiled up into his handsome face. "I can't tell you how much I appreciate your courage."

A blush of red crept across Jake's face. "And it can't have been easy reading about what my father allowed to happen to your husband." Jake looked away as he swallowed hard. "Knowing my father stood there doing nothing as his friend's life was taken has been hard for me to accept."

Putting her left hand over Jake's hand, Nelli gave it a squeeze. "I'm sure none of this could have been easy for you, Jake. But in the end, you must know it took a great deal of courage for your father to put down in writing what happened over there. He could have taken his secret to his grave, and none of us would have been the wiser."

Nelli reached up and touched his face. "I know one thing for sure. Your bringing this letter to us honored your father."

Eyes glistening, Jake squeezed Nelli's hand. "I can't tell you how much it means to me for you to say that after what I've done to upset your life."

Nelli smiled. "You did what you had to do."

With her hand still in his, a look of understanding passed between the two of them. At the sound of Nicola clearing her throat, Jake released Nelli's hand.

"I'm sorry, Nicola," Nelli said, wiping a tear from her eye. "I almost forgot you were here."

Nicola put her hands on her hips. "Thanks a lot, Mama!"

Nelli laughed. "I didn't mean it in a bad way."

Nicola grinned. "It's okay."

"Did you forget about me too?" Jilli asked.

Nelli looked over to see her youngest daughter standing just inside the front door. She beckoned to her. "How long have you been standing there? Come here and bring that sweater."

Jilli put the sweater around Nelli's shoulders. "Not too long, but I could tell you and Jake were having a moment. I didn't want to disturb y'all."

"Don't you think it's time to share Jake's father's letter with us, Mama?" Nicola asked.

"We have a right to know what's in that letter," Jilli added.

Nelli smiled at her daughters. "Of course. You each need to read the letter, but I want you to do it while you're alone, not together. Kalli is reading it right now. I gave it to her when I got back. When she finishes, you can read it, Nicola. Then it'll be your turn, Jilli. Going by birth order seems the right thing to do."

Jilli shrugged. "If you say so."

Ignoring her youngest daughter's comment, Nelli turned to Jake. "It's getting late. We'd love to have you join us for supper, Jake. It won't be anything fancy, but I can promise you it'll be filling."

Jake hesitated for only a moment before answering. "Thank you, Mrs. Hart. It'd be my pleasure to join you and your daughters for supper."

Kali stared down at the letter her mother had placed in her hand, feeling the weight of it. She could see what impact the letter had on her mother from the pain in her eyes and the raw emotion in her voice. Her heart ached for her mother. She shouldn't have to suffer the loss of her husband twice in a lifetime.

The first time her mother had been told of his death, it had almost killed her. Kalli wondered in what way learning how her husband had suffered a different death would affect her. Would her mother give up on living once again and crawl into the darkness of her room?

Kalli shook the thought from her mind. Her mother was a strong woman. She'd fought through that difficult time and came out stronger for it. Mama had run a successful business while raising three daughters and taking care of her aging grandmother, father, and brother. There was no way she would ever give up on life now.

She looked down at the letter in her hand and wondered how learning the truth of what happened to her father in Vietnam would affect her. Could she be as strong as her mother? Taking a deep, calming breath, she unfolded the letter and began to read.

A rush of anger stormed through Kalli's body as she read the last paragraph of Steven Albright's letter. She threw the letter to the side and leaned over; sure she was going to be sick. Instead, a mournful sob came up from the pit of her stomach and escaped from her throat. Her mind was flooded with images of the fear and horror her father must have suffered when he realized the man he believed to be his friend stood by watching as a machete came down on his defenseless body time after time until his life was ended. Folding her arms around herself, she rocked back and forth with her eyes closed, hoping to shut out the letter's revelations.

Suddenly, disturbing thoughts came to Kalli. *How do we know Steven Albright is telling the truth? Maybe this letter doesn't reveal the actual truth. What proof does he offer besides a letter written by a man who could have been mentally disturbed?* She stopped rocking and opened her eyes. She picked up the letter she'd tossed aside and began to read it again.

A quiver ran through her body. Kalli stood and began pacing. She held the letter up. "These are only someone's words. There's no proof of truth in here."

Kalli stopped her pacing. How was she going to find the truth? She knew what she had to do. Shoving the letter back into the envelope, she started for the front porch to confront Jake Albright. She needed to know what he had to say about this letter and the man who'd written it. As she rounded the corner of the front porch, she could see Nicola and Jilli were still sitting in the swing. Jake was sitting in the white wicker chair next to them. They all looked calm and congenial.

Knowing she needed to calm down so she wouldn't upset her sisters, she took a deep breath and swallowed the lump of anger in her throat. She did the best she could to fix a smile on her face as she walked up the porch steps.

"Where have you been hiding since you stormed out of here?" Nicola asked.

Kalli held up the envelope. "I've been reading this letter our guest brought to us."

Jilli stood. "And?"

"And it's something you both need to read."

Jilli pursed her lips. "I meant, what did you think of it? We could tell Mama was upset by it."

Kalli raised her eyebrows. "I can understand why she's upset. That is, if you believe it all."

Raising an eyebrow, Nicola asked, "What do you mean by that?"

Jake turned to Kalli. "I'd like to know what you mean by that too."

Kalli ignored Jake's comment and held out the envelope to Nicola. "Here, read it for yourself."

Nicola stood up from the swing and reached for the envelope. "I will."

Jilli snatched it out of Kalli's hand. "I will too."

"Why don't the two of you read it together?" Kalli suggested.

Nicola looked to Jilli, who nodded in agreement. The two started back toward the swing.

Kalli put out her hand. "I think it'd be better if y'all read it in private. It's not an easy letter to read. I promise you won't want an audience."

The two sisters turned and walked down the porch steps. Kalli watched as they turned the corner. She sat down on the swing. Her plan had been to confront Jake with all the anger and outrage she'd felt as she read the letter. She'd demand he prove that what was written in the letter was a truth they should accept. But her throat suddenly went dry when she saw concern and compassion in his warm blue eyes. The words she'd planned to say fell away.

Jake asked in a soft voice, "You don't believe what's in the letter?"

Kalli couldn't meet his eyes. "I'm having a hard time believing when there isn't any actual proof, only your father's words."

Jake leaned back in his chair and folded his fingers together as he slowly nodded. "I understand why you might question my father's words. He wasn't a reputable man. Growing up, I can tell you he wasn't a man I ever trusted to tell the truth."

"It's just that I find it hard to believe some of what he says in that letter."

Jake leaned forward, looking intently into Kalli's face. "Like what?"

His question took Kalli by surprise. She'd expected she'd be the one to confront him. She blurted out the one question she wanted answered most of all. "Well, like what kind of man stands there holding a deadly weapon in his hand without making a move to stop the man killing his friend, then runs away?"

Kalli watched as a darkness passed over Jake's face. His shoulders slumped as he stared down at the porch floor. Too late she realized she'd asked a question only his father could answer. She was about to apologize when he began to speak in a low voice.

"A man like my father could let a thing like that happen to a friend." Jake looked up, his eyes glistening. "In fact, to me his not helping your father and running away is the most believable part of the whole letter. The parts I have a hard time believing are the ones where he portrays himself as a friend."

Hearing the hopelessness in Jake's voice as he spoke about his father tore at Kalli's heart. She wanted to reach out to comfort him. Instead, she sat silently, sensing his words were ones he'd held back for a long time. Words he needed to say.

"I've read stories and heard personal accounts of soldiers who went through hell in Vietnam. Some found their hell on the battlefield by being ordered to kill or be killed. Some found their hell in a POW prison. Any way you look at it, being a soldier in Vietnam had to change a person, but most learned to live a good life despite all they'd gone through. I don't know what kind of man my father was before he went to Vietnam, but I know what kind of man he was when he came home. He made a choice to not try to save your father. You and I can sit here on the front porch of what once was your father's home and judge my father's actions as the most horrendous, selfish choice any human could make."

Staring into Kalli's eyes, Jake continued. "But we weren't there, Kalli. We've never gone through anything close to what our fathers went through in Vietnam. We can't know for sure what choices we would have made. We like to think we'd make a better choice than he did, but we'll never know for sure. His choice ruined his life. If he believed your father was his friend, then Nick Hart was the very last friend my father ever had. After he got back, the only friend my father had was a bottle of liquor."

Running a hand through his hair, Jake leaned forward again. "I wish I could give you something concrete to prove what my father wrote in his letter was the truth, but I don't have anything. The only thing I can give you is my experience of a lifetime of living with his lies. When he placed that letter in my hand, the look on his face gave me all the proof I needed to believe. For once in his life, he'd given me the truth. For over fifty years, he couldn't admit to anyone, most of all himself, what he'd done. He could have died without ever telling the truth, but he didn't. I never knew my father to do anything courageous, but by putting in writing what he did to your father, I believe, was his one true act of courage. That's the only proof I can offer you, Kalli."

As Jake spoke, tears began to gather in Kalli's eyes. She hadn't known what proof she'd wanted from him, but she no longer had any doubts about the letter giving a true account of what happened to her father. She didn't know if she could ever forgive Steven Albright for standing there watching as her father's life was taken by another, but she was thankful he'd had the courage to finally tell his story. Most of all, she was thankful his son had the courage to bring his father's letter to her family.

CHAPTER THIRTY-TWO

Nelli left Nicola and Jilli on the porch with Jake while she went to the kitchen to prepare their supper. Her daughters had offered to help, but she'd finally been able to convince them she could handle the preparations by herself. The truth was she wanted to be alone without anyone wanting to talk to her about the letter. She wanted to do something that felt normal and not have to think about anything other than what was the next step in fixing supper.

Nelli went out to the back porch to get a chicken pot pie and one of her peach cobblers she kept on hand in the freezer in case she had company or needed to take something comforting to a grieving family. When her Hart & Soul Inn had been in full swing, she'd gotten in the habit of making several main dishes and desserts at a time. She'd serve one main dish along with dessert that day and freeze the others for a future meal. She found the practice continued to serve her well even though the Inn had closed years ago. She liked being prepared.

As Nelli pulled the pot pie and cobbler from the freezer, she glanced out of the window that looked onto the back yard. She'd expected to see Kalli sitting on the back steps, but the steps were empty. She quickly scanned the area, but could see no sign of her. She'd felt the letter would upset her. Being the oldest, she had more memories of her father than the other two.

It had been obvious to Nelli from the moment Kalli was born that she and her father had a special bond. It could have been because she was his first or maybe it was because she was the one most like him. Whatever her reaction to finding out how her father died, it'd be something she'd have to work out for herself.

Taking the chicken pot pie and cobbler into the house, she set them down on the kitchen counter next to the stove. She removed the plastic seal from the pot pie, brushed the crust with the egg wash she'd prepared, put aluminum foil around the edges of the crust so it wouldn't get too brown, and placed it in the preheated oven. She'd just taken Topsy's mixing bowl out of the cupboard—the one she always used to make her mouth-watering biscuits—when she thought she caught the sound of Kalli's voice coming from the front porch. She stopped to listen more closely. After only a few seconds, she knew for certain it was her oldest daughter's voice she was hearing.

Wiping her hands on the towel she'd slung over her shoulder, Nelli turned to go out to the front porch to make sure Kalli wasn't giving Jake a hard time. She hoped her daughter would realize the poor man shouldn't have to suffer her wrath for the mistakes his father had made. Then she stopped and reconsidered. Deciding this wasn't her problem to solve, she turned back to the counter. She gathered her ingredients for the biscuits and got to work mixing and kneading. After all, Kalli and Jake were both adults. They could handle the situation without her getting involved.

While the pot pie baked, Nelli made a fresh salad and steamed some broccoli. After setting the dining room table for five, she walked out to the porch to call them all to supper. She'd expected to find all three of her daughters along with Jake on the porch. She was surprised to find only Kalli and Jake. The two were sitting together on the swing so deep in conversation they didn't seem to notice when she stepped out on the porch.

The two jumped when Nelli spoke.

"Where are Nicola and Jilli?"

Kalli put her hand to her chest. "Oh, Mama! You scared me. I didn't even know you were there."

"So, I noticed," Nelli said.

Kalli stood and walked over to her mother. "I gave them the letter. They're off reading it."

Nelli gave a heavy sigh. "Oh, Kalli, I wanted them to read the letter separately. One at a time, not together. I told them that."

Kalli put her arm around her. "I'm sorry, Mama. I didn't know, but I'm sure they'll be okay reading it together."

"I hope you're right." Nelli patted Kalli's arm. "Nothing we can do about it now."

Jake stood. "Anything I can do to help you with supper?"

Nelli shook her head. "It's almost ready. By the time y'all wash your hands, it should be ready to set out on the table."

Kalli turned to Jake. "I'll show you where you can wash up."

Nelli watched as the two walked into the house together. It was good to see that they were getting along. She turned around and stared down the driveway, wondering where Nicola and Jilli had gone to read the letter. Maybe they'd gone upstairs since it seemed to Nelli it was too dark outside to see the writing without a light. Wherever they'd gone, she hoped it was a good thing they were together.

Back in the kitchen, Nelli checked the timer. The pot pie had ten more minutes to bake, so she put the biscuits in the oven. Kalli filled the glasses with the homemade lemonade Nicola had made earlier, and Jake arrived in time to help her set the glasses on the dining room table.

When the timer sounded, Kalli took the pot pie out of the oven and carried it to the table where she set it on a trivet. Jake followed with the broccoli. Nelli put the biscuits in a basket and covered them with a napkin to keep them warm. She placed them along with butter and her homemade blackberry jam on the corner of the table.

Nelli was putting the peach cobbler in the oven to bake while they ate when Nicola and Jilli came down the back stairs into the kitchen. They both had bewildered looks on their faces. When they saw Nelli, they went to her and wrapped their arms around her. No one spoke for several minutes.

It was Jilli who broke the silence. Her voice was filled with emotion. "Oh, Mama, I can't imagine what Daddy must have gone through. It just breaks my heart to think of him suffering through the horrors of being a POW and then to be mutilated and his body left behind, abandoned, by someone he believed to be his friend."

Nelli stepped back, putting her hands on Jilli's cheeks. "I know, sweet girl. It's beyond our comprehension."

Nicola folded her arms over her chest. When she spoke, Nelli could hear anger and disgust in her voice. "I can't believe that man asked for forgiveness. How can any of us ever forgive him for what he did to Daddy? What he did was unforgivable!"

Nelli pulled Nicola to her. "Oh, Nicola, that's exactly the way I felt after reading the letter. I couldn't believe the audacity of his request. I'm not sure I'll ever be able to forgive him, but—"

Nicola jerked away from Nelli and began to cry. "But what, Mama? But we should? But we need to? But it's the right thing to do? There is no but here, Mama. We can never forgive him."

Nelli reached out to put a comforting hand on Nicola's shoulder. "No buts for now, Nicola, only supper."

Nicola wiped away her tears with the sleeve of her blouse. "Supper sounds good."

Nelli, Jilli, and Nicola joined Kalli and Jake at the dining room table. After taking their places at the table, they reached out for one another's hands. They bowed their heads and Nelli asked the blessing. "Dear Lord, we thank You for bringing Jake into our lives. We pray we will find peace through knowing the truth of what happened to our beloved husband and father. We ask You to bless this food to our nourishment and our bodies to Your service. In the name of our precious Lord, we pray. Amen."

"Kalli, please pass the chicken pot pie," Jilli said, holding her hands out.

"Jilli, where are your manners?" Kalli taunted. "Don't you think our guest should be served first?" She passed the pot pie to Jake who was seated next to her.

After Jake served himself, he started to pass the pot pie to Jilli, but Kalli reached over and took it from his hands. "Jilli can be first after me." As soon as she'd served herself with a good-sized helping, she placed the dish in Jilli's outstretched hands, giving her a huge smile. "Here you go, baby sister."

"Glad to see you're showing your good Southern manners to our guest," Jilli said as she took the dish from Kalli. "I know you're making our mother so proud."

"Enough, girls," Nelli scolded. She looked to Jake as she asked in exasperation, "Do you have sisters?"

"No, ma'am, I'm an only child."

"Lucky you! That must be marvelous," Jilli said as she passed the dish to Nicola. "I've often dreamed of being an only child."

"Me too!" Kalli and Nicola said in unison. Looking at one another, they chuckled.

"I think you three are the lucky ones. It was just my mother and me, which was often both silent and lonely. When my wife Valerie and I married, we planned on having four children—two boys and two girls. That didn't work out quite like we'd hoped." Frowning, he sighed deeply. "We were able to have only one child, a daughter we named Lisa. Not long after Lisa was born, my wife was diagnosed with ovarian cancer."

His face lit up as he continued, "But Lisa has blessed me with two precious grandchildren, Jacob and Kelly. They're the joys of my life."

"Oh, Jake, I'm so sorry about your wife," Nelli said. "Kalli knows the heartache of losing a spouse. She lost her husband in an accident a few years ago."

"I'm sorry to hear that," Jake said as he looked at Kalli.

Kalli blushed. "I think we should change the subject. We've had enough sadness for one day."

"I agree," Nicola said as she got up from the table. "I think we could all use a nice glass of wine to go with this fine meal Mama has prepared."

Nicola hurried into the kitchen. In a few minutes she returned with an open bottle of Sauvignon Blanc. She took five wine glasses from her mother's china cabinet and served each a glass of wine.

Nelli smiled at her daughter. "Thank you, Nicola." She held up her glass of wine. "I'd like to make a toast."

Kalli, Nicola, Jilli, and Jake held up their glasses as they looked to Nelli.

"To Nicholas Conrad Hart for his heroism in giving his life for his country."

Clinking their glasses together they repeated Nelli's toast to honor a husband, a father, and a friend to a father. A true hero.

CHAPTER THIRTY-THREE

After supper they gathered in the living room. Over Nelli's homemade peach cobbler and cups of coffee, the girls shared their more adventurous tales of growing up in the Hart & Soul Inn. It turned out Jake was a good listener. He laughed at all the right places, which encouraged them to continue with their stories, often embellishing certain details. While Jake and her daughters were enjoying one another's company, Nelli quietly left them to clean up the supper dishes.

It was a little after nine before Nelli finished with her work and joined them again in the living room. She listened as Jilli told yet another story of the Hart & Soul Inn. She had to admit, her youngest daughter had a gift for storytelling, which might be one of the reasons she was such a good lawyer.

When the grandfather clock in the hall struck a chord to announce it was half-past nine, Nelli made a point of stretching and yawning, hoping to call everyone's attention to the time.

Kallie must have gotten the hint. "Oh, my! I can't believe it's nine thirty all ready. It's past Mama's bedtime." Kalli stood and walked over to where Nelli was seated in her favorite green overstuffed chair. She held out her hand to help Nelli up. "Mama, I'm so sorry. I didn't realize the time. You must be exhausted."

Nelli gratefully accepted her daughter's hand. "I'm plumb tuckered out."

Jake stood as he checked his watch. "I wasn't aware of the time either. Y'all have been so entertaining, but it's time for me to take my leave. I hope I didn't overstay my welcome."

"Not at all, Jake, " Nelli said as she walked over to stand beside him. "We do appreciate your coming. I know it couldn't have been easy for you, but I can assure you what you brought to us has meant the world to me." She stood on tiptoe to kiss his cheek. "You're welcome here anytime."

Jake's cheeks turned red. "I can't tell you what that means to me, Mrs. Hart."

Nelli clicked her tongue. "I thought we agreed you'd call me Nelli."

Jake smiled down at her with a twinkle in his eye. "Yes, ma'am, Miss Nelli."

Nicola and Jilli joined Nelli and Kalli to walk Jake to the front door.

"Thank you for being brave enough to give us the truth about our father," Jilli said as she shook his hand.

Nicola patted Jake's back. "Yes, thank you, Jake, for bringing your father's letter to us. I know he would be proud of you for following through to make his dying wish come true."

Kalli stood back as Nelli, Nicola, and Jilli said their good-byes to Jake. When he opened the front door to take his leave, she stepped up beside him. "I'll see you out, Jake."

Nicola and Jilli giggled as they stared wide-eyed at one another. Nelli snapped her fingers at the two of them and pointed to the stairway.

With a shrug of their shoulders they turned and walked up the stairs. Nelli followed.

When they were outside, Kalli put her hand on Jake's arm as she looked up into his face. "I'm sorry for my rude behavior when I came at you earlier today demanding proof. I think I didn't want what I read in your father's letter to be true. It was hard enough when I believed Daddy had lost his life in a helicopter crash, but it was something I've lived with almost my entire life. I'd always found it comforting to think he died quickly, without suffering. Then after reading your father's letter and imagining what he must have suffered. . . Well, I just didn't want to believe it was true."

Jake took Kalli's hand in his. "I understand. It can't be an easy thing to find out someone your father trusted ended his life. I don't know if I'll ever get the image of your father being attacked while my father looked on out of my mind."

Kalli shook her head. "I know what you mean."

"Kalli, I may be out of line with the situation that brought me here and all, but I have something I'd like to ask you."

Kalli raised her eyebrows. "Okay, ask away."

"May I see you again?"

Kalli blinked. Once again, he'd asked a question she hadn't expected, but this time it was one she'd secretly hoped he'd ask. She smiled up at him. "I'd like that very much."

"Great! In that case, I have another question."

"I'll see if I have an answer," Kalli teased.

Jake gave her a sly smile. "I know this could be too forward and you might consider it way too soon since we've just met and all, but. . .may I kiss you?"

Looking up into those deep-sea blue eyes, Kalli smiled and closed her eyes in anticipation.

Jake put his hands on her waist and pulled her to him. When their lips met, it felt as if time stopped. She didn't know how long they lingered in their kiss, but she knew she didn't want it to end.

When their lips parted, Kalli rested her head on his chest as he held her. She wondered if he could feel her pounding heart. Leaning back to look up at him, she said, "That's the best kiss I've had in a very long time."

"For me too."

Jake smiled down at her. "I think this may be the best ending of a day I've had in a very long time."

"Me too."

Kalli took a step back. "I'm sorry for what brought us together, Jake, but I'm glad we met."

"Me too."

Taking his phone from his breast pocket, he asked, "Can I have your phone number?"

She quickly recited her cell number.

Jake once again pulled her into his arms. He whispered in her ear. "Thank you for this day."

When they parted, he turned and hurried to his car. Before getting in, he looked back and smiled. "Good night, Kalliope Hart Abbot. I'll call you tomorrow."

Kalli giggled as she called after him. "Good night, Jacob Stephen Albright. Drive carefully." She wanted to add "I can hardly wait for your call," but decided it sounded too desperate. Leaning against the front porch column, she watched as his taillights faded into the night. Sighing, she slowly made her way back into the house, shutting and locking the door behind her. After turning off the living room lamps, she headed upstairs.

As she ascended the steps, her thoughts were lost in the emotional twists and turns of the day. With all that had just happened on the front porch, it was hard for her to believe she'd started out her day filled with suspicion and distrust toward Jake Albright. The feelings she now held for him, however exciting, were totally unexpected.

As Kalli placed her foot on the top step her two younger sisters came rushing at her. Startled, she lost her footing and began to fall backwards. Just in the nick of time, Nicola grabbed her hand and pulled Kalli toward her. Falling backward, Nicola tumbled onto Jilli, which left the three of them in a tangled, giggling pile of sisters.

"Are y'all trying to kill me?" Kalli asked as tears of laughter streamed down her face.

"I think Nicola is trying to kill both of us!" Jilli said as she crawled out from under her sisters.

"I promise we didn't aim for any of that to happen." Nicola got to her feet. "We just wanted to find out what went on between you and Jake when you"—she made air quotes— "saw him out."

Kalli rolled her eyes at her sisters as she held out her hands. "First of all, help me off this floor."

Nicola and Jilli each took a hand and pulled her up.

Kalli straightened her clothes and brushed her hair out of her face. "Second of all, it's none of your business." She turned away and began walking toward her room.

Nicola groaned. "That's not fair."

"Come on, tell us something," Jilli whined.

Kalli stopped and glanced over her shoulder at her two younger sisters. "I'll tell you two things and that's it. You can't ask for more."

Nicola and Jilli nodded their agreement.

"I don't think this is the last time I'll be seeing Jake Albright." With a smile on her lips and a twinkle in her eye, she added, "And, his kiss is oh, so sweet."

CHAPTER THIRTY-FOUR

From her bedroom, Nelli listened to the laughter and playful bantering of her daughters. She'd thought about joining them in the hall, but was just too tired to make the effort. Instead, she pulled back her quilt and climbed into bed. Snuggling down under her covers, she found it gratifying and comforting to know the three of them had made new memories since their arrival only a few days before. Of course, some of their memories were sad, but she believed most of them were happy. She prayed their shared memories would become precious to each of them. Without a doubt, she knew the memory of her daughters being here to help her through this difficult time was one she'd treasure for the rest of her life. A feeling of content washed over her. She closed her eyes. After only a few minutes, she fell into a deep sleep.

The next morning, Nelli woke to the unwelcome sound of rain hitting her bedroom window. She was sure the predicted weather for the day hadn't included rain. As her eyes adjusted to the dark room, she glanced over at the clock on her bedside table. She was surprised to see it was past eight. She couldn't remember the last time she'd slept past seven. Her plan had been to be up before everyone to surprise her daughters with a special breakfast before they left for their various homes.

Nelli threw back the covers, slipped into her robe, and hurried out of her room. She stood dumbfounded when she looked down the hall to find the doors to her daughters' bedrooms closed. At this late hour, she'd fully expected to find them dressed for the day and rushing out of their rooms with packed bags. She'd assumed each one would be anxious to be away from here and back to their lives and daily routine. Instead of the cacophony of chaos she'd anticipated, she was met with complete silence.

Nelli decided that after the shocking revelations they'd all experienced the day before that her daughters must have been as exhausted as she'd been. She hoped each had benefited from a night of peaceful rest as much as she had. Breathing a sigh of relief, she went back to her room. After showering and dressing, she made her way down the back stairway to the dark kitchen. She switched on the lights and was taken by surprise when she found Kalli sitting alone in the dark at the kitchen table.

Nelli's hand went to her throat. "Goodness gracious, Kalli, you surprised me! When I saw your door closed, I assumed you were still asleep. I didn't expect to find you sitting here all alone in the dark."

"I'm sorry, Mama, I didn't mean to scare you. The rain woke me up, and I couldn't go back to sleep. So, I came down here to fix myself a cup of tea. I think the kettle is still hot. I can fix you a cup if you want." Kalli pushed back her chair to stand.

"No, don't get up. Thanks for the offer, but I need coffee, not tea."

Nelli walked to the counter. "It sounded to me like your sisters were giving you a hard time last night about Jake."

"They sure did. It reminded me of our teenage years when the two of them would be waiting for me at the top of the stairs to find out if I got a good night's kiss."

Nelli stopped filling the coffeepot with water and turned to Kalli. "Well, did you?"

Wide-eyed, Kalli stared at her. "Mama! I can't believe you'd stoop to their level!"

Nelli shrugged and resumed making the coffee. "I'm just as curious as your sisters. I always have been. I always wanted to know if the boy kissed you goodnight." She turned to Kalli, raising one eyebrow. "Or if anything else happened, but I held back from asking because I didn't want to embarrass you. I have to admit, it was hard at times not to be in the know."

"I didn't mean to leave you out." Kalli chuckled. "Truthfully, I just never thought you'd want to talk about that sort of thing."

After pushing the start button on the coffeemaker, Nelli joined Kalli at the kitchen table. "I know, and it's fine, but you might be surprised to learn your baby sister shared everything." She rolled her eyes putting emphasis on each word. "And I mean every. Little. Thing."

"You're kidding."

Nelli shook her head as she raised her right hand. "I promise it's the truth. Let me just say. Too much information can be just as bad as too little."

As Kalli dissolved into a fit of laughter, Nelli noticed the coffeemaker was finished brewing. She got up, took down her favorite cup she'd gotten on one of her many trips to the St. Simon's Island Lighthouse, and poured herself some. Joining Kalli at the table once again, she asked, "So, why were you sitting all alone in the dark?"

"I like to sit quietly in the dark sometimes. It helps me think."

"What are you thinking about?"

"Different things."

Nelli took a sip of her coffee as she studied Kalli. It was obvious something was bothering her oldest daughter, but from years of experience, she knew her best strategy was not to press her. She'd have to ease her into talking about what was on her mind.

After taking another sip of coffee, Nelli leaned back and sighed heavily. "My mind is still reeling from reading that letter. What I can't get my head around is how the Army gave us this whole other story about how your father died. For the life of me, I can't figure out why they would do that. What did they have to gain by not telling us the truth?"

Kalli leaned forward. "I don't get it either. The only thing I can come up with is that they didn't know the truth then and they still don't know now. When Whit told me there was a possibility that Daddy had been the one who got off the helicopter and stayed to help those wounded men, I have to say it sounded like the actions of the man I knew my Daddy to be."

Nelli nodded. "You're right about that. I can't imagine he'd have turned his back on his fellow soldiers in distress. It wasn't in his character to leave them there without helping, no matter what orders he was given."

"And without something more official than a few soldiers' claims, the Army had to go with what they believed to be the facts. The Army knew him to be a soldier who followed orders. Therefore, as far as they were concerned, he had followed the orders he was given to remain on the helicopter. So, when it crashed they concluded he'd been on it."

Nelli lowered her head. "I guess you're right. They did the only thing they could do."

"It may sound silly, Mama, but something has really been bothering me."

Nelli raised her head to look at Kalli. "I'm sure it's not silly at all. What's been on your mind?"

"I can't stop wondering whose ashes we spread around the pond. His family must still be wondering what happened to their son or husband or father." Nelli could see there was true concern in Kalli's eyes.

So, this was what had been bothering her daughter, keeping her awake and troubled. It wasn't at all what Nelli expected. She sipped her coffee as she considered Kalli's question.

"I don't know, Kalli, but whoever it is, he was a soldier who died in the service of his country. He deserved a memorial service, and we gave him that much. It may not have been his name we called out that day, but our hearts were true in honoring a fallen soldier."

"What about Daddy, Mama? He died a hero." Kalli's voice cracked as she asked, "Doesn't he deserve a memorial service to honor him?"

Nelli's heart broke as she watched Kalli's eyes fill with tears.

She reached across the table for her daughter's hand. "Oh, Kalli, yes, he most certainly does deserve one." Tears began to sting her eyes, but she blinked them back knowing it wouldn't help either one of them to give in to their emotions. She could almost hear Topsy quoting the familiar words from Psalm 31:24: *Take heart and be strong!* Was her grandmother trying to tell her this was a time for action, not grief? A time for hope, not despair.

Nelli squeezed Kalli's hand as a plan came to her. "And we're going to give him one. We may not have his ashes to spread, but I think I know how we can honor him and pay tribute to his heroic bravery."

Kalli took a napkin from the napkin holder on the table to wipe her tears. "How?"

Nelli gave her a smile as she stood up from the table. "I'll tell you all about it, but first we need to get your sisters up and fed. Then we can talk about my plan. It's going to take all of us working together to pull it off.'

To Nelli's relief, after three solid days of rain, Saturday morning dawned bright and beautiful. She, along with her daughters, had spent the past four weeks setting in motion her plan, which in a few minutes she hoped would be a precious memory for her whole family. If she had to be honest with herself, she'd had her doubts about it all coming together. It was a plan that had come to her mind in an instant, but it had taken a month to work it all out. She was proud and amazed how once she'd given an outline of her plan for Nicholas's memorial to her girls, they'd taken off with it, each adding their own special talent to the event.

It still amazed Nelli how in such a short time Jilli had been able to persuade one of her clients who happened to own a tree nursery to deliver and plant a Southern Live Oak in her back yard where Topsy's small cabin had once stood. She wasn't sure how old the tree was, but it was huge. It'd taken a large crew of workers and several massive machines to bring it to her house and set it in the ground. Anyone who looked at it would have a hard time believing it'd only been in the ground a few days. It looked as if it had grown up in this spot from a seedling.

Nicola had taken on the task of sending out a copy of Captain Albright's letter along with Nelli's special request to everyone in the immediate family, sons-in-law included. When Kalli had balked at sending out the heart-wrenching account of what Nicholas had gone through in Vietnam, Nelli made it clear that no matter how upsetting it would be to read, it was part of their history and their heritage. Plus, the rest of the family would have a hard time fulfilling her special request if they weren't aware of the events, along with his heroic actions, which led to his death.

The wooden hearts each family member now held in their hand had been Kalli's clever idea. When Nelli first told her daughters her plan of having a tree planted as a memorial, Kalli came up with the concept of family members writing their own special memorial messages on wooden hearts that would hang on the memorial oak tree. A local craftsman whose father served in Vietnam cut out the hearts with his jigsaw for free when he learned of the special service for a fallen soldier. He even drilled a hole at the top of each one so that a string could be tied on to hang it. As each family member arrived that morning, they'd been directed to the dining room where the hearts and permanent markers were ready for them to add their special message. Some had written their messages while other had drawn theirs.

Standing under the majestic oak, Nelli's heart filled with gratitude as her entire family gathered around her. When she'd first came up with the idea for Nicholas' memorial, she was sure the hardest part was going to be convincing her six busy grandchildren to come spend a weekend with their old grandmother. She wasn't sure how keen any of them would be to attend a memorial service for a grandfather they'd never known. As it turned out—to her complete amazement and delight—each had graciously accepted her request without hesitation. Her dear grandchildren had traveled from as far away as Berkeley, California.

Once her entire family was assembled around the oak tree, Nelli cleared her throat, signaling for everyone's attention. "First of all, I want to thank each one of you for being here today to honor a great man who gave the ultimate sacrifice in the service of his country." She put both hands over her heart. "Words cannot express my appreciation and the deep love I have for each one of you. Today, I feel as if I'm the most blessed woman in the world!"

She swallowed hard, hoping to suppress the overwhelming emotions building up inside her. "But today is not about me. It's about honoring a man who was a hero, a man who was the love of my life." As she spoke, tears rose in her throat. Lowering her head, she took several deep breaths to push down her feelings. Despite her efforts, tears began to flood her eyes and stream down her cheeks.

Just as Nelli was about to turn away, she felt the gentle touch of a hand taking hers, holding her to this place. Looking up through the mist of tears, she saw Kalli's sweet face smiling down at her. "What Mama is trying to say is, we are gathered here on this beautiful day to honor the sacrifice of a man who was not only a brave soldier, but a loving husband and father. . . Chief Nicholas Conrad Hart."

Kalli squeezed Nelli's hand. "When most people think of a memorial, they think of a man-made monument or structure built to remember a fallen hero. Mama decided that wouldn't do for her Nicholas." Pointing to the tree, she continued, "This Southern Live Oak will stand for years, possibly over a hundred, to serve as a living monument to a noble man and a courageous soldier."

Nelli smiled as her family clapped.

"You may have noticed; this oak tree has a gigantic yellow ribbon tied around it with a beautiful bow crafted by our very own Jilli. If you're wondering why we have placed a yellow ribbon around the tree, I'm going to explain. It symbolizes our support for our troops as well as for those who have been or are now prisoners of war."

Glancing around, Kalli paused. Leaning down close to Nelli's ear, she whispered, "Mama, I think you should do this part." Putting a strong hand on Nelli's shoulder, she added, "I can do it if you want, but I think it'd mean more coming from you."

Nelli knew her daughter was right. This was something she needed to do. This wasn't a time to stand back in a puddle of tears. Wiping away her tears, Nelli nodded.

"This past month has been one heck of an emotional roller coaster for me. It's caused me to question who I should believe and trust. It has forced me to revisit the devastating event that ripped apart my world. As you know, when we were first told of Nicholas's death, we were told he'd been killed when his helicopter crashed on his way to pick up wounded soldiers."

She closed her eyes, forcing back her threatening tears. Taking in a deep breath, she continued. "When I was told Nicholas was dead, I didn't want to go on living without him." She slowly shook her head from side to side as she spoke. "I curled up inside myself. I refused to come out of my room. I refused to eat. I even refused to take care of my precious daughters. That's when my grandmother Topsy, one of the strongest women I've ever known, came to me with a Bible verse that pulled me out of the hole I'd dug for myself."

Reaching into her pocket, Nelli pulled out her wooden heart on which she'd written her memorial message. She held it up for all to see. "It's the Bible verse I've written here."

Clearing her throat, she read, "'Be strong and take heart, all you who hope in the Lord.' That's Psalm 31:24."

She lowered her hand as she stared out at her family. "That verse brought me back to life. Every day since, I take heart and stay strong because I have put my hope in the Lord. If you've read Steven

Albright's letter, then you understand why I know 'take heart and be strong' is a sign from God assuring us that Nicholas is at peace with Him."

When Nelli glanced around at her family, she saw many wiping tears from their eyes. She hadn't intended for this memorial to be sad. She meant for it to be a celebration. "But as I look back on this past month, I have to admit it hasn't all been bad. My three beautiful daughters came together, which hasn't happened in ages. That in itself is somewhat of miracle." She chuckled at her statement and could hear others doing the same. "Seriously though, they've been here for me, surrounding me with their love and support."

Spreading out her hands toward her gathered family, Nelli smiled. "And I have all of you here with me today to remember and honor your father's and grandfather's selfless sacrifice!" Her smile widened. "Honestly, I couldn't be any happier than I am at this very moment."

Kalli, Nicola, and Jilli hurried to her side and pulled her into their embrace. Nelli held them close, knowing she would treasure this moment of feeling complete and unconditional love from her daughters. A part of her didn't want to end this moment, but the practical part of her knew it was time to go on with the memorial service.

"Girls, I think it's time for us to hang our hearts on the tree." Reluctantly, she stepped away. She kissed her wooden heart, stepped over to the tree, and, with great care, hung it on a branch.

Tears filled Nelli's eyes as she watched each member of her family step up to add their one-of-a-kind hearts to the Nicholas Hart Memorial Southern Live Oak Tree.

CHAPTER THIRTY-FIVE

<u>**ONE YEAR LATER**</u>

Nelli woke from a restful sleep to the sweet sound of a bird's song. She had no clue what bird it was serenading her on this glorious morning. She'd always meant to learn more about the birds who shared her world, but the idea had become one of many intentions she'd left untended. She threw off the special-made quilt that had graced her bed since the day Topsy had given it to her and put the pillows with their shams in place. She changed from her pajamas into her usual garden clothes of jeans and T-shirt topped with an over-sized flannel shirt. Making her way down the back stairs, she walked through her empty kitchen to the back porch. She stepped into her knee-high black rubber boots at the back door, took her ICHS baseball cap off the hook, and in no time at all she was standing in the glory of the early morning.

Nelli walked to where she'd gone every morning for the past year—to where Nicholas's Living Memorial stood. She put her hand on the trunk of the magnificent tree. Throughout the year, she'd watched as the yellow ribbon Jilli had tied to the tree had been taken away piece by piece by the wind, rain, and harsh Georgia sun. Looking up though the out-reaching branches, it pleased her to see many of the wooden hearts remained despite the ensuing weather. She'd put the hearts that had fallen over the year in a bowl on the mantel in the living room.

Nelli leaned down to wipe the dew from the brass memorial plaque Jake had added as his contribution to the memorial. She'd had it placed at the base of the tree. Standing in front of it, she spoke aloud the words embedded there.

IN HONOR OF
CHIEF NICHOLAS CONRAD HART
WHO GAVE THE ULTIMATE SACRIFICE
IN THE SERVICE TO
THE UNITED STATES OF AMERICA
AND TO THE FAMILY HE LEFT BEHIND
HE WILL NOT BE FORGOTTEN

Reading those words always brought a tear to Nelli's eye. Even after all these years, she missed him. She was still struggling with forgiving Jake's father for what he'd done. Try as she might, she couldn't make sense of how a man who called himself a friend could stand by while her husband's life was ended. She was praying for God to soften her heart toward Steven Albright so she could honor his request of her. She hoped someday she'd find it in her heart to forgive him.

Nelli closed her eyes and took in a deep breath. She caught the sweet scent of the blooming honeysuckle curling its way around the back fence. It was one of her favorite springtime fragrances. It immediately took her back to those carefree days of her youth when she'd thrown off her shoes and run through the woods in her bare feet. She smiled as she looked down at her thick rubber boots, realizing it'd been an exceptionally long time since she'd even walked outside barefoot let alone run anywhere. Those days were long gone. However, today felt like a good day to walk through the woods in her rubber boots.

Trekking through the woods in the cool dampness of the early morning, Nelli welcomed the warmth of the sunshine cascading through the openings of the surrounding trees. Stepping from the woods into the clearing, she stopped and stared out in silent wonder. There, floating on the surface of the plantation pond, were a flock of wild Mallard ducks. She watched their dark, iridescent-green heads tipping in and out of the smooth surface of the pond as they fed on the underwater plants below. She couldn't remember the last time she'd witnessed a flock of ducks feeding at her pond. Not wanting to disturb them, she carefully made her way to her bench and sat.

For several minutes she observed the ducks as they paddled from spot to spot dabbing for their food until, all at once, as if one had given a signal, they spread their wings and took flight. The precision and majesty of their ascension filled her heart with wonder.

She stared out over the now empty surface of the pond, watching the sun rise higher in the sky. She wished she could stay right where she was for the rest of this day, but knew it would be impossible with all she wanted to accomplish. In less than an hour, Jilli would be at her house. Knowing her youngest daughter as well as she did, she'd be more likely to be early than late. Even though she knew she should be heading back to the house, the splendor of the day held her to this place.

As Nelli sat taking in the beauty around her, she thought over the list of chores she needed to complete before her family and guests arrived. With her daughter's help, she couldn't imagine they'd have any problem getting the rooms ready for Kalli, Nicola, Alexandre, Jake, and Jake's family. She was excited to meet his daughter Lisa and her husband Thomas. Most of all, she was thrilled to welcome his two grandchildren—Jacob and Kelly—to the Hart & Soul Inn. She was excited to have young children once again as guests.

Thinking over the past year, Nelli smiled. She'd delighted in watching Kalli's and Jake's relationship grow. She'd known from the first day the two of them met on her front porch, they'd felt an attraction to one another. Now, here they were going a step further, with Jake introducing his family to hers. From what Jake had told her about his daughter, Lisa was happy her father was seeing someone who made him happy. She seemed to be as enthusiastic about meeting everyone as they were about meeting her along with her family.

Nelli knew how much Kalli was counting on her family to make it the ideal weekend for everyone. After running a successful bed and breakfast for over forty years, Nelli was confident she could make this weekend a memorable one. Nicola was doing her part by bringing the pastries to serve for breakfast and tea. She'd made an extraordinary dessert she promised would "knock their socks off." She'd even persuaded Alexandre to put on his French chef's hat and prepare his special dish of Boeuf Bourguignon for tonight's supper. Of course, she'd fix corn dogs for the children.

Noticing how high the sun was over the pond, Nelli sighed. She couldn't put it off any longer. It was time to head home. She got up and walked to the edge of the pond. She slowly turned in a circle, taking in the lush, green of the leaves on the trees behind her, the dandelions and clover poking through the grasses of the meadow beside her, and the white, billowy clouds reflected on the glassy surface of the pond before her.

As if a veil had been lifted from her eyes, she could clearly see God's blessings all around her. She was struck by a sudden realization. His blessings weren't only in the majesty of the nature surrounding her. Thinking back all the way to when she'd learned of Nicholas's death, she could see how even through the difficult times, blessings had been woven into her life, even without her beloved husband beside her.

Nelli had faced the troubles and tribulations in her life all the while clinging to the Bible verse and her grandmother's words reminding her to "take heart and be strong." It had helped her deal with pain and grief and loss and stay strong for her daughters. Had her determination to get her family through those hard times caused her to be blind to how God had all the while showered blessings on her life?

How long had she been taking the blessings in her life for granted instead of thanking God for each one?

At that very moment, a song from her childhood came to Nelli. It was one Topsy often sang to her as she put her to bed. She couldn't recall any of the verses, but the chorus sprang fresh to her mind:

> *Count your blessings.*
> *Name them one by one.*
> *Count your blessings.*
> *See what God hath done.*

Nelli began to count on her fingers. Number one; loved by God. Number two; blessed with being born into a loving, nurturing God-loving family. Number three; blessed to love and be loved by a great man. Number four; blessed to be the mother of three precious daughters who had given her grandchildren to love. Number five: She laughed as she held up her fifth finger. Blessed with way too many blessings to count.

Spreading her arms out wide and looking up into the bright, blue sky, Nelli shouted, "I see now what you've done, God! Thank You! Through Your grace You've blessed my life far more than I ever deserved!"

Nelli's thoughts suddenly turned to Steven Albright. From what he'd written in his letter to her and what Jake had shared about his father, his life after Vietnam seemed to be void of blessings. If there had been any, it appeared he hadn't taken notice of them. He'd lived a life of bitterness, all the while hating himself for what he'd done to a man he'd once called his friend. He'd asked for her forgiveness, but she'd purposefully, selfishly withheld it. Even though he hadn't tried to help her husband when he needed it most, she needed to show Steven Albright grace by forgiving him, not because he deserved it, but because it was what God was calling her to do.

Once again spreading out her arms and looking skyward, Nelli shouted, "I forgive you, Steven Albright, for your part in my husband's death!"

A smile slowly spread across Nelli's face as a feeling of complete peace and joy filled her body and soul. Taking one more look around, Nelli Hart turned toward home.

The End

ACKNOWLEDGEMENTS

I want to thank:

My husband, the love of my life.

My mother, who I will always miss.

My sisters, who know and keep my secrets.

My daughters, the good and the lost.

My son, who gives me hope.

My grandchildren, who bring me joy.

My daughters-in-law, who bless my family.

My nieces, who make me proud.

My best friends Julie, Linda, and Olivia, who keep me grounded.

My editor Ellen Tarver, who I will miss.

Thank you to EVERYONE who has offered kind words of support.

Thank you to EVERYONE who has taken time out of their day to

read my books.

Most of all, I want to thank GOD. I give Him all my praise, honor,

glory, and thanks.

May God bless each of you!
Carol

ABOUT THE AUTHOR

Carol has always been a devoted reader of Women's Fiction. However, as she grew older and wiser, she noticed the characters in her books were not aging along with her. It appeared as if most of the main characters the authors were creating were never older than forty. If there was, by chance, the mention of a character in the ripe old age of fifty or more, they were either there to support or hinder the younger main character.

When Carol retired after thirty years of teaching, she decided it was time to follow her life-long dream of writing a novel. Drawing on her disappointing reading experiences of forty-year-old main characters, she was determined to write a Women's Fiction book series about women who had aged past forty. Her idea grew into the Kerry Book Series, a four book series which features four retired, vibrant, Southern women–Layne, Nona, Dixie, Betty Jo– who have been friends for more years than they can remember. Their friendship, along with their faith in God, gives them the strength and courage they need to make it through life's trials.

After completing her Kerry Series, Carol began her second series of Hart & Soul which features Nelli her three daughters—Kalli, Nicola, and Jilli. *Take Heart* is the first book in her new series. Three more books will follow.

Carol lives near the small town of Hawkinsville, Georgia, with David her husband of fifty years in the log home that they, along with their three children, built. She thanks God each and every day for her many blessings and for the support of her family and friends.

Carol's books are available for purchase through Christian bookstores and online as an eBook or paperback. Carol would appreciate an honest review of this book.